SUCH A

GOOD

LIAR

Published in the UK by Scholastic, 2022
Euston House, 24 Eversholt Street, London, NW1 1DB
Scholastic Ireland, 89E Lagan Road, Dublin Industrial Estate,
Glasnevin, Dublin, D11 HP5F

ISBN 978 0702 31338 7

A CIP catalogue record for this book
is available from the British Library.

Typeset in Bembo by M Rules
Printed by CPI Group (UK) Ltd, Croydon, CR0 4YY

Paper made from wood grown in sustainable forests
and other controlled sources.

3 5 7 9 10 8 6 4 2

This is a work of fiction. Names, characters, places, incidents
and dialogues are products of the author's imagination or are used
fictitiously. Any resemblance to actual people, living or dead,
events or locales is entirely coincidental.

www.scholastic.co.uk

SUCH A

GOOD

LIAR

GIRL

SUE WALLMAN

■SCHOLASTIC

To my school library regulars – who bring
purpose, vibrancy and community

CHAPTER 1

Sunday

When Shannon Jones stepped off the small private ferry on to the island of Fengari, the sun was shining just as she'd imagined it would. It had sparkled on the water during the hour's trip from the mainland, and now it bounced off the concrete wall of the harbour. The masts of the sleek yachts moored in the marina further along clanked in the slight breeze, and the fringed leaves on the palm trees lining the walkway rippled.

The petrol vapour in the air was different to the salty sea smell she'd been expecting, but it didn't spoil her first proper view of Fengari; she was OK with petrol.

After waiting so long to be here, exhilaration filled her lungs, and kept them swollen for a moment. She nodded her thanks to the deckhand, as she saw others doing. He was dressed in beige shorts, a navy logoed polo shirt and brown deck shoes and was standing by to help anybody who needed it off the boat. He returned her nod, already moving forward to take the elbow of the elderly lady behind her, welcoming the lady back to the island, enquiring after the health of her dogs.

Shannon readjusted her sunglasses, hitched her pink Prada bag up her shoulder, and congratulated herself again on paying to have her luggage sent ahead to Linton Lodge, the place where she would be staying. She didn't know exactly how long she was going to be here, or exactly what outfits she'd need, and that had meant two large suitcases.

She positioned herself halfway in the queue to disembark the boat. She wanted to observe the people ahead of her, and to blend in. Looking anything less than assured was out of the question. Everything had had to be seamless from the moment she left London, taking a taxi to the airport. She'd sipped an espresso in a dark-wood-panelled Heathrow coffee shop when she'd craved a caramel Frappuccino. She'd denied herself the plump pain au raisin which looked so tempting in the basket on top of the counter, but she was no longer a person who liked raisins, or even pastries, and she had to get used to it.

A queue was forming in front of a simple wooden booth. The people at the front were likely to be those who had holiday homes here and used the small private ferry all the time, if they didn't use the helicopter service. Perhaps Shannon would take the helicopter back to the mainland if she had any money left over – the thought of travelling in one terrified her, but if she managed to carry out what she'd come to do, she wouldn't be scared of anything any more.

She took a deep breath, unzipped her precious pink bag and pulled out a passport. It wasn't the one she'd travelled to the mainland on. That would have been way too risky, but here, showing a passport was just a formality because it was basically a private island. There was a security guard, but he was there to keep the queue moving smoothly.

Still, standing next in line to be ushered forward to the wooden booth, Shannon's mouth was dry with nerves and a blood vessel at the front of her head pulsed. She wished she'd brought the bottle of water she'd had on the boat with her.

"Next," said the man in the booth. He looked stern, and had gold-rimmed glasses perched on top of his grey hair.

She stepped forward and held out her passport. Suddenly it felt too thin and the gold on the cover too brassy. She had no idea if the chip embedded in it was of the quality she'd paid for. She met his eyes and smiled.

"First time on Fengari?" the man asked her, pulling down his glasses and one-handedly typing into his computer.

"I was here once when I was six," Shannon said, pulling her bag further round her body.

3

He nodded. The information was likely to be there on the screen in front of him. "Where are you staying?"

"Linton Lodge."

"And the purpose of your visit?" he said, handing back the passport.

"Summer catch-up lessons," she said with a sigh, as if she really didn't want to be on the island at all. "Maths and English. And seeing family friends."

He raised an enquiring eyebrow. "And they are. . .?"

"The Harringtons," she told him. She pushed the passport back into her bag, next to her silver lighter.

"Lovely family," he said, pushing his glasses back up on to his head and smiling for the first time. "They're not here yet, though, are they?"

Shannon shook her head. "Soon," she said. Soon could not come quickly enough. She couldn't wait to meet the Harrington sisters, Annabel and Emily.

"So you'll have seen our famous Dennis when you were here last?" said the man.

Shannon's research into the island had been extensive, but she had no idea what he was talking about.

The man looked back at his computer screen. "Just checking what year it would have been. Yes, Dennis would have been here on your last visit. Don't tell me you don't remember?" He gave Shannon a disappointed look. "Everyone loved Dennis."

Even though every cell in her body was screaming, she looked at him with the dull, bored eyes of the wealthy

4

girls she followed on Instagram and said, "Sorry, I don't remember any Dennis. Like I said, it was ages ago."

"Right," said the man. Shannon could see the awkwardness on his face. "Dennis was a dolphin. He was in our waters for three years in a row. Came right into the harbour. A real character, he was." He glanced behind Shannon. "I'd better keep the queue moving. Have a good visit!"

Shannon walked through the open gate in the harbour wall to the taxi rank and car park, her heartbeat reverting to within normal limits. Stone troughs of vivid pink flowers edged the pavement, and it felt like a sign. Her mum loved a bit of full-on pink.

A silver four-by-four blocked the road and the passenger window eased down. "Darlings!"

A young couple who'd been on the ferry waved and rushed to get in the car. A small group of people made their way towards a white minibus, where they were greeted by a girl in a flowery sundress with a gold name badge which glinted in the sun. The digital sign on the front of the minibus read TREBAYA RESORT. Shannon knew it was over the other side of the island. Her mum had been there and said she wished Shannon had been able to explore it with her.

All at once, she felt a sort of weepy tiredness. There was supposed to be a black Mercedes picking her up, but she couldn't see it.

"Are you Lydia Cornwallis?" A woman in her fifties

with short, wispy brown hair and a thick waist, in a green belted dress and white tennis shoes, approached her. It was Helen. Shannon had seen her photo on the Linton Lodge website.

Shannon nodded. She felt faint. "Yes."

"I'm Helen, owner of Linton Lodge." She held out her hand and Shannon took it and matched the pressure of Helen's grip as instructed by a YouTube video on confidence. "You're going to have a marvellous time on Fengari, in between your studies." She smiled briskly at Shannon. "Your luggage arrived yesterday. This way. I'm sure you could do with a shower and a little rest before dinner." She pronounced shower as "shar".

Shannon followed Helen towards the Mercedes, which was parked half up on the pavement. It looked as if Helen expected her to sit in the front and make conversation. She climbed into the car, pleased that her white jeans were still pristine, although she was pretty sure people like the Harringtons didn't care as much as she did about such things.

Helen had classical music playing, the clashing, unrelaxing sort. She accelerated hard off the pavement and said, "I gather you're friends with the Harringtons?"

"Sort of," said Shannon, sitting more upright. She needed to stay alert despite her jet lag, and concentrate on her accent, keeping it posh-London for Helen. "Mummy and Rosie Harrington were at school together." She held on to the seat belt. "It's been a while since I saw the family, though, and I hardly remember anything about the holiday we had here when I was little."

"They're a lovely old Fengari family," said Helen, pushing her way into the cars queuing to leave the harbour car park.

The lovely, lovely Harringtons.

"We'll drive past their house," said Helen. They turned out of the car park. The road was wide, and the concrete was pale, as if bleached by sunshine. "It's walking distance from Linton Lodge."

Shannon nodded. She knew. It would take fourteen minutes to walk. She kept her cheek against the cool glass of the car window, her long hair – which she'd only recently dyed this particular shade of brown – falling forward, so Helen couldn't see her face. Strong emotions couldn't always be covered up, she'd learned. There were giveaway signs which astute people could read.

The Harringtons' summer property allegedly had one of the best views on the island. It was up on the cliff, looking over Fengari Old Town, the harbour and out to sea. It had a swimming pool, a tennis court, a summer house and access to the beach. Inside, it had art and furniture that had been handed down through the generations.

The red roof coming up. That was it.

"It's this one here," said Helen. "Clifftop House, one of my favourite properties on Fengari."

As the building came into view, Shannon felt a swift pain in her chest. There it was: the house where her mum

7

had been killed. The house where those responsible for her death still spent their summers. For a moment, boiling rage rose up inside her. She wanted to jump out of the car, wrench open those gates, run up the driveway and force her way inside. She would destroy their beloved house, piece by piece, before the Harringtons even arrived.

But Shannon Jones wasn't here right now. Lydia Cornwallis was.

So she turned to give Helen a polite smile and said, "It's beautiful. I can't wait to see it again."

CHAPTER 2

The evening passed in a blur of being reunited with her luggage and eating dinner in the hushed atmosphere of the formal dining room at Linton Lodge. The set menu of spicy prawns, beef and prunes with wilted greens, gooseberry tart and cream looked disgusting. The à la carte menu wasn't much of an improvement, so she asked for a burger and chips, which wasn't on the menu, and loved how the waiter murmured that he'd see what he could do. She added, "Sorry to be a pain, but, if possible, I'd like extra pickles and no bun." Lydia was fussy with food but thankfully not a vegetarian. A minute later, he came gliding back out, saying the chef would be happy to carry out her request. She felt self-conscious on her own, cross

9

that she had listened to Helen, who had said it would be much nicer to eat in the dining room than in her room. She wouldn't be doing it again. Her people-pleasing was a thing of the past.

She'd kicked off her shoes and sank fully clothed into her bed in her room on the first floor as soon as she could. When Helen had first shown her in here, Shannon had understood just how spoilt Lydia was. The ornate bed was huge, the bed linen pale blue satin, and the floor was polished, honey-coloured wood. There was so much cupboard space that her luggage fitted easily, and the standard of cleanliness in the lavish white bathroom was next level.

Helen had demonstrated how the various remotes worked, checked Shannon had enough supplies of coffee, tea, milk and home-made oatmeal biscuits, explained that fresh fruit would be left daily in her room, and pointed out a vase of delicate blue and white flowers on the chest of drawers, sent by Rosie Harrington. There was a small card next to it, which read, *Dearest Lydia – Welcome to Fengari! I'll be in touch when we've arrived. Rosie Harrington x*

Shannon looked at the flowers from her bed and thought about the ones she would have preferred. An explosion of colour. Different petal shapes. Scent that came at you like ripe fruit sliced open. Shannon had learned a great deal about flowers from working in Clarissa Cornwallis's florist shop. In fact, she'd learned about many things in the past year since her mum had died and everything changed, things she'd never even thought about before. Her teachers at her sixth-form college had no idea what she was capable of, and never would. She had slipped quietly away after missed lessons, phone calls not returned, meetings unattended, and finally a note saying she'd moved to live with her dad up north. The truth was she had no clue where her dad was, she never had. College had been useful for the fake passport, though – every type of sketchiness was catered for, if you knew the right person, or someone who knew the right person. The only thing Shannon regretted was falling out with her friend, Ela, and losing Ela's family, but it had been inevitable. Ela hadn't understood. She'd said Shannon's preoccupation with the Harringtons was an unhealthy obsession.

It meant there was no one to miss her.

The only people likely to contact her now were Lydia or Clarissa Cornwallis. In fact, a text had just come through from Clarissa: *Please let me know you arrived safely x.*

Shannon replied: *Hi Mummy, all's good. Leave me alone now like you promised x.*

Clarissa responded immediately with a double heart. There was a time – a year ago – when pretending someone else was her mum would be unthinkable. Upsetting. She'd come a long way since then. Now it was simply a means to an end.

She sent a quick, separate message to Lydia, who she'd put in her contacts as "Lyra" in case anyone saw it over her shoulder, to say she'd arrived and everything was going to plan. Lydia, who presumably had Shannon in her phone as "Rhiannon", as that was all she'd ever known her as, replied with: *This is such a hoot. Go us!*

Lydia had given Shannon her password for Instagram so they could both direct message Clarissa from the same account, which would be useful, although not a perfect system with Lydia being five hours ahead in Europe.

As she and Lydia had planned this, Shannon had always been careful to talk about the swap as something fun, or an interesting challenge at most. Like, how long could they get away with it for? She said she reckoned Lydia's parents might initially be cross when they found out, but it would blow over, and then they'd admire her daring and resourcefulness.

"Hopefully Daddy will think it was a jape," said Lydia. "He got up to all sorts at my age." Shannon had thought what a very Cornwallis word *jape* was.

Too exhausted to undress properly, remove her make-up or brush her teeth, Shannon wriggled out of her clothes. With one of the remotes, she turned out the lights, and in the darkness she held the interlocking gold hearts on her necklace, thought of her mum, and waited for sleep.

Monday

She woke early. Sunlight was already peeking through the slats of the white shutters. She got out of bed and put on the silky white dressing gown with the two entwined Ls of the Linton Lodge logo embroidered on one pocket. Her room looked out over the garden, luscious green with wide flower beds crammed with sun-loving plants with big heads of petals. There was a garden sprinkler on the lawn, arcing back and forth, hissing.

She took a long shower, checked her fake birthmark on her right shoulder, and called reception to ask for her breakfast to be brought up to her room, going all out on a full English with extra hash browns. While she waited for breakfast to arrive, she unpacked properly, hanging her clothes up, filling the drawers, placing her silver lighter in her bedside table. She'd bought it the day she got the job in Clarissa Cornwallis Flowers. It was symbolic. One way or another, she was going to fight fire with fire.

As she dunked a piece of toast into the baked beans, a message pinged through from Fengari Training College, reminding Lydia that her one-to-one tutoring session was booked for eleven a.m. that morning. Her tutor's name was Miriam, and she would meet Lydia in the entrance hall of Linton Lodge.

Shannon had come to the island for a very specific reason, and studying maths and English wasn't it. If she was going to be free to pursue her objective, she knew that keeping her time with Miriam to an absolute minimum would be essential.

She dressed in loose black yoga pants, black canvas trainers and a T-shirt with a logo saying *It's a beautiful day to smash the patriarchy*, a version of what she'd seen Lydia wear to go for brunch with friends, even though it seemed to Shannon that Lydia was doing quite well with the patriarchy. She forced herself to wait until 11.05 before she went downstairs. Clarissa had the same password for everything, and Shannon had seen the initial email she had sent the college, explaining that Lydia had failed GCSE maths a couple of times and had completely lost confidence in the subject, and did they have a suitable summer-school tutor to help turn things around? She'd added that Lydia could be disorganized, unpunctual, unmotivated and occasionally moody, but underneath it all she was a very bright child with an enchanting personality.

Shannon had snorted out loud. She hadn't seen any evidence that Lydia was very bright nor of the enchanting personality.

Nobody could have mistaken Miriam for being a Linton Lodge resident. She wore an unflattering navy dress – the neckline was too high, the length too long and it bagged round her bum. Her fluffy blonde flicked-at-the-ends hair needed a reboot. She greeted Shannon with more squeaky excitement than was necessary and led her into a small meeting room where they sat at an oval table.

"We'll study here this morning," she said. "Tomorrow we'll meet at college. You'll love the atmosphere there. It's buzzy, and oh my, the view from the conference room at the top is in*credible*." She did a little wiggle of her shoulders

14

as if hanging out in conference rooms was what every seventeen-year-old wanted to do.

"Cool," said Shannon. She needed to keep Miriam on side if she was ever going to extricate herself from lessons in the future.

"You're going to be having so much fun on the island too," said Miriam. "But let's get started on your studies." She placed her hands flat on the table to signify she was grinding down a gear in the excitement levels. "Now, do you have a pencil case and a notebook? I think you would have received an email about that."

"Oh no!" said Shannon. "I completely forgot." It's what Lydia would have done.

"No problem!" said Miriam, all smiles. "I brought this with me." From her bulging tote bag, she produced a clear-plastic zip-up folder. Inside was an A5 maths exercise book, a black, blue and red biro, two pencils, an eraser, a maths instrument set and a scientific calculator. It reminded Shannon of the pack she'd been given at school when she'd had to admit to her head of year that her mum didn't have any spare money to buy equipment.

She pulled out the exercise book and flipped through it. She'd always loved stationery – but she knew Lydia would keep her face expressionless and bored.

"I know maths is daunting," said Miriam, elbows on the table, leaning towards Shannon. "I'm here to help. We'll take it step by step. I promise you'll feel much more confident about your retake by the end of the summer."

15

She paused and pulled out a textbook from her bag. "Shall we make a start?"

Maths was Shannon's favourite subject, after computer science. She'd probably have got an eight or nine at GCSE if her teacher hadn't left midway through year eleven and the supply teacher had taught them the right units. Maths homework was soothing with its patterns, and right and wrong answers. Maths in the real world was less soothing but far more exhilarating – working out how much Lydia's mum, Clarissa, would notice if she siphoned off some money here and there from the floristry business, for instance.

Shannon had worked for nine months at Clarissa Cornwallis Flowers, Clarissa's high-end store in Kensington, before her ultimate plan had presented itself. Clarissa floated in occasionally to look at the flowers and remark on how fabulously the business was doing, when in reality Shannon had much more of a clue about the finances. The business was owned jointly by Clarissa and Rosie Harrington, but neither took much interest in the accounts. Rosie had merely invested because it was her friend's business and had no involvement, and Clarissa liked having something to do – when it suited her. There was a manager, a friend with less money than the other two, who kept things going.

Shannon had sought out the business on purpose. She was really gunning for Annabel and Emily Harrington, but their complicit mother could foot the bill. At first, the plan had been no more sophisticated than to steal money here and there towards a plane ticket to Fengari, but the gods of revenge had been on her side.

She still didn't have a detailed plan. How could she, when she didn't know what opportunities would present themselves here on the island? She just knew that Annabel and Emily would pay heavily for what they'd done.

In the meeting room now, it was hard to feign difficulty with the graphs Miriam was showing her, but Shannon made herself muddle up the x and y axes, and doodled in the margin of her exercise book as Miriam spoke. These classes were going to be torturous. At last Miriam said, "That's all we've got time for today. You've worked so hard, Lydia. I'm very proud," and Shannon wanted to lean back, arms folded, and say, "Proud? Really?"

Although it was a stunning day outside, she would have lunch brought up to her in bed, and go over her accounts. She might come down later to sunbathe when there were fewer people around, not because she was particularly self-conscious about her body but because she wanted as little interaction with other people as possible.

At the bottom of the stairs, Helen came bustling up to her. "How were your lessons, Lydia?" she asked. "Made a good start?"

Shannon nodded.

"Smashing. I heard the Harringtons arrived on the island today."

Shannon's heart beat a little faster. "Oh," she said.

"That's great." She jabbed a finger at her phone screen expectantly. No message.

Helen said, "I'd give them a little while to settle back in. I'm sure they'll be in touch very soon."

Damn, she mustn't be so obvious.

"There's a small crowd going to the beach this afternoon," said Helen. She pointed at a group of people about twenty years older than Shannon who were having dessert brought to their table. One of the men was laughing like a squeaky dog toy. "Would you like to join them in the minibus?"

Shannon shook her head. "Absolutely not," she said, and made her way up to her room, knowing that Lydia would have been with her on that decision. She messaged Lydia as she ate her fancy sandwich and fruit platter: *You would have hated the lessons. The woman is insanely boring.*

Lydia messaged back: *Phahahahaha. So glad I'm not there!*

After she'd gone through her expenses spreadsheet, and had sunbathed by the pool for an hour and a half with headphones in, listening to motivational talks on getting what you wanted, the text message finally came through. She was lying in the bath with a fresh mint tea next to the Aesop toiletries, which smelled amazing.

Finally, finally, the invitation she'd been waiting for: *Dearest Lydia, we're on Fengari and we'd love it if you came for dinner at Clifftop House tomorrow evening.*

CHAPTER 3

Tuesday

Miriam had severely overpromised on the buzz of Fengari Training College. There were three other students there when Shannon arrived the following morning in a taxi organized by the college, two being tutored in a small, glass-fronted room by a man with corduroy trousers and a check shirt, and one napping on a sofa in the common room who rolled over and burped when Miriam and Shannon walked in.

"Here's the library," said Miriam, pointing at a lone shelf. "It's more of a book swap, but it's very popular." The room led outside to a small courtyard with benches.

"This is where you can relax during breaks if you need some fresh air."

The conference room at the top of the building was the only interesting part. You could see the whole harbour – where the ferries came in, the fishing boats, and the yachts in the marina. The main ferry was coming in, much larger than the private one, and tourists were leaning against the outside railings, taking photos and pointing. Coming to this private island was a big trip, even though it wasn't so far from the mainland; tourist numbers were strictly controlled, and accommodation and eating out were expensive. This wasn't a place backpackers came, unless they had a trust fund.

The two of them went back in the lift to a ground floor classroom, and began work. After a while, Shannon found herself getting angry because Miriam was so patient and able to explain a maths problem in a variety of different ways, as if she had all the time in the world. It felt so unfair Lydia had access to all this, and she didn't even care.

"I think you're losing concentration. We'll take a fifteen-minute break," said Miriam.

Shannon got a mocha for herself from a machine in the kitchen area of the common room and took it into the courtyard to get away from Miriam.

She sat on a wooden bench, which made her think of Ela and the last time they'd sat on a bench in Pigeon Park. Ela had asked her if she was depressed. They had been uncomfortable being around each other since their last row about how Shannon was obsessed with the Harrington family.

"No," said Shannon.

Ela coughed slightly. "Mum says if you don't want to move away to live with your dad, she can go to the council with you and help you find accommodation." So that was why she'd come. Her mum had made her. "I get that you want to drop out of college," she said, standing to leave now she'd said what she'd come to say, "but you used to love drama club. And you've got your job at that florist. And you've never wanted to see your dad before. You've never even talked about him."

Shannon had shrugged.

"You should go out with a group of us before you go away," said Ela, as a final afterthought. "Come to Spoons tonight?"

Shannon shook her head. She had to get everything ready before she left for Fengari. There was no time to do anything fun and nothing to be gained from sentimental goodbyes or looking backwards.

"I feel sorry for you," said Ela as she was walking away. "You used to be clever and fun, and now you're kind of a bitch."

The words should have stung, but she'd hardened herself in the months since her mum's death, and cutting Ela loose was part of what she had to do. It was for the best.

Shannon spent the afternoon trying on outfits for the

dinner at Clifftop House. Weeks ago, she'd planned a dress for this first encounter: red clingy fabric with puffy sleeves. She'd wanted to make an impact. In the shop, the red dress had seemed appropriate; but now she was on the island among people with money, it seemed too over the top. She finally settled on a boring black minidress that wasn't so mini the Harrington parents' eyes would pop. It looked good with her fake tan, though. She'd had the tan done professionally and bought a top-up mist for an extortionate amount. There was no way she was going to be accused of having orangey tones.

She had a few maths questions to do for Miriam – given with an apologetic smile and an explanation that her mother had paid for the package which included the marking of homework. Shannon sat on the bed and did it carelessly, like Lydia would have done. Next, while soaking in the bath, she checked her bank account, and the amount she'd spent on Lydia's credit card. It was linked to Clarissa's, and notified Clarissa with a text whenever it was used. Shannon had told Lydia she'd use it sometimes for things on Fengari so Lydia's parents would assume she was there. She also had her own credit card, and fictional Margot Bonvalier's debit card, in whose name she'd applied for a small loan – and, astonishingly, received it. Shannon had a thing about French names. She'd had a crush on her French teacher, Mr Walker, who changed from a hunched, downtrodden teacher to a person of sophistication whenever he would *parle francais*. He'd once said the words

22

Gare du Nord with such impressive intonation that she still occasionally said it to herself in exactly the same way, like favourite lyrics.

After her accounts, Shannon accessed the revision notes she'd made about the Harringtons and the Cornwallises. She'd saved them on the cloud so they were always available, but she'd been over them so many times, she could visualize them at will. She was about to have her first, big test, and the adrenaline was fizzing through her veins. She breathed deeply in and out, like she used to before exams, and wished she was back in the cosy flat, teaching her mum dance moves in the kitchen, debating whether to have mash or pasta with their sausages.

As she stepped out of the bath, she told herself she didn't have to do this. She could make an excuse this evening and leave the island tomorrow or the day after. There was an out, if she truly wanted it. She rubbed her hair on a soft towel. No. She hadn't come this far to give up now. This was something she had been working towards for almost a year and every fibre of her being hummed with anticipation.

Shannon knew Clarissa was sending the Harringtons a hamper from Fortnum's as a thank-you for "keeping an eye" on Lydia while she was on Fengari, but she didn't want to arrive empty-handed. It was vital for her plans that the Harringtons came to like and trust her, and first impressions were everything. She'd bought some chocolates in a duty-free boutique at the airport. They were moulded like small flower heads, little works of sculpture, and had cost about the same as an entire carrier bag loaded with Cadbury's Dairy Milk.

Rosie had sent a follow-up message to say that she would send a taxi to Linton Lodge to pick up Lydia at seven p.m., and Shannon had walked downstairs at 6.45 p.m. to sit in the leather armchair in the entrance area. She was happy with the admiring double takes she got from other guests. She knew the dress suited her, and her hair and make-up were on point. Everything was subtle and understated. It wasn't how she would have looked if she'd been going out with Ela – when they were still friends – but apparently old-money families liked the dull aesthetic. At first she'd found it confusing, seeing photographs of insanely wealthy people wearing clothes that looked as if they'd been bought in a charity job bundle, but she'd realized there were secret codes to it. Like, you had to have at least one very expensive brand on you, preferably one which looked as if it had been kicking around for years.

She messaged Lydia: *Wish me luck. Leaving for Clifftop House any minute! Please keep your phone nearby in case I need you.*

Lydia came back immediately: *Good luck Rhiannon!! Yes, I'm standing by. Don't forget to message me later and tell me EVERYTHING!*

The taxi was scruffy and smelled of cigarette smoke, and after establishing the driver didn't have air-con, she slid open the window. It seemed silly to be driven when she could have walked it in fourteen minutes, though maybe not in her beloved glittery silver Jimmy Choo sandals, an over-the-top present to herself after she'd booked her flight and ferry crossing.

They arrived at the gates of Clifftop House before she had completely composed herself. With a horrible jolt, she realized she'd left the flower chocolates in her room. She told herself to keep calm. *That's it*, she told herself. *That's the one mistake you're allowed to make this evening.*

The taxi driver said the company he worked for had been paid by the Harringtons, but it was clear he was expecting a tip, so she gave him a generous one. She wanted to ask him if he'd known her mum. She'd first come to Clifftop House in a taxi too, arranged by Rosie Harrington, but after the driver had taken the notes, he turned up the radio to dismiss her. She stepped out of the car, and without the breeze from the open car window the air suddenly felt humid and stifling.

Shannon had been given the biggest opportunity of her life and here she was, ready to meet the Harringtons.

The first time they had discussed the swap, the real Lydia had come to the shop to drop off some bespoke ribbon for a customer, moaning as usual about having been asked to do a minor chore by her mum. Shannon was used to it by this point. Lydia had sat in the corner of the store, on the display-only high wooden stool for flower arrangements, which Shannon had been expressly told never to sit on.

Then Lydia had moved on to a new beef, which was that her whole summer was about to be ruined: she was being sent to Fengari to get privately tutored for maths.

Shannon had stopped snipping eucalyptus stems.

"It totally sucks," Lydia had said, her hands either side of her oval face, dark brown hair falling forward. "I want to go travelling with my boyfriend, but my mum is being aggy about it, even though it's my holiday. How am I going to last that long without seeing him?"

"I'll go to Fengari for you," said Shannon automatically, her mind spinning at the possibilities opening up before her. Here it was: the outrageously perfect opportunity for revenge, and she was up for it. "I'd pretend to be you."

Lydia laughed.

"Seriously," said Shannon. "We could make it happen. Our faces look kind of similar. Don't you think?"

"You'd have to hang out with my mum's friend and her family," said Lydia, rolling her eyes.

The breath caught in Shannon's throat, threatening to come out as a coughing fit, but then she was able to speak. "I couldn't pretend to be you with them, could I?" The *could I* was quiet but sharp. Everything hinged on it. If this plan didn't work, then Shannon would think of some other way to get to Fengari ... but if it worked, it would be the answer to everything. Deceit was becoming second nature to her. It was almost as if she was discovering her true talent, and she got such a rush from it. It felt like proof she wasn't a nobody.

Lydia frowned. "Actually, I bet you could. I haven't seen them in years."

"All I'd have to do is dye my hair darker, lose a couple of kilos, and invest in some brown-coloured contact lenses, right?" said Shannon.

Lydia stared at her. Had she gone too far? The contact lens comment had maybe been a little creepy. You didn't normally go round noting other people's eye colour unless you fancied them or it was particularly unusual, but Shannon's fantasy had gone spiralling into the practicalities already.

"How funny would that be?" said Lydia, stepping down from the stool, laughing. "Rhiannon, you're wild."

Lydia didn't even know Shannon's real name. She took everything at face value. Yes, this could work.

All these months later, Shannon could still hear that laugh. Lydia had believed in her. Did believe in her.

Close up, Clifftop House was even more imposing. The brick was a paler red than the roof, almost pink in the soft evening light. The double front door was white, with bright red flowers growing around it. Shannon's knowledge of plants only extended to the ones sold in Clarissa's shop, but she thought it might be bougainvillea.

Her mum had been excited to come here. Before she came, she'd never been outside the UK. It was supposed to be the beginning of their good fortune. The turning point.

Shannon breathed out slowly and loudly, and clenched

her fist until her immaculate red nails dug deep into her palm. She rang the doorbell and heard it echo loudly. The door opened and Shannon held back a gasp. She'd been expecting Mrs Pushkin, the housekeeper, but instead was looking at a face she knew well from staring at it for hours online.

Annabel Harrington.

Shannon forced a smile. Annabel, younger than her by a month, was in dark jeans and a lavender-coloured crop top with white piping round the neck. Her narrow feet were bare. Shannon had misjudged the dress code, but she couldn't dwell on that now. Annabel's slightly wavy, dark blonde hair was damp, her skin make-up free, her nails unvarnished and her expression set in a sneer.

"Hi," said Annabel, making no attempt to hide that she was looking Shannon up and down; and Shannon made sure to do the same. Annabel was bang-average to look at in real life. The sort of person who wouldn't merit a second glance where Shannon lived in south-east London, if she'd been in joggers and Nikes. Her face was blemish-free and her eyebrows were well-shaped, but she was unremarkably featured. The only sharpness to her face was her eyes.

Shannon kept the smile. "Annabel?"

"Yeah." There was a brief faux-smile from Annabel before she waved Shannon inside with a hand which held a half-eaten apple. "Come in, I guess. Mrs P, our housekeeper, usually answers the door, but she's not arrived on the island yet and God knows where Mum is."

Shannon stepped into the wide hall, on to a rug which looked ancient, all deep reds and blues, and worn to beige thread in one corner. She clutched her pale pink Prada bag. Annabel had recently answered a silly question-and-answer thing on social media about herself, and in reply to *Someone would steal my heart if they bought me a . . .* she'd answered, *Prada tote*.

For a moment, it looked as if Annabel was going to wander off and leave Shannon alone in the hall, but she gave Shannon's bag a closer look. "I was thinking about getting one of those. I would have got the blue one, though. Pink is a brave choice."

Shannon smiled and sucked up the insult. Lydia would probably have laughed and made a joke about the bag matching Peppa Pig sweets, or done a stupid twirl with it, but Shannon couldn't bring herself to do that.

A woman with hair in an artfully messy bob and fringe came down the stairs, all floaty layers over wide-legged trousers and bony feet in flat sandals. Shannon's stomach twitched inside with nerves, but Rosie didn't falter when she saw her. She kissed her on both cheeks, saying, "How lovely to see you, Lydia! Annabel and I have just been for a swim on the beach. Glorious! Come into the kitchen and tell me how your mama is doing. It's been ages since I've seen her. And the tutoring – is it frightfully dull?"

Rosie was putting on a performance, and the way she said "mama" was silly. Shannon knew that she could be cold and cutting. She had experienced it herself via email

29

at the worst time in her life. She watched her flutter about, reaching for a wine glass. "Let's get you a drink. Douglas has opened rather a good bottle of red. You'll have to forgive us. It's just a very basic kitchen supper tonight. Our darling Mrs P stayed behind to pack up Birch Hill – I always leave things in such a mess – but she'll be here tomorrow, thank God. We usually have an extra member of house staff, but this year we thought we'd see how we got on without."

Extra member of house staff. That had been her mum, last year. Bex Jones.

"Staff can be so much work, can't they?" said Rosie with a laugh.

"Especially the thickos and weirdos we get sent by the agency," said Annabel. She rolled her eyes. "You wonder where they find them."

Shannon wanted to pick up a heavy-looking lamp and hit her over the head with it.

She was ushered into a large kitchen. It felt familiar and strange at the same time. Her mum had taken a short video of it when Mrs Pushkin hadn't been there, to show Shannon how rich people lived. The cupboards were made from a light-coloured wood and managed to look simultaneously old and new. There were two double ovens and a large island with four bar stools at one side. At the other end of the room, by bifold doors with a sea view, were two white sofas and a table which would easily seat twenty people. Shannon turned and saw, high above the door into the kitchen, a huge old dark wooden beam

30

which her mum had said was the family's pride and joy because there was some story or other attached to it.

"Douglas, Clarissa's daughter is here! Lydia Cornwallis."

Shannon was introduced to Douglas Harrington, who was reading a newspaper at the table. His hair had gone grey either side of his face but not on top, making his hairstyle look more radical than it was. His eyelids drooped a little, as if he was only half awake. He said hello as if he was used to meeting people and immediately forgetting them.

"This room is pretty," said Shannon, accepting a glass of red wine from Rosie. She took a sip and was unprepared for the sour, woody taste of it.

"It really is, isn't it?" said Rosie. "We adore this house. We love Birch Hill too, of course, but, well, Clifftop House is magical. That big beam up there was part of the boat Doug's ancestor came over in when he first bought the land here in seventeen. . ."

"Seventeen eighty-six," called Douglas. "There's authentic graffiti scratched into the wood from that voyage." He grunted and went back to reading his paper.

"Take a seat at the island and tell me everything," said Rosie. She began cutting tomatoes on a wooden board with a knife that had a white handle. It might have been plastic, but Shannon would have bet on it being bone.

Annabel sat on one of the sofas nibbling at her apple, smirking at Shannon as if she found her black dress ridiculous for a "kitchen supper" or as if she'd spotted the wince when Shannon had tasted the wine.

31

Shannon imagined herself snatching the knife from Rosie's hand and plunging it into Annabel's heart.

Patience, she told herself. *All good things come to those who wait.* It was one of Nan's sayings. "It doesn't mean you sit around and wait for things to come to you, Shan," she had said once. "It means you take your time before you pounce." And she'd winked. Nan had probably been talking about relationships, to be fair; not that Nan had had a good track record.

Where was Emily? She needed to hold back on asking too many questions, on seeming too nosy, but she had to know. Nothing could happen without Emily here.

"How's the floristry business going?" began Rosie. "It's one of my favourite investments."

"Really well," said Shannon. She certainly didn't want Rosie to start looking into the finances. "But Mummy..." It was weird to say *Mummy* out loud. "She did something to her knee when she played in a tennis tournament, so that's slowed her down." She'd practised that sentence a few times, but her voice sounded odd. The accent was OK, but it was too hesitant.

Rosie didn't seem to notice. She nodded and leaned forward. "And tell me about Henry. I hear he has a new job and a new boyfriend."

Shannon felt a twist of terror as Rosie pushed for more information about Lydia's brother's boyfriend. In the end she did a slight shrug. "Well, I ... to be honest, I don't know much about him. You know what Henry's like."

Rosie nodded and took a neat sip of wine.

There was a growing smell of roasting chicken from one of the ovens. She watched Rosie slide the tomatoes into a pale green bowl and grind a small amount of salt over them. There would be an elaborate salad dressing next, she was sure of it.

"I wish I remembered being here," said Shannon. The boldness of that statement made the hairs on her arm stand up.

"You were what, five? Six? It's been far too long since your mother was out here," said Rosie. "I'd love her to see the garden."

"Summer's busy for the business," said Shannon. "All those weddings." She looked at the garden through the glass doors. She could see the fountain her mum had taken a photo of, when she'd seen a multicoloured bird perch on the edge. It seemed bare, bleak almost, without that bird.

Rosie looked at a clock on the wall. "Twenty minutes until we eat. Annabel, show Lydia around. See if she remembers the house."

Shannon's stomach did a kind of flip. Excitement or nerves, she wasn't sure which.

Annabel's eyes narrowed. She looked at Shannon's silver sandals. "You'll have to take those things off. They'll dent the flooring upstairs and Dad will be livid."

Douglas looked up. "What's that, Annabel?"

She ignored him and got off the sofa, hitching her jeans up, showing off her toned, flat stomach. Flexing. "So this is the kitchen," she said as she walked across the room, and

Shannon, hastily removing her Jimmy Choos, followed. "Next, we have Dad's study. It has two doors – one in here and one in the hall." She was over-explaining to make the point she'd rather be doing anything else than showing Shannon around.

"For God's sake, Annabel, don't go in there!" Douglas shouted.

"Too late!" Annabel called back, strolling in.

There was an enormous desk and a filing cabinet with four drawers, papers in wire trays and piles of books on the floor as well as crammed into bookshelves. Annabel felt a muscle in her neck loosen. Judging by the way this family operated, she bet there was all sorts of incriminating stuff about the Harringtons in here.

"Annabel!" called Douglas from the other room. "I don't want people in there."

"Relax, Dad!" Annabel shouted back. "It's only—" She paused and her not-reaching-the-eyes smile appeared. "What's your name again?"

"Lydia," said Shannon, the humiliation swiftly converted to another layer of anger.

"Lydia!" shouted Annabel. She stood by the desk, picked up a silvery metal paperweight in the shape of a dolphin, and said, "Which school do you go to?"

"Walton House."

"Wallys? D'you know Millie Montgomery?" Annabel asked.

"Yep, she's in my year," Shannon answered smoothly.

She'd spent two evenings being coached by Lydia in how to be her. Having Lydia's password for Insta had helped Shannon get into Lydia's head too. Lydia wasn't close friends with Millie Montgomery, but Shannon wasn't sure where she fitted into the school hierarchy. Annabel had sounded scornful, maybe even pissed off. "Millie, hmm."

"Oh, you can tell me," said Annabel. There was an edge to her voice which told Shannon she didn't like Millie, and an eyebrow raise which was inviting her to start a bitch-fest. This must be how Annabel bonded – a shared dislike or ridiculing.

Shannon took a chance. "She's a cow."

Annabel smiled. "Really? Come on, I'll show you the rest of the house. You'll love it. We all love it."

"OK," said Shannon, breathing out slowly. This was going well.

CHAPTER 4

After Douglas's study, Annabel showed Shannon a formal dining room. There was a large open fireplace, a tapestry on the wall and a shiny dark wood table with matching rectangular-backed chairs. Very medieval. The glass-fronted display cabinets caught her eye immediately and she went to peer at them. They only had glassware in them, though. No mythical animal "monster" statue like the one her mother had described. It felt cold in here. Like a showroom. In her family, there'd never been a separate dining room. They ate meals off their laps on the sofa.

"We only really use this room if we come here at Christmas," said Annabel. "But we hardly ever do. We're usually in Val d'Isère."

Shannon nodded. She hoped there wouldn't be much skiing talk, although she'd learned the jargon and knew Lydia had broken her ankle skiing in St Anton.

They moved on to a TV room Annabel called the "garden room" with a corner sofa and mountains of cushions, and a lounge she called the "drawing room" which was much more formal with oil paintings – portraits of pale double-chinned people with pheasants and dogs – and another she called the "sitting room", which was floral. So many places to sit down in this house. Annabel pointed out a doorway that led to Mrs Pushkin's bedroom and bathroom. "We used to go and visit her in there when we were little, but it's sort of out of bounds now." Next there was a downstairs toilet, a shower room, laundry room and the back stairs. By the sink in the shower room, Shannon glimpsed liquid soap embossed with a gold hexagon. She didn't know that brand: she'd look it up later to see if it was absurdly expensive or a budget brand that only looked like the genuine article. Knowing these things had become important.

They went upstairs. The banisters had ornately carved vertical bits. There was a name for them – spindles or something. Shannon hadn't grown up in a house. She'd always lived in a flat. It had been rented, and when her mum died, there'd been enough money to keep it going for two months, and then she wangled another couple when she said she'd pay but didn't, before paying her elderly neighbour on the next floor down to live in her spare room with money from Clarissa Cornwallis Flowers until she came here. All the time she'd had to dodge phone calls and meetings from social services, people wanting to know if she had relatives to stay with, talking about foster care options. Eventually, through a combination of avoidance and lying that her neighbour was an elderly aunt, she slipped down the priority list for the overworked, constantly changing team handling her case. She was seventeen, nearly an adult, after all.

"Millie Montgomery made a move on my boyfriend, Seb," said Annabel as she started up the stairs. "Like blatantly. At a party. I don't even know why she was there. Then I *accidentally* ripped her top with a corkscrew and she backed off."

Shannon tried to look as if she found this amusing. "She's so inappropriate."

"For real," agreed Annabel. "Who does she think she is? She is so boring. Me slashing her top was probably the most exciting thing that's ever happened to her. As if Seb would be interested. Such an insult." Annabel's hair had completely dried now. It hung in clumps and made her look about twelve. And innocent. If there was one thing Annabel and Emily Harrington weren't, it was innocent.

All the doors on the landing were ajar. Annabel pushed one open. "You probably stayed in here when you came. It's our family guest-room suite."

The guest room suite was two bedrooms, and a shared, enormous en suite bathroom with a claw-foot bath.

Shannon nodded. "It feels familiar," she said. It did. Her mum had sent a photo of that bath because the claw feet had amused her. In the second bedroom she walked over to the window and stopped abruptly. In a wooded area, set back from the formal part of the garden, she could see a one-storey brick building. The bunkhouse, rebuilt since the fire. "Is that where your other staff live?" she asked.

Annabel was on her phone. "What?"

Shannon repeated her question. Her face was flushed and she needed to be calmer.

"Yes, the randomers who are here for the summer live there," said Annabel.

Randomers. She wanted to spit in Annabel's face. If she wasn't so enraged, she would ask more questions to see how she reacted. She'd ask why the building looked so new, for a start. Now, though, she walked out on to the landing to get her anger under control. Three deep breaths. She glanced through an open door. It looked like Annabel's room. There was a suitcase on the floor with clothes spilling out of it.

"Go in if you want," said Annabel behind her, so Shannon did. Everything was carelessly placed, from her make-up on the white carpet to her laptop balanced on the edge of a chest of drawers. There was a cardboard box in front of a bank of fitted wardrobes, with brightly coloured fabric in clear plastic sleeves spilling out of it. There were other boxes against the wall, stacked up in an untidy pyramid. She was pretty sure it was the beachwear Annabel was selling last summer through Instagram.

Annabel sat on the huge bed, then shuffled up against the headboard, her bare feet on top of the plain white duvet. She didn't suggest Shannon sit down. "Seb is coming out here next week. He hasn't been to Fengari before. Can't wait." She brushed sand out from between her toes on to the floor. "Sometimes I sprinkle sand around to wind the staff up. Gives them something to do."

Shannon thought about the times her mum told her she'd had to sweep or vacuum up sand. There was vomit on occasion too, left for her to deal with.

"Mum said you'd just split up with your boyfriend," said Annabel. "Spill the details." She was animated at the thought of gossip.

"I dumped him," said Shannon. It's what she and Lydia had agreed to say.

"Why?" Annabel.

"I wasn't feeling it any more," said Shannon. She pictured Lydia's boyfriend, Crispin. He was fit, but not her type. Too wide-necked and rugby-player-like. But she owed him. He'd persuaded Lydia to take the leap.

He'd come into Clarissa Cornwallis Flowers to meet Lydia one time. It had been eight agonizing weeks after she'd had that first conversation with Lydia and nothing more had been said. Shannon was determined not to rush things, in case it freaked Lydia out, and had concentrated instead on getting to know her better, making her laugh to put her at ease and listening to the endless moans. She had made Crispin a mug of tea while he waited for Lydia to finish gathering flowers to take wherever they were going to next. As she handed it to him, she said, "Has Lydia told you about our wild idea of swapping places – me going to the maths lessons in Fengari and her going travelling with you?"

"That's sick, Rhiannon," he'd said with a huge grin. "I love it." He squeezed Lydia's shoulder as she bent down to select three gerbera stems. "Why didn't you tell me, babe?"

"My stupid parents would never fall for it," Lydia said. "And how would the money work?" She looked at Shannon, who shrugged. And waited.

Crispin made a thinking-humming noise, then said, "Your mum would buy the ticket which Rhiannon could use – changing the name doesn't cost that much. The two of us have got enough money to go travelling for the summer."

"True..." said Lydia. She stopped wrapping the ribbon round the flowers.

"Just think about it," he said, warming to the idea. "You, me? Travelling around without anyone checking up on us?" He wrapped his arms around her from behind, and she leaned back, smiling up at him.

Shannon had to steady her breathing. She shook her head. "No way, *no way*. Your mum would totally work it out. She messages you, like, ten times a day!"

Crispin looked thoughtful for a moment, but then, it was as if a light bulb flipped on above his head. "But, Lydia, if you share your Insta account with Rhiannon, she can post pics and stuff about Fengari to convince her you're there and you can message too and answer any awkward questions! Oh my God, I think I might actually be a real-life genius. If we could pull this off, we'd be *legends*."

"I mean. . .?" Lydia said, her smile widening. "Wow. Yes, this *could* work! I'd still be in touch with Mummy, but I'd tell her I wanted to be more independent, to stop her getting over-involved or sending too many messages. We could give you a little spending money, Rhiannon."

Shannon hoped her smile looked gracious enough. She was already siphoning off money from the business, but every little bit helped. "That *would* be incredible, I've always wanted to go somewhere like Fengari. . . But no, it would be too much. I wouldn't want you to ever think I'd, like, take advantage of our friendship." She was pleased how she'd slipped the word *friendship* in there.

"What are you talking about? You'd be doing *us* a favour!" Lydia wriggled with excitement. "Oh my God, Crispin. It would be *A. Mazing.*" She turned and placed her arms round his shoulders.

"OK," he said, pumping the air. "Let's do this."

Annabel made a snorting noise and Shannon's attention snapped back to Clifftop House. "You'll like Seb," said Annabel. "He's a laugh. But you're not having him."

"Who d'you think I am?" said Shannon. "Millie Montgomery?"

It worked. They laughed at the same time. Shannon pointed to the pile of clothing in front of the wardrobe. "Big online order?" She waited for Annabel to look embarrassed, but there was no trace of it on her face.

"Oh," said Annabel. "No, I run a little business. Beachwear. Bikinis and wraps."

"Awesome. Sounds fun!" Shannon picked up one of the thin packages. "Did I see your bikinis on Insta?" She hoped she didn't sound too stalkerish. There had been an official account for Annabel's beachwear last summer until it got taken down but she still had photos of it on her private account.

"Yeah, you might have," said Annabel. "It was so busy for a while. I'm focusing on other things now."

Lydia had only recently become online friends with Annabel and her sister. One time, when Lydia had come into the flower shop to stock up on the handmade soy wax candles they sold, Shannon had said, "I'd feel much more comfortable about going to Fengari if I knew a little bit more about Emily and Annabel Harrington."

"It's weird if I friend request now," said Lydia.

"You've got a few mutuals," said Shannon. "It's not weird." She'd already made two fake accounts in case she needed them, and tempted Annabel and Emily's more careless friends to accept friend requests so the accounts showed the right connections. Afterwards, she erased Shannon Jones from social media completely, and it had been a relief not to be out there any more, pretending to be getting over her nan, and then her mum.

In Annabel's bedroom, Shannon picked up a framed photo on a bookcase. "That's your sister in the blue dress?" Emily was a year older than Annabel, blonder, taller, equally as vile. She took in a slow breath. "When does she get here?"

Annabel glanced over at the photo. "Yeah, that's her. Who knows?"

Shannon fought to prevent the disappointment from showing on her face. Emily had to be here. She couldn't risk making her deadly move before both sisters were on the island.

"Where is she?" Shannon's voice wasn't casual enough.

"St-Tropez." Then Annabel added, "She says the nightlife is better there." She shrugged. "She's right, but she'll be back when she's burned through her summer allowance."

Shannon nodded. *It was fine*, she told herself. She had time on her side. Emily would show up eventually. She'd always spent at least part of the summer on Fengari. She was as sentimental about this house as the rest of them, even if the nightlife was rubbish: "Sounds morbid," she'd announced on TikTok recently, "but when I die I want my ashes to be scattered in the garden of Clifftop House on Fengari." There had followed a slew of photos of "fun" times in the garden and summer house. Shannon had thought, *How prophetic*, and a little shiver had climbed up her spine.

Annabel got off her bed and rearranged her crop top in the long mirror by the door. "We should go downstairs. I'll take you down the back staircase. There's the *best* portrait of Emily along there by some famous artist. It makes her look completely awful."

The painting was simplistic and depicted Emily with a receding hairline and an elongated face.

"The only reason she doesn't mind it," said Annabel, "is that it's worth a ton of money and it'll be hers one day."

Shannon saw it then, the monster in a display cabinet near the back stairs. It was a strange terracotta animal about eight centimetres high. It had horns, fangs and wings, and it was exactly as her mum had described it to her. It stood next to two grey vases, with fierce mythological creatures painted on them.

"This stuff looks interesting," she said, her accent almost slipping. She stood next to the cabinet, even though Annabel had started down the stairs.

"Yeah," Annabel said. "That creature looks like someone made it for a primary school project, doesn't it? But it's hundreds of years old. It's Dad's favourite. He hates anyone picking it up."

Shannon pressed a hand against the glass, as if she could touch the monster through it. This beast had played a big part in the terrible events of last summer.

"Come on," called Annabel. She did a sort of skip down the first few stairs.

Shannon's arms suddenly ached from longing to hug her mum. She wanted to hold her tight and tell her it was OK. She was going to make things right. She was going to bring down the Harrington sisters.

CHAPTER 5

Shannon's mum was only seventeen years old when she had her, and didn't even know she was pregnant until she was in the back of an ambulance giving birth. So Shannon and her mum always had to figure out stuff together. With Fengari she and her mum had made a catastrophic mistake, but at the time it had felt like a no-brainer. As if their luck was finally about to change.

Her mum was interviewed by Rosie Harrington and told that, subject to references, the summer staff job for their house on Fengari was hers if she wanted it, starting in a week's time; she'd had one evening to decide whether to take it.

Three months on an exclusive British island off the US

coast. All costs, including flights, accommodation and food paid for, plus earning enough money to pay off a substantial amount of the debt that had built up after the rent increased and Shannon's mum's work hours decreased. In addition, they could sublet their flat to a neighbour's family who were coming over to London for the summer from Nigeria.

They'd looked at Fengari on the internet – it was the shape of a fluffy cloud. They saw the houses, the weather, the dazzlingly blue sea. Shannon's mum was on a zero-hours cleaning contract, which meant she didn't need to give notice.

No one would have turned it down. Shannon often told herself that.

"I can't leave you for the whole summer," her mum had said. She'd twisted her high ponytail round and round, letting go before starting the twisting routine again. Shannon loved how young her mum looked, and how she dressed. She was always on the lookout for new accessories.

"It's fine. I can stay at Ela's," Shannon had assured her. "Her parents won't mind." She wished she'd been able to go to Fengari too. She could have helped her mum; they'd often worked as a team.

"We'd pay them rent," her mum said. "We're not freeloaders."

Ela's parents had wanted the bare minimum, just for food. Shannon and Ela made plans together, to visit all the charity shops round London, buy student theatre tickets, and to sneak off and drink in the graveyard and sunbathe in Pigeon Park.

Shannon had gone by coach with her mum to the airport a week later, to help her with her suitcases and wave her off, both of them exhausted from cleaning the flat from top to bottom, ready for the neighbour's family.

She hugged her mum goodbye, hanging on to her neck and inhaling the smell of her skin mingled with the Beyoncé perfume she'd given her for Christmas.

"Let go of me a sec," her mum said, then she'd taken off the necklace she always wore and placed it carefully round Shannon's neck. It had two interlocking hearts, one of them studded with what Shannon had always thought were real diamonds when it had been Nan's. Now she knew better, but it was no less precious.

"You can't," said Shannon as her mum fumbled with the clasp. "You'll feel lost without it." Ever since Nan died, it had been her mum's most treasured possession.

"I want you to have it," her mum said. "It's to remind you that you come from a long line of strong women who don't take any shit."

Her mum took photos and videos of the house when the old housekeeper, Mrs Pushkin, wasn't around. She said the Harringtons acted as if she was invisible and the housekeeper had exacting standards, but that was to be expected. Shannon could see the main house was amazing, but her mum lived in a basic wooden building called the bunkhouse, divided into two tiny bedrooms with a tatty kitchen and bathroom, which she shared with a young gardener called Bobby who was also there as a summer worker. Her mum said she wasn't in the bunkhouse much so it didn't matter. She was either working or out exploring on foot or by bus. The island looked beautiful, and the weather was stunning. "The only thing missing is you," her mum said on a video-call, and Shannon joked, "Have you double-checked they don't want me to come out to assist you?"

It was the daughters who really interested Shannon. They were totally unrelatable but immensely fascinating. Annabel was Shannon's age and she already had her own beachwear line. Emily, a year older, was being privately tutored to get into a top university in the States. Hearing about them from her mum was like dipping into a private reality show.

Shannon also heard about Bobby. There were two gardeners. An old guy, Ted, who'd been there for years and lived somewhere else on the island, and this young one called Bobby who was there to do the heavy lifting. "He's twenty-one, Shan, but he seems much younger," her mum explained when she first told Shannon about him. "Vulnerable. The girls are really mean to him, but not in front of the adults. Just me. I guess I don't count. I've told him he needs to stand up for himself."

Three weeks after she'd been on Fengari, her mum

phoned up in a rage. "I'm going to tell you what those girls have done," she said, her voice shaking with anger. "They were bored. Bored! Their friends were busy, so they told Bobby he had the afternoon off and they were taking him to a beach the other side of the island. Sounds nice of them, doesn't it? But wait until you hear what they did."

Shannon had just come back from a party with Ela. She lay on the sofa to listen while Ela raided the kitchen cupboards for snacks. She could tell her mum was pacing, which she did when she was agitated.

"He's only just come back," said her mum, "and I can't tell you how furious I am. Emily drove them all there, then she and Annabel told him to go swimming, and when he was in the water they left him behind, taking all this things, including his clothes and suntan lotion. They drove home! He walked barefoot all the way back – sunburnt but shivering because he was in nothing but his swimming shorts. Said he couldn't find any buses and he didn't know any taxi numbers. He's in a terrible state."

"Poor guy," said Shannon.

"I told the girls what I thought of them and they just laughed." Her mum gave a long sigh, and Shannon caught the Coco Pops bar that Ela threw at her. She was missing her mum, but it didn't sound too bad out there, and spending the summer with Ela's family was fun.

The next time her mum phoned she said she'd told Rosie Harrington that Annabel and Emily were bullying Bobby, and Shannon's stomach turned uneasily.

"Was that wise?" she murmured. Bad stuff went down all the time at college, and anyone who dared wade in got caught in the crossfire.

Her mum was indignant. "Shannon, you don't turn a blind eye when that sort of thing happens right under your nose. You don't let people get away with bullying, especially when it's someone you care about."

Shannon thought about the time her mum had lost a job for being outspoken. Bex had a mouth on her, as Nan used to say. There were in-your-face people at college who went on marches and stuck posters around the building, and talked passionately about things that were unfair. That's what she imagined her mum had been like, until she'd got pregnant with Shannon and dropped out of education. Sometimes Shannon felt guilty for coming along and making her mum's life hard. She'd told Nan that once, and Nan had laughed and said, "You daft thing."

"What did Rosie Harrington say when you told her about the bullying?" Shannon asked.

Her mum tutted and exhaled loudly. "Said it was young people having a joke, or something."

Over the weeks, Shannon stopped answering the phone when her mum rang in the early hours, forgetting the time difference, to mouth off about something the girls had done. Shannon would listen to the voicemails in the morning and wonder if her mum was becoming too fixated on the girls' behaviour.

One afternoon as Shannon was leaving college, her

mum video-called to say the girls had taken the ladder while Bobby was up on the roof fixing a loose tile. He hadn't been able to get anyone's attention, so he'd attempted to ease himself down to a window ledge, lost his footing and fell. "He had to have stitches in his arm, Shannon," said her mum. "He was lucky. He might have broken his neck."

Shannon sympathized, but told her mum to keep out of it. The girls were clearly nasty, but she needed to look out for herself and focus on the job. Besides, Bobby wasn't some child – surely he should be saying something?

But then Bobby went out one day and didn't come back. Shannon's mum couldn't reach him on his phone. She told Shannon that she thought something was very wrong but the Harringtons didn't seem bothered, although they were annoyed he hadn't shown up for work. Rosie said sometimes staff did that – left without the courtesy of handing in their notice. Shannon's mum said Bobby hadn't taken anything with him apart from his phone, although he wasn't answering it, but Rosie had merely shrugged. Four days went by and on the fifth Bobby's body washed up in a cove. Shannon's mum went to the police.

And everything spiralled.

CHAPTER 6

Shannon knew the conversation was too stilted when she sat down at the large table for dinner with Annabel, Rosie and Douglas Harrington. The real Lydia would have kept it going better. Been more charming and amusing, asked more questions and pumped Annabel for more information about her friends to look for connections. She'd seen Lydia chatting with customers of all different ages. It came easily to her. She exuded the confidence of someone brought up to believe that people should listen to whatever she had to say.

Being on Fengari, seeing the bunkhouse out of the window, the terracotta monster, sitting in the same room as the Harringtons, thinking so hard about her mum – all this was messing with her concentration. She had to sharpen up.

"I'm think I'm still jet-lagged," she said to explain herself, but immediately it sounded pathetic. The Harringtons travelled all over the place.

Rosie nodded and offered her a second helping of the roast chicken and layered creamy potato dish, which Shannon turned down. Her stomach was too unsettled to eat. She watched Annabel scoop tomatoes from the salad with the long-handled salad spoon and mop up the juices on her plate with a chunk of fresh crusty white bread, noting the cutlery she wasn't using, the way she delved into the salad to retrieve another slice of tomato with her fingers. If Shannon had done that as a guest, would that have been bad manners?

"How often do you go to your little place in Scotland?" grunted Douglas. He was red in the face from the wine. "Where is it again?" His tone was dismissive.

Good question, Shannon thought, struggling to remember that detail. *Keep it vague*, she decided.

"In the middle of nowhere – the Highlands." Shannon rolled her eyes dramatically for comedic effect, as she'd seen Lydia do many times. "Trust my parents to buy somewhere where it's less sunny than London."

"What do you even do up there?" asked Annabel.

"Stay in bed to keep warm, and eat haggis. The haggis part is a joke. I can't stand it," said Shannon. It was a quote direct from Lydia herself. She looked at Annabel. "I mean, the scenery is amazing, and our cottage is pretty, but it's so boring."

Annabel said, "If my parents made me stay in a cold holiday cottage, I'd die. Unless we were skiing, of course."

Rosie put her cutlery down with a smug look. "We're so very lucky to have Clifftop House. It's such a cherished bolthole for us." She focused back on Shannon. "When you were here last, you were all very excited about your cousin getting a part in a West End show. I was trying to remember what it was."

Cousins. Shannon had learned the cousins' names. It must have been Tilly or Mia, but neither was acting now. They both had upmarket catering jobs – she could have told Rosie all about those, right down to Mia's recent promotion. She felt hot under the armpits as Rosie frowned.

"I know it was one of your uncle Graham's daughters," said Rosie. "Was it Tilly? You were going to see it as soon as you got back to London."

"Oh yesss," said Shannon. "I'd forgotten about that." She had to swerve the conversation but nothing came to her. She was left with no option but to knock over her glass of water. She leapt to her feet while Annabel looked at her as if she was a total idiot.

After Rosie had found a tea towel to mop it up, Shannon excused herself to go to the loo, remembering not to use the word *toilet*, acting flustered although there wasn't much acting required. She quickly texted Lydia, and Lydia sent back a laughing emoji face with *Tilly. Les Misérables. Played*

Cosette for about three months. Everything else OK? Are they falling for it? Give me all the deets!

Shannon messaged back: *Thanks! Yes I think so. It's funnnn! More details later.* Then she stood, leaning against the back of the toilet door for a couple of moments, catching her breath, letting the heat in her body dissipate against the coolness of the wood.

Back at the table she said, "Sorry about that. It was Tilly, by the way. *Les Misérables.* I can't believe I'd forgotten about that. Everyone was so excited about it at the time. She hasn't done any acting for ages. She teaches cooking to people working in ski chalets now."

"How wonderful!" said Rosie, and she reminisced about the cookery course she'd been sent on by her parents after finishing school.

Another bottle of wine was opened. Shannon had poured half of hers away into the sink during the bustle of getting things on the table at the beginning of the meal and Douglas losing his glasses. Now, as Rosie tried to top up her glass, she murmured, "I'm fine, thanks." Where she came from, people under eighteen didn't drink with parents. They drank to get drunk with their mates. If Shannon started drinking, everything would be lost. She bit her thumbnail, then stopped. She had to remember where she was.

Show me a sign that you're here with me, Mum. I need you.
Nothing.

When Rosie got up to make coffee, Douglas stood up

57

with his wine glass and walked towards his study, telling Rosie to bring his coffee to him there. She nodded and said, "OK, Doug. Roll on darling Mrs P getting here so she can look after you."

Annabel yawned, and looked towards her phone on the work surface.

Panic fluttered in Shannon's chest. If she didn't reel Annabel in soon, she might be lost for ever, Lydia relegated to "daughter of a friend of her mum's". A sad little add-on to the occasional family dinner. She had to wriggle her way into the Harringtons' world and become accepted, at least until Emily got here and she could finally execute her plan. She knew the moment would come. She *deserved* it.

"I saw there was a place to get pedicures in Fengari Town," she said, focusing on her enunciation, imitating Lydia's lilting, rolling way of speaking. "The Turtle Dove?" She hadn't seen it yet, but she'd researched the most expensive place to get beauty treatments done. "I'm going to check it out tomorrow afternoon. You want to come with me, Annabel? My treat?"

Annabel propped herself up on one elbow. "The head massages there are good," she said.

"Really?" said Shannon. "We should have one of those as well." She watched Annabel straighten up.

"Yeah, sure," said Annabel, shrugging.

Shannon gave a brief smile. If she was too friendly, Annabel would take it as a weakness. "OK, I'll book and let you know what time to meet." She added, "I'd better go.

I need an early night," and could sense Rosie and Annabel were relieved.

"We'll call you a taxi. Annabel, darling, would you use your app? Marvellous to see you, Lydia. Come for a swim next time?"

"Yes! Thank you." Shannon made herself sound more enthusiastic than she felt about the prospect of a swim. She would be fine if she didn't go out of her depth. Lydia, of course, was a confident swimmer. She'd been in a swim squad lower down the school. "Thanks for a nice evening. I'll tell Mummy all about it, although –" she made a big thing of lowering her voice – "I've asked her to give me some space. I don't need her breathing down my neck."

"Of course," murmured Rosie.

"Ten minutes for the taxi," said Annabel, looking at the app. She continued to scroll through her phone with her long skinny fingers, silver rings on most of them. Shannon could see she didn't look after her nails.

Shannon looked out at the garden. The light was beginning to fade. What she could see of it was immaculate. All neat edges and flowers in bloom. No brown or yellow leaves, not a single straggly stem. She wondered if there was a new summer gardener.

What if the Harringtons thought keeping an eye on her meant one dinner and the occasional text to check she was OK, and she was never invited back here?

"Annabel, show Lydia the summer house while you're waiting," said Rosie. She gave her tinkling, affected laugh.

"That's where the young folk like to hang out when they're here, Lydia. I don't ask questions."

"God, Mum. You sound ancient. 'Young folk'." Annabel rolled her eyes but stood up and opened the door to the garden. There was a sharp smell of earth from where the flower beds had been watered. Rosie glanced down at Shannon's silver sandals.

"I'll take them off," Shannon said hurriedly. She slipped a finger through each back strap and held them up in one hand. Walking around barefoot with expensive sandals dangling as if they were worth nothing was a straight-up Harrington move, even if hers were too blingy.

Rosie indicated some brown Crocs near the door. They were big enough to be Douglas's, and one of the inner soles was folded over. Yuck. Shannon unfolded it, put her feet inside and resisted grimacing.

"I'll say goodbye now," said Rosie. "By the time you've walked there and back, the cab will be here. Give Doug's Crocs back to Annabel when you've finished with them."

Ew, so they *were* Doug's. Shannon sensed Annabel making an I-can't-believe-you're-making-me-do-this face to her mum behind her back. She picked up her pink tote and went down the steps to the path, feeling for her necklace, pushing the pointy end of the biggest heart into her thumb until it hurt. She'd seen from the upstairs window which way the bunkhouse was, so veered left. Annabel caught up with her, her feet in scruffy Birkenstocks.

Shannon stiffened as the brick bunkhouse came into

view between the trees. Her stomach rolled at the thought of her mum being burned alive in the old wooden bunkhouse. She could feel her vision blur.

Her mum was inside her head now. *You come from a long line of strong women.*

"We call it the bunkhouse," said Annabel, as Shannon took deep breaths. "You should see the gardener who's living in there at the moment. Oh my God." Annabel was suddenly animated, pushing both sides of her hair behind her ears. Shannon could see the dark holes where her lobes were pierced but she hadn't bothered to put earrings in. "He. Is. Fit. As."

It was hard to smile, but Shannon managed it.

Annabel pointed at a different path. "The summer house is up here."

Shannon stumbled after her, her vision better now. The summer house had its own decking and outdoor furniture. Inside there was a huge room with two sofas, which Annabel said turned into beds, a table and chairs and built-in floor-to-ceiling cupboards. Leading off from it on one side was a small kitchen, and off the other side there was a shower room and toilet. The furnishings were simple but solid. The kitchen was a glossy pale grey and looked like the showroom of some flats Shannon had visited with her mum one Sunday afternoon when they had nothing else to do. It was a totally different league to the bunkhouse, which she'd seen in her mum's videos.

"It's basic but it's away from the house and no one

hassles us here," said Annabel. She opened one of the cupboard doors and there were two stacked-up boxes with *CAUTION* stamped on them. "Fireworks. We had an amazing end-of-summer party last year. Invited pretty much everyone we know on the island. Emily and I did the whole thing ourselves. We're going to do it again this year."

They'd had a party after everything they did? Shannon stepped outside and crushed a fallen yellow flower head under a brown Croc, grinding it into the decking. She imagined smoke filling up inside the summer house, flames reaching higher up the walls.

Annabel's phone pinged as she pulled the door closed behind them. "Taxi's here."

"Don't you lock the door?" asked Shannon.

Annabel looked surprised. "The crime rate on this island is really low. When there's a fight over a parking space, it makes the Fengari news app." She pointed at a large shed tucked back against a fence. "We don't even lock that, and the new ride-on mower cost a fortune."

They walked past the pool, which was fenced off with black metal railings. It was as big as the lido where Shannon had paddled when she was little, but that's as far as the comparison went; the water here was clear, and Shannon could see the blue-and-white patterned tiles at the bottom. A steady thrum came from the building where the boiler and changing room must be. Lights in the pool suddenly came on, and it looked magical. Like a photo shoot – or a scene in a Netflix thriller.

Annabel said, "Tell me if that gardener isn't hot."

Shannon turned and saw someone not much older than them walking out of the changing room in swim shorts that clung to his muscly legs. His resting face was intense, as if he was thinking about something, his body pretty much what you'd expect from a guy who was doing physical work all day.

"He's allowed to swim in the evenings if we're not using the pool," said Annabel, as they watched him dive elegantly into the deep end. When he came up to the surface, he flicked his head to one side in an attempt to shift hair out of his eyes, and he saw them. He nodded in acknowledgement before plunging his face back into the water to front-crawl to the end. He didn't seem intimidated. Not at all like Bobby, then.

"We're going to have fun with him," said Annabel.

"What d'you mean?" asked Shannon.

"Show him around Fengari," said Annabel. "Summer's for having fun, isn't it?"

Shannon wanted to swipe her sandals round Annabel's head. She imagined a sharp heel slashing her cheek.

"That's the tennis court," said Annabel unnecessarily as they walked past it to the side gate. "That net needs mending. You'd think our gardeners would work on their own initiative, but they're really thick. I'll have to add it to their list."

The taxi was waiting for her in the driveway. Shannon stepped out of the gross Crocs back into her sandals, holding on to the gate for support. She had a flashback to getting ready for a night out with Ela, holding on to each other as they changed into their heels. But Shannon could tell Annabel was the type of person who would pretend to be there for you and then let you fall. Before Shannon got into the back seat, Annabel gave her a brief, automatic hug, the sort where there was barely any touching involved.

"I'll let you know what time to meet at the Turtle Dove tomorrow," said Shannon.

Annabel nodded. "Sure."

Shannon climbed into the back seat and exhaled. She was exhausted. Being Lydia for hours at a time required more mental effort than she'd realized. There'd been several moments when she might have given herself away and she couldn't be that sloppy again. She was here for one purpose only and she was going to make sure she achieved it.

Whatever it took.

CHAPTER 7

Wednesday

Although Shannon called the Turtle Dove during her first break in lessons, she kept Annabel hanging, and only messaged her at one p.m. to say she'd managed to get an appointment for two fifteen p.m. She didn't want Annabel to think she was too eager. It was a risk, but Annabel responded straight away and said she'd see her then. Having studied Annabel's social media, she knew Annabel enjoyed crushing people if they didn't act tough enough with her, but she also took offence if she felt not enough respect was being given to her. It was a fine line to tread. She had to stay close to Annabel, at least until Emily showed up.

The Turtle Dove was a set of treatment rooms in shades of teal and beige, where staff whispered and everything was calm. Apart from Annabel. She sat in a chair, her feet being scrubbed and massaged, while she recorded a voice-note for her friend Maddie, who was also on Fengari, and complained about someone called Piglet. Shannon, meanwhile, was locked in a brief Insta exchange with Clarissa Cornwallis.

Clarissa: *Delighted you had dinner at Clifftop House yesterday*

Shannon/Lydia: *Annabel & I are having spa treatments today*

Clarissa: *Have fun darling! Send photos x*

Shannon looked down at her bare feet, soaking in perfumed water. Would a mother know her seventeen-year-old daughter's feet? Possibly. Shannon's toes might look too chubby. She took a sneaky shot of Annabel instead, and sent that.

Shannon/Lydia: *You can have a photo of Annabel*

Clarissa: *Lovely! I must make time for a pedicure this week. What was the name of the therapist you rated when you went to the salon on Hooper Street?*

Shannon had to hope that Lydia would chime in soon. The previous evening, the two of them had messaged back and forth for about an hour when she'd returned from Clifftop House, even though it was in the early hours for Lydia. Shannon told her about the house and the Harringtons as if it was one big joke. In turn, Lydia gushed about Italy and how special it was to be spending time with Crispin.

Shannon needed to make sure no one on Fengari posted any photos of her on their socials in case anyone showed the Cornwallis family. Lydia and Crispin had promised to be careful too, and had made a big thing of going on social media breaks for the summer. Lydia had tried to make her hashtag #NoSocialsSummer trend, which defeated the point, and illustrated how stupid she was.

Mario, Lydia replied. *He's like the head person.* Clarissa responded with three kisses. Via iMessage, Lydia sent a laughing emoji and Shannon sent back a thumbs up. Her heart sank as she saw the dots that told her Lydia was typing something else, but she was the only person Lydia could confide in – Shannon had insisted nobody else could be in on the deception – so she had to act like a supportive friend. The last thing she needed was for Lydia and Crispin to come home early. She needed them to be having the time of their lives, their secret adding excitement to their relationship.

Lyra/Lydia: *OMG can you believe it? Crispin's mum WhatsApped him to say she was glad he was on*

holiday with the boys because she reckoned I am too high
maintenance!!! What a bitch!

Shannon smoothed it over, assuring Lydia that she was the perfectly normal amount of maintenance, until a beauty therapist asked if she and Annabel would like their head and shoulder massages in the same treatment room. Before Annabel could answer, Shannon said, "Why not. We can chat."

The two of them got comfortable on the luxurious towels on top of the massage tables, which had been placed side by side, and Shannon hoped they were bonding as they murmured to each other how they both didn't want their hair to get oily.

"Ahh, I so need this," said Annabel as her therapist started by straightening her head. Shannon couldn't resist imagining a sudden twist of the neck. "This was a good idea."

"Definitely," said Shannon, who couldn't allow herself to completely relax. Being Lydia required so much effort, especially this reeling in of Annabel. "I'm starting the summer how I mean to go on. We should do this regularly."

Annabel grunted. "That sounds good." She closed her eyes. "Last summer was so lame..."

Don't react. Shannon's head felt hot. She clutched the towel with her clammy hands and took a deep breath and waited for Annabel to continue.

"There's, like, a group of us whose families all have

houses here. My family has had a house on the island the longest of anyone we know, which practically makes us Fengari royalty. Anyway, not everyone comes each summer, and last year Mads was on the island but too loved up with her boyfriend, Zander."

Shannon concentrated on breathing slowly as she turned on to her stomach for the next part of the neck and shoulder massage.

Annabel had already turned over and her voice was muffled now. "Mads and I want to do a girls' night out with our friend Piglet tomorrow at George's Shack. Just the three of us. But Piglet has gone and booked an area and invited a load of people. So selfish."

Shannon had read about George's Shack. It had been the first café-bar on Fengari and had achieved celebrity status. The walls were lined with photographs of George, squat and bearded with an enormous grin, with his arm round every celebrity who'd ever been to the island.

"What did you do last summer without your friends?" It slipped out before she could check herself.

"Hung around with my sister and got monumentally bored," said Annabel, then yawned. "But we always find entertainment eventually. We're resourceful."

Shannon clenched her jaw. Her masseuse said, "You're so tense. Lots of knots in your neck and shoulders."

Annabel didn't say any more until the staff left them to relax in the room for ten minutes.

"The one who was massaging you had awful skin,

didn't she?" said Annabel. "I shrank away from her when she came into the room to let her know I couldn't bear her touching me."

"Her skin was grim," agreed Shannon, hating herself for it. This was clearly the sort of chat that Annabel lived for.

"She shouldn't be working here. They should keep her in a back office or something." She shuddered dramatically. "How could you bear it?"

"I had my eyes closed," said Shannon, "and imagined she was Seb." She paused for dramatic effect, then made sure by her expression that Annabel knew she was joking.

"You wish," laughed Annabel, delighted. "He's all mine."

"I don't even know what he looks like," said Shannon. "Show me a photo."

Annabel pulled one up on her phone, and Shannon nodded approval and decided he looked exactly how she thought he would. As if he thought he was better than everyone else.

They settled into silence and Shannon thought about her finances. She'd amassed a good sum of money, but there'd been a lot to pay for, including the fake passport and a whole new wardrobe of clothes. Thank goodness these beauty treatments would go on Lydia's credit card to be paid for by Clarissa.

"Super kind of you to pay," gushed Annabel as Shannon tapped in the PIN in the reception area. "We should have got a discount because of that woman's gross skin, though."

Shannon laughed, wincing inwardly.

Annabel's phone pinged and she said, "Oh! Mads is here." She rushed to the front door and, as it closed behind her, Shannon could hear her shout, "Maddie Morgan-Foster!"

Shannon left a hefty cash tip and went outside to join them.

"Mads, this is Lydia," said Annabel, not bothering to do the introduction the other way round. Maddie was tall and skinny, with brown hair streaked with pink and a mini sundress in a very colourful floral material. In her hair she had a huge fabric flower attached with a clip.

"Hi," said Shannon.

"Wait. You're Lydia Cornwallis?" said Maddie, in a way which made Shannon's heart thump in panic. She nodded.

"From Walton House?"

"Yep."

Maddie frowned. "That's odd. Perhaps I'm muddling you up with someone else." She spoke in a slow, drawn-out way, as if she was formulating her thoughts as she went along.

"Lydia's mum was at school with my mum," says Annabel.

"Family friends," Shannon said firmly, her heart beating faster now.

"I met a Lydia at Christmas," said Maddie, the flower in her hair flopping forward. "From Walton House. But it wasn't you."

Shannon's mouth was dry. "Yeah, I'm not the only Lydia at Wally's." She wasn't sure about this. She'd memorized everyone in Lydia's year group, but she hadn't seen a list of all the girls in the whole school. She pretended to catch a bug crawling along her arm.

When she looked back, Maddie had lost the quizzical look and was wiggling her hips, singing, "Just a few hours to go!"

"You must be excited," said Annabel.

"My boyfriend Zander's coming over on the six p.m. ferry," explained Maddie when it was clear Annabel wasn't going to. "He's at Portland. He knows a few Wally girls. He probably knows which Lydia it was I met."

Damn. Portland was a boys' school a short distance from Walton House. Lydia had spoken of joint ventures – plays and debating clubs.

"Cool," said Shannon. "Can't wait to meet him." She had a sense of inevitability. She'd known something like this would happen. It would be OK, she told herself. She could handle it.

"I'll see you soon, Lydia," said Annabel, dismissing her. "You've got the number of the taxi firm to get back to Linton Lodge, yeah?"

"You should come to George's Shack tomorrow night," Maddie said, tucking a few strands of pinkish hair behind her ear.

Bingo.

"A friend of ours has booked an area there from eight."

Maddie looked at Annabel. "She should, shouldn't she, Bels?"

"Sure," said Annabel. "Good place to meet the right sort of people."

People like her and Maddie, she meant. Posh, white people. She thought of the corner of London she came from, of the many different cultures and nationalities. Of Ela, who identified as seventy-five per cent Bangladeshi and twenty-five per cent English even though she'd never been to Bangladesh.

"If you're sure. . ." said Shannon with a little smile. "I'd hate to gatecrash."

"Not at all," said Annabel. She glanced at her pedicured feet. They looked a million times better than they had when she'd turned up at the Turtle Dove. "Stick with me. I'll show you a good time."

"Thanks," said Shannon. "I'll see you tomorrow, then." She turned away, the smile still on her face.

CHAPTER 8

Thursday

Before going to Fengari Training College the next morning, Shannon nibbled on one of the flower chocolates she'd forgotten to take to Clifftop House and sent a message to Lydia.

Shannon/Lydia: *Are there any other Lydias at Walton House? Someone (Maddie Morgan-Foster) said they met a Lydia from Walton House at Christmas. Also, do you know a Zander from Portland? Help!*

She hoped it sounded jokey enough. She finished

straightening her hair so she looked more like Lydia, popped in her brown contact lenses and left her half-eaten chocolate on the bedside table. It tasted bitter.

During her lessons, she considered what to wear to George's Shack. It meant she wasn't concentrating and some of the mistakes she made in her maths were genuine, which was a bonus.

She knew from looking at photos online that it was the tourists who tended to bling up for the restaurant, not the wealthy locals. Her plain burgundy jumpsuit might be the thing – with her silver Jimmy Choos, which would be the only ostentatious part of her outfit.

There was no reply from Lydia when she went back to her room. That was fine. It wasn't an emergency.

In the afternoon, Shannon went back to the Turtle Dove and, thanks to the tip she'd left the previous day, she managed to get an immediate appointment with a hairstylist to pin her hair up in an intricate chignon. The make-up she could do herself. She'd been addicted to YouTube make-up tutorials since for ever, and, with this crowd, less was more anyway.

There was still no reply from Lydia. It was making her jittery now. Lydia wasn't travelling anywhere without phone signal. They'd agreed to check in with each other at least once a day even if they had nothing to specific to say.

On her way back to her room, Helen stopped her to ask what time she wanted a table for dinner.

"I'm sorry, I should have told you earlier," said Shannon

with a look that she hoped was apologetic enough. "I'm going to George's Shack this evening with Annabel Harrington."

"Splendid!" said Helen. "They're such a lovely family."

"Oh, and is there any chance I could have room service in future? I'd find it easier," said Shannon, glad to have got that out of the way. She had no idea if she'd be eating at George's Shack, but she wasn't hungry.

"That's fine," said Helen. "As long as you're happy, I'm happy, and I know your mother will be too."

When Shannon arrived at eight, neither Annabel nor Maddie was there. There were only two guys, chatting with a petite girl. Great. She was waaaay too early.

She skirted round the cordoned-off area to sit on a stool at a different part of the bar and ordered herself a non-alcoholic cocktail. The "shack" was a deluxe wooden structure, with roofs at different heights, and a relaxed, moneyed vibe where lots of people knew each other. She checked her phone – still nothing from Lydia – then watched the clientele by looking in the mirror behind the bar. Did her jumpsuit fit in? She was pretty sure it did. She rubbed the heart on her necklace until it felt warm.

"Lydia?"

She'd sunk into a daydream, imagining her mum on the bar stool next to her, bemused by her drab clothing but admiring her bravery. She swung round to see a boy in a navy jacket with an amused expression on his face at having startled her. He'd been one of the guys in the cordoned-off area. He had intense dark eyes, neat eyebrows, dark brown hair which was one trim away from looking too sharp, and standard posh entitlement, although he reminded her of an Algerian boy from college who definitely wasn't entitled.

"Yes?"

"So you *are* Lydia! Piglet wins. Those two had a bet." Without much of a pause, he shouted, "It *is* Lydia!"

Was that a French accent?

The petite girl with reddish-blonde hair curled round her shoulders and a black body-con dress danced from side to side with exaggerated glee, then rubbed her thumb and forefingers together in a money gesture. The boy next to her, in a boring pale blue shirt and beige chinos and similar coloured hair, shook his head slowly and fiddled about with his Apple Watch. Was he transferring money to Piglet?

"Nice," said Shannon, hoping the guy next to her caught the sarcasm.

"Apologies, that was rude. Of them, and me. I am Victor de Courtois." He leaned in for a posh hug, which she wasn't ready for, but he smelled nice. If she'd had to guess what it was, she'd have gone for sandalwood. Clarissa Cornwallis Flowers had a range of diffusers and he smelled like one of those. "From Paris. I'm a friend of Ollie's. He's her brother." Victor nodded in their direction. "Come and join us. They are waiting." He sounded impatient. Arrogant.

"Well, we wouldn't want to keep them waiting, would

we?" said Shannon. He would not make her feel inferior. Her eyes flickered to the mirror and she saw Victor check himself out in it, adjusting the edge of his navy jacket. Underneath there was a crisp white shirt, with a trim of turquoise where the buttons were.

"Jacket looks fine," she said, making the sarcasm clearer this time.

He stood up straighter, embarrassed at having been caught. "It's one of my favourites," he said. "Bespoke."

There was the noise of a group of people arriving, chatting and laughing. Shannon heard Annabel before she saw her. Pre-drinks had definitely been consumed. "We need a photo to mark the beginning of summer. Me and you, Mads, with Piglet. Is George here tonight? I want a photo of us with George." She caught sight of Shannon. "Lyds! Darling – you made it! Come here and meet everyone. Everyone's dying to get to know you!" Her glow up was unreal – she wore a fitted purple sleeveless dress, her make-up was subtle, her hair was shiny and her ears flashed with diamonds, and probably not the fake sort.

Shannon took a deep breath and got down from her bar stool. "Bels!" she called back, and went in for a light hug. "Love the dress."

"FYI," said Annabel, "this is one of the places where as long as you're with locals, you don't need ID to drink alcohol. Just don't do anything to ruin the Shack's reputation." She made her way to the wall of

78

black-and-white photographs, her arm looped through Maddie's. Maddie, her pink-streaked hair in loose curls, was in a dress which looked as if it had last been worn to a tea dance in a distant era.

Someone told Annabel that George wasn't in, and she pouted. "That's not fair. He's usually here on a Thursday night. Pigs? Where are you, Pigs?" She pulled Piglet to her and angled her phone for a selfie. "It's going to be an amazing summer."

Victor popped up at the back, photobombing.

Piglet turned and started giggling.

"Whoever you are, butt out," said Annabel, her face switching from fun mode to annoyance.

"He's Victor, Ollie's friend," said Piglet.

"Oh," said Annabel. "OK. But you can still butt out." She took a few photos, then said, "Next photo – Fengari old-timers. Only people who have houses on the island, please. Come and line up. Ollie, that's you." She shouted out other names, and Shannon had never seen such a bunch of people so pleased with themselves.

Shannon turned away, and almost spilled her drink over a boy with a round, red-flushed face and receding hairline. He looked seventeen going on thirty-five.

"Are you Lydia Cornwallis?" he asked.

"Yes," she said. "And you're..."

"Zander, Maddie's boyfriend," said the boy. "I probably know a load of your friends. Isn't Pippy Rogers one of your best buddies?" He shot out a hand for a formal handshake.

She took it, firmly aware of a slick of sweat in her armpits and behind her knees.

"Pippy, yes, she is. . ." she began. Lydia had coached her on her group of friends, none of whom were in on their secret. Pippy, Pippy. . . Shannon's mind went blank. Was she the one who was into horses? "Pips is a real sweetheart."

"Isn't she?" said Zander approvingly. "So who do you know at Portland?"

"James Mortimer is hilarious," she said. She'd practised different scenarios over and over in the shop with Lydia, who assured her that everyone would have a story about James.

"James? He ate five pages of *Macbeth* during an English exam," said Zander.

Shannon laughed. "Were you at the party where he knocked over the ice sculpture? I only saw it when it was in a billion pieces!" Lydia had told her that most Wallys and Portlanders in their year had been at this party, along with so many other people, no one would have been sure exactly who or hadn't been there.

Zander's eyes were almost sucked into laughter lines as he recalled the incident.

Victor came up to them as Zander was impersonating James Mortimer apologizing for the ice sculpture incident. "Sorry to barge in," Victor said loudly, "but Annabel says she wants everybody in a group shot, and I've been ordered to round up everyone."

Zander laughed. "Annabel turns into a terrible bossyboots when she's had too much to drink."

Shannon wondered whether he ever called boys bossyboots. "I'll take the photo," she said quickly, before she was made to be *in* the photo.

"Eyes on Lydia," said Victor loudly to the small group posing in the middle of the room. He leapt in front of them and lay on the floor, propped up on an elbow. "If everyone smiles nicely, Lydia will turn round and we can all see the price tag on her jumpsuit."

"What?" Shannon felt behind her and sure enough there was a price tag. Her body flooded with heat. She remembered it had been marked down in H&M and there was a red sticker on the tag. How did these people feel about H&M? Would they think her bargain hunting wasn't the right sort of bargain hunting? *That she couldn't be Lydia?* "Why didn't you tell me before?" she wailed.

Everyone laughed, and she took a few shots.

"See?" said Victor. "Laughing faces. Perfect. And at least your jumpsuit wasn't from ... how do you say it? Primark?"

Shannon took a deep breath. "I'll have you know Primark do very good Christmas pyjamas!" She'd seen TikToks with posh people showing their bargains as if they were astonishingly clever for having unearthed them.

There was another ripple of laughter, which felt reassuring. She hadn't misstepped too badly. Piglet lurched forward and tugged at the label to remove it and Shannon murmured, "I'm so embarrassed. Thank you."

"Oh hun, I do this all the time," said Piglet soothingly.

Shannon gave her a grateful smile, and took shot after shot with different people's phones.

Her own vibrated in her pocket. When she checked it discreetly she saw it was a message from Lydia.

Lyra/Lydia: *Having the best time. There's a Lydia in the year below. Lydia Talbot. Don't remember Zander, but Crispin knows his friends and says he's a rowing bore.*

Shannon quickly did an online search for Lydia Talbot. She looked nothing like Shannon. Next she searched up Pippy. She could see Zander coming towards her, a bowl of glistening olives in one hand, a drink in the other. "So good to have a Wally to chat to," he said.

He held the bowl out next to her and she took an olive, popping it into her mouth and holding her hand up so he couldn't see her talking with an open mouth as she said, "Aren't you into rowing? I've definitely heard your name before."

Zander looked pleased. Shannon let him talk about a recent regatta at length, asking questions when the conversation flagged. After a bit, Maddie came over and entwined herself around him. The vintage dress had an amazing brooch pinned to it of a tiger face made from jewels. She saw Shannon look at it. "My family owned a tea plantation in India back in the day," she said. "So I have a thing about tigers."

"But tiger print is tacky," said Zander firmly. "I don't

let her wear it."

"I thought I'd met Lydia at Christmas," she told Zander, stroking his ear. She sounded pretty drunk. "I told Annabel that we'd done Jagerbombs together, but it wasn't the right Lydia."

"It must have been Lydia in the year below," Shannon said quickly, not giving a surname in case Maddie remembered and looked her up. "So how did you two meet?" she asked, moving on.

They looked at each other and smiled, and Maddie went on about a party given by a mutual friend and something to do with a hot tub and an Uber discount, and Shannon smiled and nodded, and looked at them both and thought, *If you hadn't been so wrapped up in each other, perhaps your friend and her sister wouldn't have gone looking for fun by tormenting their staff.*

CHAPTER 9

The evening began to float in front of Shannon's eyes. She drank soda water with ice and lime because it looked like gin and tonic, batting away offers of more drinks, implying that she'd already had plenty to drink. The amount of people grew, and the noise expanded. Everyone's hair was shiny, teeth dazzling, skin glowing. Compared to south-east London, where she was from, it was also undeniably very white, apart from Victor and the two guys behind the bar. Ela would be sighing in Shannon's ear if she was here.

She mingled, her head aching as she worked at staying in character, matching everyone's energy, their loudness and their easy entitlement. She wanted to be part of

Annabel's world for a while, to experience what it was like to live like her and Emily before she watched them squirm like maggots on a fishing line.

Questions came at her.

What school do you go to?

Which part of London are you from?

Do you know X (where X was someone who either lived in London or had a connection to Walton House School)?

Cornwallis – was your father something to do with Cornwallis and Mather, the law firm? No?

It was easier sometimes to pretend to be airy and hopeless to wriggle out of the tougher questions. People seemed to expect it, even like her for it. One guy even patted her arm and said, "You're such a charming little thing," and as he bored on, she hissed insults at him in her head for being so patronizing when she was stone cold sober, and he was drunk and stupid.

Everyone was searching for a connection, a way to check she was sufficiently one of them. She smiled and listened and caught sight in a mirror of the little fake diamonds on her necklace, twinkling like frantic fireflies. She had to admit, she felt intoxicated on surviving so far on Fengari. She felt like a Somebody.

She took a photo of the crowd and sent it to Lydia, telling her she was having a good night, and Lydia sent back a kiss emoji.

As the night wore on, people drifted away, on to somewhere else, or back home. Shannon found Annabel and said she was going to buy a round of drinks for everyone and then she was calling it a night.

"There's still quite a crowd here," said Annabel, looking around her, unsteady on her feet. "Are you sure?"

"Yes," Shannon said, swaying a little to match Annabel. "It was so nice of you guys to include me tonight."

Annabel said, "I'm glad you're here, Lyds. My friends really like you. Stay a bit longer."

That was worth a round of drinks.

Around forty-five minutes later, Zander told her that he, Maddie, Annabel and a few others were going to buy patties in Fengari Old Town and sit on the beach awhile, and she should join them. "The meat is organic and properly cooked, in case you're worried by street food," he said. "They do vegetarian ones too."

"Sure," she said, wincing at his pomposity as he carried on explaining about hygiene ratings of street food. She'd never had a patty before, but she guessed they were like spicy Cornish pasties.

"There you are!" said Maddie, coming over and grabbing his hand. The curls in her hair were dropping. "Lydia – you're coming with us, aren't you?" She beckoned over Piglet and Piglet's brother, Ollie, blandly beautiful in a men's perfume advert kind of way. Whenever Shannon had seen him during the evening, he'd been nodding at something someone else was saying and drinking steadily, his face devoid of much thought or emotion.

"I'm so hungry," said Piglet excitedly in a high-pitched

86

voice. "Ollie, is Victor coming with us? And where is Bels?"

Shannon reached for the soft, grey cotton wrap, which was tightly rolled in her bag, and draped it round her shoulders. It was from an organic stall in Borough Market (very popular with girls from Walton House, according to the Insta accounts Lydia followed). She left George's Shack with Annabel, Maddie, Zander, Victor, Ollie and Piglet, gasping quietly at the sight of the huge full moon.

They jumped into taxis which were waiting outside the bar, and it was a short ride to Fengari Old Town. Nobody paid at the other end, because such trips were put on parents' accounts.

They walked down a small pedestrianized street. Shannon's feet were tired in her sandals, but every time she looked down at them, they brought her a little glow of pleasure. The shops were closed but brightly lit. They all had beautifully styled windows. The toy shop window had a sweet display of soft toys playing board games.

"Bet you have to play a lot of board games in Scotland," said Annabel, next to her. Her breath stank of sweet alcohol.

"Yeah," said Shannon with a fake little laugh. She walked closer to the window of the little jewellery shop her mum had told her about – it had been her favourite place to window shop. "Nice things," she said. "I need to come back here."

"It's one of the best shops on the whole island," said Annabel. "Everything is gorgeous in there."

87

"Those gold bangles are cute," Shannon said. "I love the ones with the leaf design etched in."

"Yes, me too. There's a matching necklace," said Annabel. She turned to Shannon. "What's the story with that?" She pointed at Shannon's gold-hearts necklace.

Shannon touched the hearts. "Sentimental value. I never take it off." She had a lie ready.

Annabel glanced at the others, who were moving further up the street towards a takeaway food shop. Not proper street food, then. "Nice, if you like that sort of thing."

Shannon could shove her hard and Annabel might hit her head on the stone paving. She could claim Annabel was drunk and had tripped. Annabel's sandals weren't as precarious as hers, but it would be totally plausible.

"Come on, you two!" called Piglet, waving madly at them. "Get a wriggle-piggle on."

"Piglet's called Piglet because she's small, right?" asked Shannon.

Annabel giggled. "Yes, she's always been little and pinkish. Don't you think her face is a bit like a pig's?" She giggled again. "She's always been ugly."

Shannon smiled as required.

They caught the others up and the smell of the yellow semicircles of dough and meat lifted her mood. Victor appeared to be buying a huge selection for everyone, and Shannon wondered if he was doing exactly the same as she had when she'd bought the round of drinks – inveigling his way into the group. It was his first time here. He carried the cardboard box ostentatiously to the beach, Piglet squealing that he was like the Pied Piper. At the edge of the beach, Shannon took off her sandals and felt the warm, silky sand between her toes. Even the sand was beautiful here. It was the colour of expensive vanilla ice cream, the sort without added colour.

"This is where we like to sit," explained Maddie when they arrived at a group of large rocks. She'd taken off her shoes too, and Shannon saw her toenails were painted all different bright colours. She wondered if Zander had given the go-ahead on those.

The rocks were smooth and still retained mild heat from the day's sun. Shannon sat on the edge of the group, next to Piglet, who was already tucking into a beef patty, holding it in its individual square of greaseproof paper, and Annabel, who was necking water from a bottle. The box of patties was passed round, and Shannon sunk her teeth into a chicken one, the spicy flavour so delicious she ate slowly to savour it. Maddie sat between Zander's bent legs, and Ollie and Victor sat at the highest point, Ollie explaining to Zander that he'd met Victor earlier in the summer when they'd done a sailing competition together.

"And now I'm having a little holiday," said Victor. "To get over the disappointment that I got silver."

"And I'm having a little holiday to reward myself, because I got gold," said Ollie, laughing in a fake, self-deprecating way, looking round to check everyone had heard him.

"Heard you're in the Maritime Hotel, Victor," said Maddie. "Can we come visit?"

Victor said, "Of course. They have a huge infinity pool. You people should come over for a swim. I'll get you passes."

"Which school do you go to?" Zander asked. There it was – that ridiculous question again.

"An international school in Paris," said Victor. "My parents run an art investment company there." He brushed crumbs off his precious navy jacket.

Shannon took another patty, vegetable this time, and listened to the girls talk about somebody they knew who'd gone to Paris to do a fashion course that summer.

She wiped her hands on a napkin, leaving it next to her bag and sandals, and walked across the sand to the water's edge. Holding up the trousers of her jumpsuit, she placed one foot, then the other, in the cold water, wincing only a tiny amount because she was aware the others were watching her.

She moved round in a little circle, taking in the shadowy light, the sea which stretched on until it merged with the ever-greying clouds and, on the shore, the properties adjoining the beach. Who from Broad Lee Academy in south-east London would ever believe she was here among these people? None. It had taken hard work – studying the island, the Harringtons, Lydia and her family and friends, working out the codes she'd need in order to pass as a person of status here, living and breathing the accent which would have caused everyone to ridicule her at college but made people accept her here.

A male figure in shorts and a T-shirt wandered through the shallow water in line with her, flip-flops in hand. In a few minutes one of them would have to move for the other.

It wasn't going to be her. Her days of standing back for someone were over, unless it furthered her goal.

When he came towards her, she recognized his face but couldn't place him. He gave her a brief smile. As he walked round her, it came to her: he was the gardener she'd seen in the Harringtons' swimming pool. His hair looked shorter now it was dry.

She walked back to the rocks, sand clinging to her feet, like sugar on a wet teaspoon. The others were laughing when she reached them.

"You so fancy Annabel's hot gardener!" said Maddie. "You were rooted to the spot!"

"I was working out how I knew him," said Shannon, more indignantly than she meant to.

"Hot but awkward, don't you think?" said Annabel. "We need to bring him out of his shell. Get him to live a little. He'll be a nice little project for this summer."

There was a general babble of conversation until Piglet said, "Didn't something happen to your gardener last year? I think my parents said he'd drowned."

Shannon tensed.

Everyone was silent. "Yes," said Annabel. "He did. There was something wrong with him. He wasn't right in the head; he even stole an ancient sculpture of ours."

There was a photo on Shannon's phone of Bobby with her mum, standing outside the bunkhouse, holding mugs of tea in the early morning sunshine, Bobby in his gardening uniform, her mum in her house staff uniform of black trousers and white top. Bobby was big. He could have knocked out Annabel with one punch. He should have done.

"Sounds as if he had big problems," said Maddie, plaiting her hair on one side absent-mindedly.

They didn't even know his name. Annabel was dabbing her mouth with a napkin, unperturbed by the conversation. Nobody mentioned the bunkhouse fire. Had it been hushed up? Did anyone other than the Harringtons and a few officials know that someone had died?

"Let's make some summer plans," said Piglet brightly.

The smell of the remaining patties in the cardboard box made Shannon feel sick. She wanted to grind them into everyone's smug faces for moving on so quickly and dismissively from Bobby's death.

"I've got a list of bars on the mainland that don't do ID checks," said Annabel.

Ollie explained to Victor and Shannon, "The best beaches are on Fengari, but the nightlife here is terrible. It markets itself as a family island so they get the right sort of tourists. Locals can sometimes get a little frustrated by that."

"The late-night ferry is brutal after a night out," said

Piglet. "Especially when you've drunk too much."

"Don't you ever stay the night on the mainland?" asked Victor.

"We should do that," said Shannon. "An overnight stay on the mainland..." She looked round. "I'm in." As everyone agreed, she realized she'd done it: she'd integrated into Annabel's group. They were discussing an overnight trip to the mainland and she was part of it.

"Oh my God," said Victor. He was on his phone. "Listen to this, it's on the Fengari tourist information app: *Weather warning. Please be aware that severe weather is on the way. Hurricane Rex may make landfall on Monday evening. Fengari authorities will keep you up to date with travel and other information.*" He looked up. "What the hell? It's Thursday evening. That's four days away."

"It's hurricane season," said Ollie, looking up the information on his own phone. "They rarely hit."

"How scared should we be?" asked Zander.

"Don't worry," said Piglet. "Most houses on the island are hurricane-proof." She beamed. "I love storms, don't you?"

Zander shook his head. "Not on my summer holiday, and not if I might die."

Maddie wrapped her arm around him. "Babe, you're not going to die. We get these warnings all the time. We'll hunker down in my basement on Monday."

"But what if the hurricane's for real? I don't want Seb to be delayed," said Annabel. "He's due to arrive on Monday.

93

That's so unfair."

And I want Emily to come soon, thought Shannon. What if she stayed in St-Tropez all summer to avoid a bad hurricane season?

Maybe she would have to get rid of the girls separately after all. She picked up the napkin she'd left by her bag, squeezed it into a tight ball and walked across the sand to a litter bin, where she threw it in with such force her upper arm throbbed.

CHAPTER 10

Friday

Before everyone went home, Ollie and Piglet had suggested meeting on the private beach below their house the next afternoon to make the most of the weather before it broke. They'd become a group of seven in a surprisingly short period of time. It gave Shannon a thrill when she woke the next morning and contemplated the day ahead.

While Shannon was sleeping, Clarissa had sent her a message asking if she'd heard there might be a hurricane on Fengari.

Don't worry Mummy, Shannon had typed back. *Linton*

Lodge is hurricane-proof. She assumed that was true – she'd have to speak to Helen.

Lydia added another message a few moments later: *Remember I went on that survival course with school? I know what to do!!*

Shannon googled what she was supposed to do in a hurricane. Stay indoors away from glass, basically. The idea of the hurricane excited her. It was as if she was being given a helping hand in shaking up the island. During her lessons she fantasized about turning up at the beach wearing a turquoise beach wrap from the range Annabel had clearly ripped off just to annoy her, but she knew that even if she'd owned one, she wouldn't do it. For now, she had to play at being friends.

She'd taken a taxi back to Linton Lodge from the training college and asked it to wait while she rushed up to her room to get changed into her bikini and a loose dress over the top, and grabbed an apple from the fruit bowl to eat as she packed a new bag.

"Hi, Lyds!" called Piglet, spotting Shannon first as she approached the small group lying on white sunloungers. "Maddie and Zander decided to go out for the day. It's just us five."

The others waved at her from their loungers. Annabel lifted her sunglasses up to look at her. "No labels hanging out this morning?"

"You wouldn't think there's bad weather on the way," said Shannon, looking at the calm water and the heat shimmer above the sand, through which the cliffs at the far end of the beach appeared distorted.

"Visitors are always surprised by the unpredictable weather patterns," said Ollie, rubbing suntan lotion on to his forehead. He began mansplaining climate change and rising sea levels.

Shannon nodded and laid out the beach towel she'd taken from Linton Lodge on to a lounger, although she saw she needn't have. There was a basket of towels next to an open cool bag of drinks and fruit. She'd seen the outside of Ollie and Piglet's house, called Hideaway Lodge, as she'd done the combination code on the lock to go through the gate which bypassed their garden. It was huge and modern, built from wood and steel. There were very few windows looking out to the front. A large, wavy piece of metal looked as if it was the door to a big garage. The place looked like some kind of arty prison. She hoped she'd get to see the inside of it at some point.

She wriggled out of her dress and glanced at her shoulder as she lay down, at the fake birthmark, the size of a ten-pence coin. She'd surreptitiously photographed Lydia's shoulder for reference when Lydia had worn a sleeveless running top. Telling Lydia she planned to recreate it would have taken what they were doing beyond a joke. A tattooist had refused the job, saying the request was so odd it made him uncomfortable, so she'd settled for Sharpie pens in two shades of brown. The problem was the colour faded over just a few days and she had to keep reapplying it, and it wasn't the easiest place to reach.

"Are you OK?" asked Piglet. Her skin was a sort of pinkish colour. She could have done with a bit of self-tan.

"Yes, thanks. Need to chill after my lessons this morning," Shannon said.

"Emily was tutored last summer," said Annabel, putting her hands behind her head. "She didn't want to be a total dimwit at uni. Maybe that's why she's staying away from here. Bad memories of having to do something." She laughed.

Shannon laughed too, hatred burning through her veins. The two of them *should* have had bad memories of what had happened to her mum and Bobby. She trailed her hand in the sand beside her lounger.

"Have you seen all the boats in the harbour bringing everything across in case we get cut off by the hurricane?" asked Piglet. "I'm scared we're going to run out of paprika crisps. I'm not sure if the packets I ordered are going to get here in time."

Ollie grunted, "I think my protein shakes are more important, Pigs." He looked better without his boring clothes on, although his swim shorts were a classic mid-blue check. Victor's were flamboyantly floral and had a logo on the side which she couldn't quite read.

"Stop whingeing," said Annabel. "I'm the one who's actually got something to complain about because of this stupid hurricane." She turned to Shannon with the news the others had obviously already heard. "Seb's had his flight cancelled."

"Oh, I'm sorry," said Shannon.

Annabel sighed heavily.

"Maybe everyone will go feral when the hurricane hits," said Victor, and she saw, with a jolt of embarrassment, he'd seen her tilt her head to look at his shorts. "That might be fun." He reached for a banana from the cool box.

"Are you not tempted to take the ferry to the mainland?" asked Shannon pointedly. "Get out while you can?"

He gave a look of surprise. "No. I'm not ready to go home yet. I have confidence in the Maritime not to blow away. And, hey, I'm enjoying everyone's company so much." He put down his auction house magazine. "And Ollie says there'll be skinny-dipping tomorrow evening at Annabel's. Can't miss that."

Ollie laughed. "I didn't." It was interesting to see him with a different expression on his normally inscrutable face.

"Sorry, what?" said Annabel.

"Aren't I invited?" said Victor. He made a tragic face.

"It's my parents' drinks party," said Annabel. "Of course there won't be skinny-dipping, but you lot are welcome to turn up to keep me company and talk to all the old people. It'll be boring as hell."

"We need a group chat for the summer," said Victor. "You can delete it when I've gone," he added, winking at Annabel. "Come on, everyone, get your phones out. I know you island girls have got your own group but we need one with Lydia, Ollie, Zander and me on it as well."

As Shannon reached for her phone, she saw a message from Clarissa telling her to take care. She closed her eyes briefly. For a moment, when she first read it, it had felt nice, having someone worry about her, and then she'd rolled her eyes at herself for being so stupid.

"Everyone needs cheering up," said Victor. He took a small white cardboard box from under his lounger and took off the lid. "Mini muffin, anyone?" he asked, and tipped the cardboard box towards Annabel. Shannon saw rows of plump little cakes which, although they were sweating slightly in the heat, looked delicious. "Blueberry."

He was eager to please, she'd give him that. Her initial evaluation of him as an idiot had maybe been hasty. He was perhaps just a little socially inept.

Everyone took a muffin except Shannon. She could almost feel the blueberries in her mouth, sweet and juicy, but Lydia loathed them. "There's something about blueberries which makes me squirm," she said. She held her hand up to her mouth as she mimed a squirm, allowing the bangle she'd bought fifteen minutes previously, on the way to the beach, to be properly seen.

"Oh," said Annabel, surprise in her voice. "You went back to buy it?"

"Oooh," said Piglet, her mouth still full. "Pretty! Let me see."

Everyone leaned in to admire it, and Shannon knew they were dying to ask how much it had cost, but old-money people, like the Harringtons, were squeamish about mentioning the price of things. Only Annabel had seen how much it had cost, and she was the one who mattered.

"I couldn't resist it," murmured Shannon. "It was an impulse buy."

That was true – and she didn't have unlimited funds. She needed to be careful; after all this, she would have to reinvent herself somewhere else, and she couldn't risk taking any more out of the floristry business. Ever since she could remember, money had been a vein of worry pulsing through her body. Before, the struggle had been about whether she and her mum had enough to get by, and now it was about how long the money would last. "You have to buy some things when they catch your eye, don't you?" she said. She touched the leaf, which was etched deep into the smooth gold, and then, like a reflex, she touched the only jewellery that would ever truly matter: her double-hearts necklace.

The phone call to say her mum had died in a fire was from a shaken police officer from the mainland. By then her mum had been dead for a few hours and they'd gone through the agency to find Shannon's details. Shannon had been pouring own-brand Cheerios into a bowl in Ela's house, and her phone had vibrated in her hoodie pocket, over and over. And when she saw it was an international number, she knew it was bad news. She had finished the call having hardly spoken, sinking to the floor with a howl that had brought Ela's family running, and caused the neighbours to hammer on the front door to see what was wrong.

There was very little information about what had happened until a long time afterwards, but when she heard the fire had been started by a cigarette, Shannon knew her mum was not to blame. Nan had been a smoker and had died of lung cancer. Shannon's mum had never smoked in her life, and had become rabidly anti-smoking after Nan's death. She'd been furious when she once found Ela's cigarettes in Shannon's coat pocket.

After everything Shannon had heard about the way they'd treated Bobby and hounded him to his death, she knew who was to blame: Annabel and Emily Harrington. Rosie and Douglas were complicit: they hadn't listened to her mum's fears, and the smoke alarms in the bunkhouse must have been non-existent or faulty; otherwise, her mum would have woken up as the first tendrils of smoke activated them. The building was one-storey; she should have been able to escape, and, on top of all that, Rosie and Douglas had lied, saying they'd regularly seen her mum smoking, and they were convinced she had tampered with the alarms herself so she could smoke inside.

Shannon had become obsessed with Annabel and Emily. Social media was her friend, and she scoured the internet for mention of the Harringtons. She knew where Douglas worked, and where Rosie shopped. She discovered Douglas came from a family which had made its money in cotton mills in the Industrial Revolution. Rosie came from a big landowning family.

Shannon didn't have a hope of gatecrashing any parties and meeting them in person. When the Harringtons weren't on holiday, they lived in Birch Hill, a house in Oxfordshire. She'd seen it on Google Maps and once took a day trip there. For six solid hours, not a single person had gone in or out of the gates, which were heavily monitored with two CCTV cameras.

On and on she went with her research. Rosie invested in her friends' businesses. She had a fifty-per-cent share in Clarissa Cornwallis Flowers, which was an hour away by bus and train. She had other stakes in an interior design company, a wine-tasting business and a high-end chain of sushi bars. Shannon had no issues with putting time and effort in. The family would pay. She would take their money and go to Fengari as soon as she had enough to get there. She kept asking about weekend jobs in Clarissa Cornwallis Flowers, said she was desperate to go into floristry, that working in that particular florist's was her dream. As soon as there was an opening the manager called her in and asked Shannon – or Rhiannon, as she had decided to be – to put together a bunch of flowers together for £80.

Shannon was good at maths, adventurous with colour, and she soon discovered that she was brilliant at being somebody other than herself. She could be the sort of person clients would like. Polite, well-spoken, with a dash of spirit. The sort of person they thought they were themselves.

She got the job, and within a few weeks had infiltrated the finances. She met Lydia. She was on her way.

"Oh my God, Lydia," said a voice beside her. "Did you forget to put suntan lotion on your nose? It's going red." It was Annabel.

There was a pause. "Earth to Lydia?" said Piglet.

"She looks hilarious," said Annabel. "Like a tourist."

Shannon sat up, snapping herself out of her memories. She needed to pull herself together. When she was with these people, she had to stay focused.

CHAPTER 11

Saturday

Shannon woke the following morning to the news on the group chat that Emily had flown into Fengari at 11.30 p.m. the previous evening. Annabel said her parents' drinks party had turned into a Return of the Prodigal Daughter event and it was starting at 6.30 for 7 p.m. A hurricane watch had been issued, but the weather would remain mild for the next twenty-four hours, so the plan was still to have it in the garden. Dress code: summer evening vibes.

Emily is on Fengari. Shannon flopped back against her pillow and allowed the news to sink in. Her breathing was all off, and her stomach felt dodgy. It was impossible to stay still, so she got up and, for distraction, practised a natural make-up look for later.

Google told her that "6.30 for 7 p.m." meant she shouldn't arrive later than 7 p.m. She would bunk off her lessons and go for a walk in Old Town. It would help her gather her thoughts. It was also a solid Lydia Cornwallis thing to do. Shannon had been too diligent so far. It was ridiculous to have lessons on a Saturday. Six days a week of tutoring was over the top, and now that Emily was on the island, they were more irrelevant than ever.

She messaged Lydia to tell her she'd awarded herself a morning off lessons and Lydia responded with, *Don't blame you. They sound so bad! Crispin and I are loving Italy.* She sent through a couple of photos, one of them grinning at the Colosseum, with a filter which had turned them into gladiators, and another of them in a fancy little pizza restaurant.

As Shannon waited in the hallway for a taxi, Helen came bustling up. "Morning, Lydia. I do hope you're not anxious about the severe weather warning. I can assure you this building has hurricane certification. No need for you to worry about a thing! Have a good morning at college."

Shannon nodded and hurried out to her taxi, asking the driver to drop her the other end of Fengari Old Town from the college. After a walk, and a smoothie in a café, she headed towards the expensive boutiques, where a gorgeous wrap-around silk dress with a leaf design on it caught her eye. It was perfect with her new leaf bangle. She already had so many clothes, but when she tried it on, this dress made her feel rich and powerful. The neckline plunged low, so she bought a new bra in the exact shade of green required. She wouldn't get this through Clarissa's credit card, so she handed over her "Margot Bonvalier" card.

When she arrived back at Linton Lodge for lunch, Miriam came running up to her. She must have been waiting in the entrance hall. Ugh. She hadn't wanted to face her so soon. "Oh, Lydia, there you are! I was so upset you didn't turn up today. What happened?"

Shannon winced. The bag with her dress in was so large it was pointless hiding it behind her back. "It's hard, you know. This is my summer holiday."

"I know," said Miriam with an overly sympathetic eye blink. "But you're on the intense programme. We know that six mornings a week work better than three full days. I'm sure you don't want to let your parents down."

Miriam was probably scared of Clarissa. "I think I'd cope better if I didn't have to do so many hours of lessons," said Shannon. "You're great, but I find having someone with me all the time too intense; it's just a lot of expectation and pressure. I learn better when I go over things on my own, in my room. I've done all the homework so far. If you quiz me, you'll see I'm learning loads from it." The homework took Shannon minutes. That wasn't the problem. Not spending enough time with the Harringtons was. She mirrored Miriam's worried face. "I don't want to let anyone down, and I am trying. Would it be OK if I message you when I'm not feeling up to lessons? Mummy doesn't have to know, but she won't mind as long as I'm working hard and learning."

Miriam's face was glitching. She wasn't sure how to play it. After a bit she said, "Well, perhaps, as long as you don't miss too many sessions. I mean, if there's a hurricane, that's one thing, but dipping out for other reasons, you need to let me know. Promise?"

"I promise. Let's not tell Helen either," Shannon said. "She fusses too much." Miriam frowned. Shannon felt for her – she was only doing her job. "It'll be fine," she said. "I'll do all the homework and I'll tell Mummy how much I'm enjoying the lessons."

Miriam sighed and said, "All right. Let's see how it goes, Lydia."

When Shannon stepped out of the taxi, the air felt more comfortable than it had last time she'd been at Clifftop House, but she wondered if the low neckline had been a bad move. An older couple who had just arrived at the front door wore clothing that screamed old money: a slightly faded navy linen dress for the lady and beige trousers, white shirt, navy blazer and striped tie for the man. The diamond on the woman's ring, though, was enormous on her wrinkled, tanned hand as she pressed the doorbell.

Shannon touched her necklace and readjusted her neckline.

A thin woman of about seventy in a plain black dress

and flat lace-ups, with short grey hair and a wrinkled face, opened the door. Mrs Pushkin. She greeted the couple and told them to head through the house to the garden. Now she stared at Shannon.

"You're a friend of. . .?" she said, as if she was trying to place her. Her face was angular, triangles and straight lines.

Shannon's pulse quickened. Was she noticing a resemblance to her mum?

"I'm Lydia Cornwallis, family friend," Shannon said.

"Of course. Do come in." Mrs Pushkin forced a smile. She was the type who prided herself on good manners but rarely made people feel at ease. "I'll show you the way through to the garden."

"Don't worry. I was here the other day," said Shannon. "I know the way." It was almost impossible to keep her voice even. This woman had been in charge of the summer staff. She could have helped Bobby and her mum but chose not to. She'd looked the other way – the very thing her mum had refused to do. Shannon burned with guilt when she remembered how she'd encouraged her mum not to get involved.

She walked down the hallway towards the kitchen because that was the only way she knew how to get to the garden, unless she'd gone through the side gate. The kitchen turned out to be busy with a large number of caterers and waitstaff, and Shannon apologized as a girl showed her a way to the garden through a door near the downstairs toilet.

Where was Emily?

"Lydia, darling! Good you could make it." Rosie stepped forward and kissed her on both cheeks. Her perfume was powerful, and her deep pink dress well-tailored, with matching wedge sandals. "Meet two dear friends of mine..." Shannon nodded and didn't listen to the names. All she wanted was to see Emily. There were too many people, all bunched up together.

A waitress came up to her and offered her champagne. There wasn't a non-alcoholic alternative on the tray so she took a glass. She allowed herself one sip. For courage. It fizzed down her throat and unsettled her stomach.

"It seems Emily didn't know that Fengari is about to be hit by a hurricane," said one of the women, as Rosie turned away to greet someone else. "But it's a marvellous surprise for Rosie and Douglas."

"Such a lovely family," said the other woman.

"Lovely," echoed Shannon, slow-twirling the champagne glass in her hand as she followed the woman's gaze.

Emily. There she was with Maddie, Zander and Victor, laughing at something. She was taller in real life than Shannon had expected. Her blonde hair was half up, half down, artfully casual. It had gone lighter in the south of France, or maybe she'd had some good highlights done. She wore a floppy white dress, her skin already tanned, her feet in plain black flip-flops. She looked completely at ease.

"Excuse me," Shannon said to the woman. "I'd like to go and say hello to her."

She walked slowly, past the fountain. Emily was in the middle of an anecdote now. When the others laughed at her punchline and she was looking pleased with herself, Shannon stepped forward and said, "Hi, Emily. I'm Lydia Cornwallis. Our mothers are friends." She added a lilt at the end, like a question, to see if Emily had heard from Rosie or Annabel that she was on Fengari.

"Oh, right. Yes," said Emily, looking her up and down just as Annabel had that first time. Her eyes were lighter than Annabel's, a prettier blue, but the set of her jaw and her mouth made her look harsh.

Shannon held her breath. She had the sense that Emily was remembering something.

Emily said, "My friend knows your boyfriend. Crispin, right? Apparently, Crispin was full of some secret adventure that was going to happen this summer. Sounded all very hush-hush." She was smiling, but it wasn't a kind smile.

Shannon should have hammered home to Crispin more thoroughly the importance of keeping his mouth shut. She hadn't clocked this attention-seeking side to him. She'd have to message Lydia to make sure he wasn't in touch with anyone now they were travelling.

Annabel was there, suddenly, next to Shannon, in a black dress. It looked extreme, her in black and Emily in white. Shannon stared at them both. The two sisters. Together. Strikingly similar, although Emily drew the eye more with her height, blonder hair and tan. Shannon's stomach churned, but she was excited. She – ordinary

Shannon Jones – had managed to get herself to Fengari to face these two.

Annabel said, "Lydia's split up from Crispin."

Shannon swallowed. "Crispin and I did have plans," she said. "But, well, yes, we split up. We're still friends, though. It's all fine." The champagne glass felt slippery in her sweaty fingers.

Emily grinned at her awkwardness. "Oh, he's so over you. Sorry to break it to you..." She looked at the others to check they were listening. "But I heard he went travelling with a mystery girl instead of you and is *completely* loved up." She watched Shannon, who bit her lip. "Don't let it upset you, but I believe there was some..." She lowered her voice to a stage whisper. "... *overlap* with you and this girl. Boys can be brutal. Especially if they think you're a tiny bit needy. Not that I'm saying you are." She kept her head slightly tilted – a cue for Shannon to leap in and defend herself.

Unexpectedly, it was Annabel who did. "Em, be nice. Lyds is all right."

Shannon looked at the little bubbles collecting on the surface of her champagne, like her anger. She snapped her head back up. "I'm OK," she said. "Being here is good for me."

"Aw," said Maddie, her head leaning on Zander's shoulder. She was wearing mottled, bright blue-and-grey feather earrings. Shannon wondered if they had come from a bird on Fengari. "Is it nice to be back, Emily?"

"Not really," said Emily. "I should have stayed in St-Tropez. Nobody told me about the hurricane."

"That's because you didn't tell us you were coming back," said Annabel. "It's not our fault you ran out of money, or failed to look at the weather apps."

Emily rolled her eyes.

"Well, don't worry, I can bring France to you," said Victor. He said something in French. From Shannon's limited grasp of the language, it sounded like something along the lines of him making it an unforgettable summer for her. He was back in idiot mode. Emily bought it, though.

"You're sweet, Victor. Friend of Ollie's, right?" she said.

"Emily, everyone is my friend here."

Ew.

"Welcome to your first summer on Fengari," said Emily. "Our family has been here since seventeen eighty-six – have you seen the wooden beam in our kitchen? That was from the boat that brought them over."

"Seriously? That's impressive," said Victor, while Shannon fought the urge to roll her eyes.

Conversation moved on and Victor began an anecdote about a time he fell overboard during a sailing race, acting out how he was treading water, coming up with sound effects to make them laugh. She looked around. A few metres away, Piglet and Ollie were standing with an older couple and Shannon could hear the guy talking about the prep he needed to do for Hurricane Rex. Piglet was sipping

113

her drink through a straw, and nodding now and again. Ollie looked vacant.

She spotted a woman with hair similar to her mum's, and she had a wave of missing her so badly she wanted to sink to her knees and sob. Leaving her champagne glass on a table, she murmured about needing the bathroom, but when she was almost at the house she took the path that led to the other part of the garden. She'd go and see the bunkhouse.

Piercing sadness caught her in the chest when it came into sight. If she half-closed her eyes and let everything go blurry she could picture her mum walking out of that door in black trousers and white top. There was a grassy smell in the air; the lawns must have been freshly mown that day for the party. She could almost hear her mum sneezing. She stood like that for a while until the door opened and she was suddenly face to face with the new gardener in his gardening uniform. He was as startled as she was, but he recovered more quickly.

"Are you lost?" he asked. His manner was wary, his accent American.

It was a huge garden, but she thought it was doubtful anyone could get truly lost in it. Was he being sarcastic? "No. Sorry. I was just … I was getting away from the party for a moment." Did he know what had happened in that bunkhouse last summer? She guessed not. Who would have told him?

"Fair enough. I need to check the sprinkler system. There's been a problem with it."

"You don't want any guests to get soaked, right?" Shannon said.

"That would be bad," he agreed.

"But funny," she persisted. She wondered how much he hated the Harringtons.

"But, yeah, maybe funny," he said, his mouth twitching slightly.

"Hello!" Victor emerged from the path. "I wasn't expecting to find you here, Lydia, and. . .?"

"Finch," said the gardener. He held Victor's gaze. "Hope you both have a good evening," and he set off towards the side of the house.

"What are you doing, Victor?" she said, irritated that her conversation with Finch had been interrupted.

"I wanted a break from the drinks party conversation." He flashed his charming smile and her irritation subsided a little. "Are you interested in gardens?" He grinned, as if to say he suspected she was more interested in the gardener than the garden.

"Actually, my mother has a floristry business," she said curtly, "so I know a bit about flowers." She hoped he wasn't going to test her on any of them – although, thinking about it, the real Lydia wouldn't have a clue.

He nodded. "Ah." For a moment, she thought he was lost for words, which didn't seem very Victor-like, but then he said, "To be honest, I'm finding this party quite ... well, boring. I'm not sure I can talk about weather systems and the refurbishment of the golf club

115

with those old people for much longer. I think it's time for a swim, don't you?"

Now? Shannon had thought the swimming conversation the previous day had been a joke. "I don't have my swimming things." She thought about the forty-five minutes she'd spent styling her hair just right.

"Oh, I'm sure Annabel has a billion swimwear items you could borrow," Victor said smoothly. "You know, since she's insisting we have to wear them." He had already turned towards the house, and she sensed it was easier to go with him.

He walked with a slow confidence, as if inviting other people to look at him, and when they were in sight of everyone else, a few of Rosie and Douglas's friends did turn and gaze at him, at them. Shannon found herself quite enjoying it. Did people think they were a couple?

"The architecture is unattractive from the back, don't you think?" Victor said, and it occurred to Shannon he was testing her to see how disloyal she'd be.

The back of the house did look haphazard. The windows were a variety of shapes and sizes, and the kitchen and garden room jutted out in an extension of different coloured brick to the rest of the house. "It's been rebuilt a lot since seventeen whenever it was the family first arrived," she said. "The Harringtons are very proud of it."

"I guess it's been in the family for over two hundred years and they have the bit of wood to prove it," said Victor. He led the way to where Annabel was standing with the others. "Have we done our socializing duty now?" he asked her. "Is it time to have fun yet?"

There was a small plastic basket of spare swimwear in the changing room building. By the time Shannon had found a bikini she was happy with and changed into it, the others were in the pool, joking around. She lowered herself into the shallow end, dipping down quickly into the water so that it covered her shoulders.

"Race everyone to the other end!" shouted Ollie.

Shannon stayed where she was and watched everyone else pound the length of the pool. She'd never had swimming lessons when she was young, apart from six sessions with school when she'd been ten, and they had been cold, miserable experiences, being shouted at in an echoey, smelly place. More recently, she'd paid for three expensive swimming lessons knowing that she would have to go in a swimming pool or the sea on Fengari. She hadn't learned to swim properly, but she could do a splashy doggy paddle and didn't fear being in the water any more.

Someone said the race wasn't over, people had to swim back to the other end, and suddenly she had to move out of the way. It was too late. Maddie swam into her.

"Oh, hey," Maddie said, standing up in her knitted-style bikini. "Sorry. Weren't you racing?"

"No," said Shannon, rubbing her shoulder.

"I thought all Wallys could swim at a hundred miles per hour. You've got that amazing pool at your school."

117

Shannon held on to the side rail. She pulled her leg back as if she was doing a stretch. "Just had a cramp," she said.

Maddie circled round her, like a shark, and dread lodged in her stomach. "You've got a dead leaf or something on your back? What *is* that?"

The fake birthmark. Shannon hadn't re-coloured it in. She hadn't tested it in chlorine either. She wished she had a mirror so she could check it properly. Had the colours run? She twisted round to see what had happened.

Annabel was there now. "Is it a bruise?"

"It's nothing," said Shannon, dipping down into the water again to hide it. "A birthmark. I'm self-conscious about it. I sometimes put make-up over it." She was pleased with that. It explained why the mark might look different in future.

Her eyes unintentionally met Victor's. He was pushing back his black hair. He looked sleek, like a sea animal, completely at home in water. He made her feel on edge, but in a different way to the others. He was an outsider too, and the way he looked at her as if he was trying to work her out didn't annoy her – in fact she quite liked it. She felt somehow seen.

But she wasn't here to feel anything other than rage.

She heard the conversation drift on to waterproof make-up and Emily said she needed to buy some new mascara and she'd wanted to get some in duty-free but there hadn't been time. Her voice was an entitled whine. Shannon floated on her back, looking up at the sky. She put her hand out to hold on to the side of the pool. Floating was only relaxing if she knew she could put her feet down on to firm ground. "Hey, Finch or Fitch. Whatever your name is!" It was Annabel's voice.

Shannon pulled herself upright to see Finch walking past the swimming pool fence.

"You want to join us?" called Annabel. "Our parents will be OK with it if we tell them we invited you. You won't get into trouble."

"No, thanks," he said, carrying on walking.

"We like it when people play hard to get!" Emily called, as he disappeared from view.

"You two are terrible!" laughed Zander. "He was basically running away from you."

"Nobody can outrun us," said Emily. She looked at Annabel. "Come on, admit it, Bels. You're pleased I'm here."

Annabel smiled. "OK, OK. It can be boring here without you."

Those girls think they can get away with anything. Her mum's words echoed in her head.

Well, very soon those girls were going to be stopped.

CHAPTER 12

Sunday

The group chat – the one Victor had set up – was silent when Shannon woke the following morning. Everyone was probably still asleep or doing their own thing. It was Sunday, which meant a proper day off from lessons. She ordered pancakes, syrup and fruit for breakfast in bed and browsed TikTok, and then looked at the Fengari app. It said residents should make storm preparations, although it was still unclear if Hurricane Rex would make landfall in thirty-six hours. The ferries and helicopter had stopped running. The island was cut off.

As long as Lydia and Crispin stayed out of sight and

Clarissa stayed clueless, Shannon had all summer to put her plan into action. She went to the window. The sky was overcast and a breeze was buffeting the more delicate plants in the garden. She went back to bed, the hours stretched out in front of her. Looking at the app again, she saw the buses were still running. She'd visit a place she knew her mum had been to – there was a bus which went to Little Trebaya on the other side of the island, where there were tiny art galleries, a pottery and vegan cafés.

She slipped out of Linton Lodge, managing to avoid Helen, who might try to persuade her to stay inside or push her into a group activity. The bus stop was a good twenty minutes' walk and although it was windy, the air was warm. Shannon wore a Lydia-style outfit (a loose, short linen dress with scruffy Nike Airs) with a Shannon-style hairdo – her hair pulled back tightly and piled high on her head. When the bus arrived, there were a couple of tourists already on it, but everyone else was either old or people in work uniforms. The uniformed workers were predominantly people of colour. There was a very obvious racial divide on Fengari, and Shannon bet that it was rarely discussed – or even noticed – by the likes of the Harringtons.

She settled in a window seat and looked out at the beautiful big houses and hotels which, after a while, gave way to more modest homes. Then the bus took a detour off the main road into an area of low-rise blocks of flats where more workers got on. There were signs of hurricane preparation everywhere – people removing dead branches from trees, bringing outdoor furniture inside, and installing shutters on windows. The bus rejoined the main road and went past a stretch of farmland, followed by dry scrubland, before the houses and hotels reappeared again as they neared the coast an hour and a half after setting off. The island was small. No wonder everyone knew the lovely, lovely Harringtons.

The bus turned off its engine in a market square. This was Trebaya, and the tourists got off. Shannon knew to stay on until the next stop, further along the coast to Little Trebaya, the artists' community. She was the only one to get off the bus there, but the place was bustling despite the threat of imminent severe weather. A shopping mall and a nail bar would normally be her sort of thing if she wanted to relax, but she breathed in the smell of fresh bread, sugary things and sea air, and was pleased she'd come. There was a fretful anticipation in the air too, as locals were starting to board up the glass fronts of shops, and the wind was whipping up the waves out at sea.

She wandered the main street, turning down alleyways when she saw a shop or gallery that interested her. After walking round an exhibition of pictures made from strips of newspaper, she settled into a café with a view of the choppy sea across some wild tufts of grass on sand that wasn't as white and fine as the other side of the island. She ordered a fresh mint tea and a small square of brownie (even if Lydia rarely ate pastries, she did like chocolate) and watched two local boys playing cards at the next table, a tired dog spread out underneath it. Every now and again, one of the boys stroked the dog with his bare foot, and it grunted happily.

She didn't notice Finch come into the café because one of the boys had won the card game and the dog had woken up and was wagging his tail against a chair leg. He must have been sitting at the table next to her for quite a while before she saw him because when she did, the black coffee in the clear glass was half-drunk. Perfect. This was a way to get to know him better – there was every chance she might need his help later down the line. He looked up from his phone and gave her a startled smile, as if he'd had to think for a split second who she was.

"You're the Harringtons' friend?" he said, shifting his chair more towards hers.

No. "Yes," she said. "They were being stupid last night, though." She rolled her eyes. "They shouldn't have embarrassed you."

Finch shrugged. "It's OK. It didn't bother me." He seemed genuinely unfazed.

"That's good. They can be ... full on."

"Yeah – I'm getting that vibe from them." He gestured at the view. "The storm's coming in."

She liked how he'd changed the subject. "You think the hurricane's going to hit Fengari?"

He shrugged. "It's looking that way. I came to take some photographs. It's beautiful out here and today the light is unusual."

"So you're into photography?" Shannon wondered what it would take for him to trust her.

"Yeah, as a hobby," he said. "I'm a biology major, so I take photos of plants, mainly."

She nodded, to encourage him to talk.

"I wanted to spend some time on Fengari this summer to see some of the indigenous species and being a gardener was a good way of doing it." He took a gulp of his coffee. "So what are you doing out here? Shopping?" It sounded dismissive.

"I'm checking out the island," she said. "It's my day off. I do lessons at the training college by the harbour."

"First time here?"

"Yes," she said without thinking. That was stupidly reckless. She was supposed to have been here when she was little. "First time on this side of the island, I mean." She sat up straight, digging her thumbnail into the palm of her other hand.

"I go all over the island. It's good to get away from my accommodation block," said Finch. "I find it depressing." He was looking at her, almost challenging her to say something because he'd dared to say the bunkhouse was depressing.

If only he knew, he'd find that place worse than depressing. "It must be lonely," she said, then almost closed her eyes in embarrassment. It had come out unintentionally flirty. He must know how good-looking he was.

He paused, probably considering how to react. "I'm happy with my own company most of the time..."

She was impressed with his measured response, and unsure if he was hitting on her or not, but she had a sudden urge to protect him. "Yes, stay away from Annabel and Emily."

"What d'you mean?" he asked.

"You've seen what they're like," Shannon said. She couldn't let herself be distracted. "They can be..." She couldn't find the right word, and looked out at the sea, where the high waves were white as they crashed on to the shore. She knew the water wasn't actually white; it was the way the light was bouncing through the individual droplets. She felt sure Finch knew that about waves too.

"Reckless?" suggested Finch.

"Yes," she said. She needed to project Lydia more. "They're family friends. I know what they're like, but yes, reckless."

He nodded as if he was thinking it over. "Yeah, I can see that. But don't worry, I can look after myself." He stood up. "You should visit the gallery further down this street. They have some old photos of the island. You can see what Old Fengari looked like when it was a fishing village. It's interesting. I'll show you if you like. I'm heading that way." He picked up a camera bag. "I'm taking photos further along the coast."

"Sure." She put the last piece of brownie in her mouth and went to pay. She'd be careful – she couldn't get too close to Finch, because that wouldn't go down well with Annabel and Emily.

They didn't talk as they walked up the road together, but it wasn't awkward. Shannon matched Finch's stride and looked at the boutiques and the delicatessen with the window display of beautifully packaged food. How rich would she have to be to be able to afford the best-quality produce all the time, knowing that everything she put into her body was organic and locally produced? She could sense her mum smiling at that, telling her there was nothing wrong with Cadbury's Dairy Milk.

The gallery was tiny, with an open shopfront which hadn't yet been boarded up, and the photos were big and dramatic. "See, they're good, aren't they?" said Finch, leaning against the wall as she stepped inside. A girl sitting in the corner on her phone briefly flicked her head up in a greeting. There were photos of fishermen, cigarettes hanging from their mouths, looking straight into the camera; women dressed up in hats and long dresses outside what looked like a hat shop; there was a cart of hay with a couple of young boys sitting on top of it, and shots taken inside and outside big houses.

"That's Clifftop House," said Finch, pointing at a photo of a garden party with a brick house in the background.

Shannon looked more closely at it. The kitchen extension hadn't been built, but the fountain was there. The people were dressed in seventies clothing with flared trousers and waistcoats and A-line skirts.

"Douglas Harrington's father owned the house then," said Finch.

"Really?" said Shannon. She could have given an hour's lecture on the history of the Harrington family with the amount she knew.

"Ted, the permanent gardener, told me about it," said Finch. "He's been working for the Harringtons a long time, like Mrs Pushkin." He pointed at a photo of the harbour and was about to say something, but was distracted by a sports car pulling up. The roof was down and Victor was in the driver's seat, smirking at them.

"Well, look who I found!"

"Hi," said Shannon, then found herself desperately trying to explain the situation Victor had stumbled upon. "We're not really together. We bumped into each other in a café and Finch told me about these amazing photos. There's one of Clifftop House about fifty years ago."

Victor raised an eyebrow. "Is that so?" He didn't make any moves to park up and look at it.

"Yeah," said Finch calmly. He lifted his camera bag to Shannon. "Anyway, I've got things to do." And off he walked.

"Oooh," said Victor. "Sorry for interrupting. I didn't think he'd walk off in a huff."

Shannon rolled her eyes. "He's not in a huff. He's gone to take some photos. What are you doing out here?"

"Looking at some artwork for my family's art foundation, but I'm heading back now. The rest of the gang are meeting at my hotel for a swim – you've obviously been far too busy to look at the group chat for a while. Fancy the infinity pool?" He indicated the passenger seat next to him.

Shannon liked the sound of "the gang" but not the swim.

"I'm too tired for a swim," she said. "But I'll come and hang out with you lot at your hotel." She looked up at the sky. "Not that it's very sunny."

"It's still warm, though," said Victor as she got in. He put the car into gear and moved it out into the slow-moving traffic.

"So what's the deal with you and the gardener?" he asked.

"His name is Finch."

"So what's the deal with you and Finch?" he said. "Are you trying to annoy the others? I think I'm the only one who doesn't fancy Finch." He looked at her. "You know Ollie's gay and Zander's bi?"

"Of course I know," she said, although she hadn't. She needed to sharpen up and get more of a handle on these people. "But believe it or not, I did just bump into Finch here."

"Hmm," he said, and turned left on to the main road away from the coast. He sped up, which thankfully meant it was hard to have a conversation because Shannon had had enough of him. She leaned an elbow on the door and let chunks of hair come loose from her updo, whipping round her face in the wind.

At the Maritime, Victor left the car at the entrance,

and nodded at a valet as he got out. It took Shannon a split second to realize that the valet would be parking the car, but Victor had already noticed and asked if she was daydreaming.

"You caught me," she said cheerfully as they made their way into the lobby. "What time is everybody meeting?"

"After lunch," said Victor. "We can have a sandwich up on the roof terrace, if you like." He gave a casual shrug. "Or maybe you'd prefer lunch on your own with a magazine? A bit of peace and quiet? That can be arranged too."

She placed a finger on her chin, jokily pretending to think about it. "I'll eat with you, I suppose."

"Wonderful!" His smile seemed genuine and she smiled back. "Very good answer," he said. "By the way, I reckon I'm a much better lunch date than Finch." He nodded towards a sign showing the way to the lift.

"I told you – it was a coincidence he was there," said Shannon.

Victor narrowed his eyes dramatically. "If you ask me, there is more to you, Ms Lydia Cornwallis, than meets the eye. You are so jumpy."

Her mouth went dry. "Jumpy?"

"Yes. Whenever I mention Finch, but other times too. As if you aren't enjoying your holiday." He was nudging her to be indiscreet again, like the previous evening when he'd asked her if she thought the back of Clifftop House was unattractive.

"This isn't a holiday," she said, immediately annoyed at

her knee-jerk reaction, adding, "How could it be when I have lessons six days a week?"

He was looking at her more intently than she found comfortable, and she was grateful when the lift arrived. The views from the high roof terrace were one hundred times more dramatic than the conference room in Fengari Training College. The one that drew her eye the most was the pool on the floor below. She'd heard about pools which were built to look as if they went on for ever but had never seen one in real life. The way it was positioned, it looked as if it merged with the sea.

On the terrace itself there were sofas with white cushions, exotic plants everywhere, their leaves fluttering slightly in the breeze, and metal-and-wood tables and chairs. It was only half-full, maybe because the sky was darkening.

"A magnificent spot to have lunch," said Victor. He pronounced *magnificent* in his French-accented way. "And very pretty at night with lots of lights. When there isn't an incoming hurricane."

Shannon could picture herself here at night in a short tight dress and dramatic acrylic nails. If she'd designed the seating, though, she'd have added brightly coloured, fluffy cushions.

A waiter greeted them, gave them a prime spot overlooking the pool, and handed them a couple of menus.

Victor's phone rang and he glanced at it, frowning as he cut the call. "My cousin," he said. "I'll call him back later."

"Tell me about your family, and the art business," Shannon said to Victor. "I want to know all about them."

"Why waste a lovely lunch talking about my family and the foundation? That's too much like work. Let's imagine we are two people enjoying each other's company on a beautiful roof terrace," he said. "Tell me, what sort of food do you like?"

Shannon decided she'd tell him about her love of burgers, turning it into a joke. There was no harm in relaxing, just for the duration of lunch.

CHAPTER 13

By the time everyone else turned up, Shannon and Victor had finished lunch and had moved down to the pool level. They sat on loungers in the sticky heat, flicking through a pile of magazines that had been placed on a table at the entrance. Victor had been up to his room to change into swim shorts that had a photograph of a beach scene printed on them.

"Nice shorts," said Shannon. She'd messaged Annabel, asking her to bring a spare bikini for her to sunbathe in. For now she'd taken off her trainers and hitched up her linen dress to expose her legs, so she didn't feel too overdressed around everyone else.

"I like swimwear that makes people look at me," he said,

and he seemed to have reverted to the brash personality he displayed around the others. It was confusing, but she shouldn't be using up energy thinking about it.

The others turned up in dribs and drabs, Maddie and Zander in matching tie-dye shorts they'd bought for a bet, with Piglet and Ollie, who were bickering because they had forgotten to bring a special type of suntan lotion with them. Annabel and Emily were late because of a tennis lesson. Victor didn't mention Finch when he said he'd seen Shannon in Little Trebaya and had given her a lift back, but his eyes lingered on her afterwards and she wondered if he expected anything in return for his discretion.

After establishing that the two of them had had lunch together, Emily widened her eyes dramatically as she sat on a lounger, and said, "Moving on from Crispin already, are we? Did you post a photo to show him what he's missing?"

"It was just lunch, and no," said Shannon giving her side-eye.

"Ah, don't be so touchy, Lyds," said Emily with a mocking laugh.

While the others swam, Shannon attempted to change into the bikini Annabel had brought for her. It was uncomfortably small for her, so she went back to her lounger in her dress, which by now was glued to her back with sweat from the humidity. She listened to the squealing and shouting from the pool, closed her eyes, and thought about the water fights she and her mum used to have in the garden of her nan's house on hot days. The memories brought a burrowing loneliness that focused the mind: she was with the Harrington sisters now. She had a plan to enact. She just needed the right moment.

After a while, Annabel came over, having stubbed her toe on the side of the pool. She sat on the lounger one over from Shannon and inspected her toe.

"Hurts like hell," she said.

"Bad luck," said Shannon. A stubbed toe was the very least of what she wished Annabel.

"Didn't like the bikini?" asked Annabel.

"It was the wrong size," said Shannon. "But no worries." Annabel had probably done her a favour. At least she definitely didn't have to swim now, although the water looked cool and inviting.

"Shame." Annabel kept hold of her foot and rolled on to her back, so that her knee was bent at a right angle to her body, as if she was doing yoga. "Word of advice," said Annabel in a low voice. "I saw your face when we were teasing the gardener yesterday. You need to lighten up. "

"Finch?" Shannon said lightly, straightening the soft towel she was lying on. What about his name was so hard to remember?

"Yeah, whatever. No hate, but you're so serious, Lydia. I know you're doing catch-up classes here, but you should chill more. Have some fun!"

Victor had called her jumpy. Annabel was telling her to lighten up. Shannon had to up her game.

"And what could be more fun than a hurricane?"

said Shannon. "Actually that probably *is* more fun than my lessons. Don't tell your mum, but I've convinced my tutor that it would be OK to start skipping some. She's so gullible."

Annabel laughed. "That sounds good." She stood up again, the mood lighter.

Shannon tried to tune out all the splashing and laughing, and the smells of chlorine and suntan lotion, and concentrate on Nan's garden. She remembered the back fence at a wonky angle, the grass with bald patches and the smell of roses, and the almost-taste of mint when she rolled a leaf from a pot between her fingers. Most of all, though, she remembered Nan sitting on a flowery deckchair, wanting to get up and make some food, and her mum telling her to relax and stay sitting down, and then the three of them with sandwiches. Not exactly having the best time of their lives, but content. Strong women.

She must have drifted to sleep because she was woken by a long sigh. She saw Annabel looking at her magazine, dripping water on to it. She had it open to a double page featuring accessories with a nature theme.

"Don't you love this jewellery?" asked Annabel, angling the page so Shannon could see it.

There was a series of bangles with leaf imprints that reminded Shannon of the one she was wearing. She made a calculated decision, unsnapped the clasp on her bangle, took it off and handed it to Annabel. At least Annabel knew how much it had cost, so there was no mistaking that side of things. "Here, have this," she said. "It doesn't really suit me, and I want to thank you for welcoming me here."

Annabel hesitated a moment, glanced towards the pool to check this slightly awkward moment wasn't being witnessed by anyone else, and took the bangle as if it was the most precious thing she'd ever handled. "It's beautiful," she murmured. "Are you sure?"

"Of course," said Shannon. She'd seen Lydia do this on a lesser scale – ordering a hoodie online for someone when they'd made a passing comment they liked it. Inwardly Shannon was wincing about the amount of money she was throwing away, but the money had been spent anyway whether she wore it or not, although she could hear a voice in her head reminding her that she could have sold it later on. It was gold. It was way more than she should have spent. She couldn't help visualizing her expenses spreadsheet.

And anyway, when this was over? She might take it back.

"I love it," said Annabel. "It's super kind of you." She put down her magazine and lay back on her sunlounger, angling her face towards Shannon. "You're a credit to Wallys."

Shannon twisted the edge of the towel she was lying on between her fingers. "Thanks," she said.

"You're someone who comes across as prickly to start with, but you're not like that underneath." Annabel nodded as if to reinforce this opinion in her mind.

And that was what the bangle had bought Shannon.

The others came out of the pool, racing across the terrace to reach their towels, looking up at the gathering clouds and out to sea, where the waves were gaining height. Emily noticed the bangle on Annabel's wrist. "Where's that from?" she demanded.

"Lydia doesn't want it any more and gave it to me!" Annabel beamed like a little child.

Emily said, "Lucky!" and Maddie grabbed Annabel's wrist to take a closer look. "Nice one!" Maddie raised an eyebrow at Shannon. "When's mine coming?"

Shannon laughed, surprised how much she was enjoying the attention. "I wouldn't be here if it wasn't for Annabel's family."

"What d'you mean?" asked Victor. He was distracting her, standing there with his toned body.

"Is Emily getting one too?" said Maddie provocatively.

Shannon said, "Ah, I didn't think that one through." She had, though. She hoped Emily would be sucking up to her now. She had both of them where she wanted them.

"This place is so nice, Victor," said Piglet, looking back at the spectacular pool. "Even with the weather turning."

"Yeah, not a bad hotel," said Emily.

Victor grinned. "You guys should come back for dinner. Before everything closes ahead of tomorrow night. There are three restaurants but the best is the Anchor Room. You'll love it. We can watch the first squalls of the storm out of the window. I'll call Marco and reserve a table for" – he did a quick head count – "eight of us. My treat. Everyone in?"

"Seriously?" said Zander. "We'd love to, wouldn't we, Mads?"

Everyone else nodded enthusiastically. Marco presumably was the guy who made things happen in the hotel. Shannon struggled to find the correct term. *Concierge*, that was it. A French word. Victor was on his phone now, speaking in French, wandering towards the pool. He dipped a toe in, balancing on the other leg. It didn't shake at all, which Shannon's would have done. She'd have toppled straight in.

Victor came back and said, "There's an event happening in the Anchor Room." He made a disappointed face. "I don't want to take you to the other restaurants so Marco has made a reservation for us instead at the Castle on the Hill. Eight o'clock."

Maddie whooped.

"Nice one!" said Ollie.

Shannon was impressed. The Castle on the Hill was the most expensive restaurant on the island, with its own farm and estate. She'd read that unless someone made a booking a year ahead, it was impossible to get one.

"Oh my God, the last time Ollie and I were there was aaaaages ago," squealed Piglet. "We love their food."

"Zander's never been," said Maddie.

"It's been ages for us too," said Emily, looking at Annabel. "Did you get us a table by a window?"

138

"I did," said Victor, and Shannon saw that Emily was slightly taken aback.

Shannon lifted the bottle of water which she'd tucked to the side of her sunlounger, and held it in the air. "To us!" she said.

The others looked at her in amusement, then lifted their own bottles. "To us!" they chorused.

"To a fun summer," said Emily. She rummaged in her bag and brought out a packet of cigarettes. She offered them round. "Anyone?"

Shannon's blood froze at the sight of them.

"Thought you'd given them up?" said Annabel.

"Well, they are extremely hazardous to my health..." said Emily, lighting one.

"Especially if they start a fire," said Annabel, inspecting her toe again where she'd stubbed it. She looked up and caught her sister's eye.

The temptation to push both of them over the edge of the building was huge, but there were too many people to stop her, even if she had the strength to drag them to the metal-and-reinforced-glass balustrade. She walked over there herself, looking at the dark horizon and then down the ten or so storeys, and felt giddy.

Tonight, she told herself with a rush of adrenaline. She would act tonight.

CHAPTER 14

Helen was more excited than Shannon when she heard Shannon was going to the Castle on the Hill. "I can't believe you got a reservation," she asked. "I have multiple guests who are desperate to go there. Lucky you. Maybe people didn't make it over to the island, or are starting to cancel, because of the storm?"

"Maybe," Shannon replied.

She went upstairs to her room and stood under the shower. Despite the fantasies that continually played out in her head, she knew that she would probably opt for poison in the end.

It was one of the methods she'd researched in London. She'd come to the conclusion that the easiest way would be to use Nan's medication, which her mum had shoved into a bag for life with a load of belongings she couldn't face sorting through. Shannon had brought the tablets with her in her own washbag. The challenge would be getting it into their food or drink, making sure only Annabel and Emily were poisoned, putting in just enough so they wouldn't taste it but a sufficient amount to do the job properly.

They would be rushed to hospital, where nothing could be done for them, and before the cause was discovered, she would have disappeared from the island. That was the theory. But the reality was the hurricane was due tomorrow and there would be no way off the island and she didn't know how long that would last. On the other hand, if she waited, there was a risk that her cover would be blown or she might not get the same access to Emily and Annabel around food or drink. Her mind raced feverishly back and forth, trying to come to a decision.

She would be brave. She was doing this for her mum. As Shannon faced the shower, tilting her head back and closing her eyes, the water thrashing down on her face, she decided that tonight was the best night. The whole island was bracing itself for destruction and she would deliver.

After her shower, Shannon sat on the bed, wrapped in a towel, holding the bottle of white tablets. She would grind up the amount needed and pour it into two mini plastic bags which opened easily by pushing at the corners of the opening – one for Annabel, one for Emily – and wear a dress with pockets. She scoured the website for photos of what people wore to the Castle on the Hill. The photos were mostly of weddings or functions, but there were a couple where the customers were dressed like Maddie. Safe bohemian. No high thigh slits or too much cleavage. Plenty of wavy hemlines, expensive fabrics and jewellery, which did a good job of stealth boasting.

Her phone pinged with a message from Lydia: *How's it going? Crispin and I have drunk too much.* There was a second message about a club they'd been to in Bologna and a long description about how unbelievably cool it was and how they might enrol for Italian lessons.

Shannon didn't have time for this. She sent back: *Big night here. Dinner at a fancy restaurant. Got to go.*

Lydia had no idea how big a night it was going to be.

NICE ONE, came back the reply. *Bedtime for me!!*

Having decided on a black dress with a tight bodice and loose-ish skirt (with pockets), she coloured in her fake birthmark and checked her hair would cover it most of the time, then perused the menu online, her face slackening as she saw the prices. Thank God Victor was paying. Not that she could think about eating right now.

She needed to focus – and arrive early. Shannon's taxi dropped her at the stone-pillared entrance and she was welcomed by a man who held a large black umbrella above her to shield her from the rain, which was falling steadily but wasn't yet torrential, and told her Victor was already there.

He ushered her into the bar area, where Victor was

sitting on a high stool, tapping away at his phone, with what looked like orange juice by his side. When he saw her, he jumped down from the stool and greeted her like an actual friend, but she shook off the pleasure that brought. All emotion needed to be tucked away tonight.

"This doesn't look like the sort of place we'd be served alcohol underage," she said. It was an immaculate restaurant, all stone, glass, and thick white linen tablecloths and napkins. The view was across lush farmland to the sea. Woven seascapes hung on the wall.

"Correct," said Victor.

"So," said Shannon, "I propose a round of their non-alcoholic cocktails to start with. On me." She didn't stop to ask for his approval. "There's one with raspberries which looks amazing." She couldn't have any clear drinks because they would go cloudy from the tablets. The Harringtons liked raspberries – there were countless photos online of them with berry smoothies. "I'll order them now." She pulled her credit card out of her little patent black evening bag. It gave her great pleasure that Clarissa would be paying for this.

Victor seemed surprised that she was taking over, and looked as if he was going to object, or say that they should wait until everyone had arrived. She didn't like the way he watched her order and then line up the drinks when they came. Was he ever going to look away?

"Should we take a photo of the drinks and send it to the others, telling them to hurry up?" he asked.

But then his phone rang, and he said he had to take the

call outside, where it was quieter.

She glanced around for CCTV. There wasn't any; this was Fengari, not London. Now the moment was here, she was shaking. *Mum, please help me. I'm doing this for you.* She moved two of the glistening red drinks apart from the others and fumbled in her pocket for the ground-up tablets. She waited until the staff were occupied elsewhere, then slipped the contents of a bag into each glass.

She reached for a straw and stirred them quickly. She was still holding it when Victor came back.

"Taste test?" he asked.

Treacherously, her face blushed. "Yes," she said. "They're really good. Have one." She angled her body so he wouldn't take a spiked one.

"Did you get the photo?" he asked.

She blinked. "Not yet," she said, and she made a big thing of making the shot look perfect before she took a few photos. She checked them carefully to see if the two drinks at the back looked different to the others. When she was satisfied they didn't, she sent a message to the group: *Drinks are waiting, get a wriggle on!*

Piglet and Ollie arrived within minutes, and Shannon handed them a glass each. Piglet shrieked with delight at being there, while Ollie frowned at her. Next came Maddie and Zander, Maddie more conservatively dressed than earlier in the day but still colourful in an abstract print dress, and Zander looking more middle-aged than ever in a grey suit. The minutes until Annabel and Emily arrived were excruciating, seeing the two glasses sitting on the bar, condensation pooling at their bases.

Her heart was racing and she felt as if she might vomit from nerves. But what exactly was she nervous about? Failing – or succeeding? If she was honest, she didn't know.

And then the Harringtons swept in as if they owned the place, Annabel in a grey-and-cream shift dress, Emily in tight black trousers and a black frilly top.

"Do you always wear that funny little necklace with everything?" asked Emily with a flick of her blonde hair. "Ahhh, I bet Crispin gave it to you, didn't he?"

Shannon touched it and said, "I just love it!" in that nonchalant, confident way Maddie had about her clothes.

"Thing is, it *could* look tacky," said Emily. "A bit Poundland. But you don't wear much jewellery, so it sort of works."

Victor pointed at the two remaining drinks.

"Lydia insisted on these raspberry cocktails," he said, and Shannon nodded, unable to speak.

Annabel picked up the glass waiting for her. This was it. Shannon willed herself not to throw up. Emily had hers now and held it up to the light and looked at it closely.

"Pretty," she said.

Annabel nearly had her glass to her lips.

"Wait!" said Piglet. "We need a photo. Come on, everyone! I want to remember this evening!"

Annabel brought her glass back down as they jostled together for the photo, taken by a waiter who spent agonizing minutes arranging them into a symmetrical shot away from the bar. Lydia let her hair fall forward at the last moment so her face could hardly be seen.

"I regret getting him involved. The photos are so bad," laughed Piglet, taking a long sip of her drink. "Mmm, that's delicious."

Shannon's eyes were darting between Annabel and Emily. Neither had drunk from their glass, and now Emily had put hers down on the bar counter. Zander had put his next to hers as they looked at the rain outside, becoming heavier.

After rearranging his shirt collar, Zander picked up his drink, except it was the wrong one. It was Emily's.

That spiked liquid couldn't reach his lips. Shannon shot forward and grabbed the glass. "Sorry, Zander," she said, her voice low so the others wouldn't interfere, but she knew it had a slight wobble to it. "There's a hair on the edge. There." She pretended to pull it off and drop it on the floor.

"Gross," said Zander. "You wouldn't think that would happen here of all places."

"I think it might have been mine," said Shannon. "I was standing near there earlier." She pointed outside. "Whoa – did you see that lightning?"

This was the moment. With shaky fingers, she leaned forward and switched the glasses.

It was done. Emily turned round first and picked up the drink intended for her. Shannon's head thumped so hard

146

she could barely keep it upright and everything around her was in ultra-HD.

Suddenly, she couldn't do this. She wasn't strong enough. When it came down to it, she wasn't a murderer.

She swept her small bag on to the floor, pretending not to notice. She braced herself in advance for causing a huge scene, then tripped over it, flailing her arms so that they knocked both drinks out of the girls' hands, Emily's as she stood next to Zander, and Annabel's as she was inspecting Maddie's eye make-up.

The sound of glass smashing on hard tiles, the sloshing noise, a scream and the horrified gasps – all these mingled together and reverberated in her head. Emily was saying "Oh my God" over and over and Annabel wailed, "My dress is ruined. This is my favourite dress. It cost an absolute fortune."

Shannon looked up and saw raspberry-red splashes all over Annabel's grey-and-cream dress. Like blood splatters.

Waiters came rushing over. Everyone in the restaurant stopped their conversations.

She was pulled up from the floor by Victor. "Are you OK?" His expression was hard to read. She'd just ruined his generous night out. "What happened?" There was a note of suspicion in his voice.

"I'm not sure," she said. "I fell over something." She bent down and held up her bag. The hem of her dress was damp – it was black, so it didn't show too much. The drinks were being cleaned up by a waiter who was working efficiently with a mop. The restaurant was getting back to the previous hum of conversation, and Emily, Annabel and Piglet had disappeared. Maddie, Zander and Ollie had moved out of the way to dissociate themselves from the drama she'd caused.

"The others have gone to the bathroom to clean themselves up," said Victor, handing her a white napkin. "Use this to wipe your arms." The napkin turned red as she soaked up the cocktail and ground-up medication on her arms. She couldn't stop shaking. "I'm going to the bathroom too," she said.

As soon as she entered, the raised voices stopped. "I'm so sorry!" she gushed. "I'm so clumsy. So embarrassed." The cringing was real. Annabel and Emily had no idea what they'd escaped.

Piglet said, "It was an accident. Don't worry."

"Pigs, my dress is ruined," said Annabel. She was scrubbing at the red stains with a mini hand towel, making them worse, diluting the colour but spreading it.

"I'll buy you another one," said Shannon. "It's the least I can do."

Annabel grunted. "It's humiliating. How can I eat dinner looking like this?"

Emily was looking at her make-up in the mirror with a towel in her hand. "You caused such a scene, Lyds. So embarrassing."

Shannon washed her hands. Her head was whirling. A massive weight had lifted, she could finally take a breath, but at the same time she felt a dizzy nausea: if she didn't have it in her to murder, how was she going to punish these girls? How would her mum be avenged? All these months, all this planning, all this hatred she had nurtured for so long – what had it all been for?

"Everyone?" Maddie was there now. "Our table is ready. Bels, your dress isn't that bad. Let's make the best of the evening, for Victor's sake."

They went back out together, the four girls ahead of her, talking in low voices, Annabel saying, "I can't bear everyone looking at my dress."

Victor had indeed got the best table – the huge rectangular one by the window. Rain was lashing against it dramatically. "Shame about the view," he joked.

"How did you get this table at such short notice?" asked Ollie.

"It's what happens when you stay at the Maritime," said Victor with a slight wave of his hand. As if it was obvious.

"I'm impressed," said Ollie. "Even my dad can't get a same-day reservation."

"I'm paying a lot extra to move people off this table, obviously," murmured Victor, "but it's worth it, right?"

"Definitely," said Ollie. "Why wouldn't you?"

They had their own waiter, a man with a long, thin face, who explained he would only be serving their table, and they'd have a five-course tasting menu. Shannon had no idea what a tasting menu was, but it soon became clear there would be lots of small-portioned dishes to try with foods she'd never heard of, let alone eaten.

She was hyper aware of Victor opposite her, watching as she took a small mouthful of spiced shrimp in a beetroot sauce, despite having no appetite.

"Are you all right?" he asked.

"Yes. I'm really sorry about earlier."

"Don't be," he said airily. "Don't say anything more about it."

Emily, Victor, Zander and Ollie were eighteen and so able to drink after flashing their IDs. Emily was already on her second glass of wine. "What happens in Fengari stays in Fengari. Always," said Emily. "We won't squeal about this on social media, don't you worry."

Shannon smiled weakly, battered by the swinging emotions of the past few hours. She could feel herself slipping down into a hole that only her fury had kept her from before. No, she decided, that wasn't quite right: she still had the same hatred, but now it was weighted with shame. She loathed herself for not being able to go through with it.

As she cautiously smeared truffle butter on a small square of rye bread, she was suddenly aware of everyone looking at her. "Oh, sorry? Were you talking to me?" she asked.

"You remember Miss Martin, Lydia?" asked Zander, still chewing on a piece of shrimp. He looked like a younger version of Douglas Harrington, with his wine-flushed face.

Shannon nodded. The rye bread was stuck in her throat. Miss Martin wasn't a name Lydia had mentioned. She thought of Lydia in a drunken sleep. She wasn't going to reply to a message if Shannon needed her.

"She used to come to Portland too. What a nightmare woman," said Zander.

Shannon's mind raced. Someone who went to Walton House and the boys' school. A specialist teacher maybe? She rolled her eyes to agree with him.

"She had this hilarious, high-pitched shout," said Zander.

Shannon blinked and moved her hand to her thigh to stop the slight shaking. Was she a swimming teacher?

"God, the shouting," she said.

"What did she shout?" asked Maddie. She was looking from Zander to Shannon.

"You tell her, Lydia," said Zander. He was laughing now, remembering Miss Martin.

Shannon's armpits were hot, but her mind was suddenly clear and methodical as she raced through the options of how to reply. She might have botched a murder, but she could do this. She landed on a suitable response after a pause during which she smiled to match Zander's laughter. "I bet you'd do a better impression of her," she said.

It worked. "If you can't sing in tune, *mouth* the words," he yelled. Several other diners looked at him.

Their waiter, standing at a discreet distance, came closer. "Everything all right, sir?" he murmured.

The others laughed, and Shannon felt acutely aware that they must be being regarded as badly behaved rich kids.

"Tip top, thank you," said Zander.

"That waiter is such a killjoy," said Emily loudly, within earshot of the man.

Shannon exhaled. The next course arrived – a chilled cucumber soup which tasted as if someone had added water to a vegetable drawer in a fridge and swilled it around for a bit before pouring it into bowls. Just the smell of it made her want to gag.

She could leave, just say she felt ill, but she'd already caused enough drama. She would sit quietly and endure the meal.

The next course was beef in a blue-cheese sauce followed by tiny fish, all gazing up at her with their dead white eyes, served with little bowls for them to wash their fingers in, and the softest of cloths to wipe them afterwards.

There was a trio of tiny but intensely rich desserts, and cheese, oozing and smelling of something dug up, and brittle crackers with black bits embedded in them, coffee and little triangles of marzipan dipped in chocolate. The bill eventually came and Victor patted his jacket pocket, froze, then sighed and said, "I don't believe it. I left my credit card at the Maritime," and everyone glanced at each other in the silence. First the scene with the drinks, and now this.

Victor ran his fingers through his hair. "So. Yes. What an idiot." He pronounced *idiot* with a strong *t* at the end.

"I'll ask them to send the bill to the Maritime." He went off with the waiter to speak to the manager, and came back still embarrassed. "Will someone get it and I'll pay them back? It's just over one and a half thousand."

"Oof," said Zander, taking a sip of wine. "That's quite a chunk."

"This night is cursed," said Maddie. "We'll probably be blown away in our taxis on the way home, or a tree will fall on top of us."

"Don't say that, babe," said Zander.

Emily said, "Lydia, your mum won't mind if you put it on her credit card, will she?"

Would Clarissa mind? Possibly not, but she didn't want to have an unnecessary argument with her over it. She might try and curtail Shannon's other spending.

"I'll do the honours," said Ollie, gesturing for Victor to hand him the bill.

"Well done, Ols," said Piglet.

"I'll pay you back tomorrow, my friend," said Victor, and the two of them did a fist bump, then Ollie looked round and said, "What can I say, guys – I'm a legend both on and off the water!"

Annabel twisted the leaf bangle round her wrist as the waiter took Ollie's card and Shannon thought about how the bangle would have looked on her dead body. How close it had been.

"I'd better go back to boring old Linton Lodge now," Shannon said.

"What's it like there?" asked Maddie, stroking Zander's bright pink ear.

Shannon sighed. "I'm the youngest person there by about thirty years, and the woman in charge, Helen, is on my case the whole time."

Emily was drunk. "Sounds deathly, Lyds. Come and stay at Clifftop House for a bit."

Shannon felt a ray of hope open up inside. The chance of staying in the same house as the Harringtons was one she'd never dared consider. Perhaps she could find another way of exacting revenge?

"As long as you don't go smashing the place up," Emily added, with a cruel smile.

Shannon imagined *her* lifeless body by the bar, and it made her feel both powerful and weak at the same time.

"You are very clumsy," chimed in Annabel.

"Not usually, I swear," Shannon said, putting on her most apologetic smile. "But that's really so sweet of you. I mean, I would *love* to get out of the Lodge. But only if you're sure..."

"We're sure," said Annabel. "Move in tomorrow! You'll have a blast with us."

CHAPTER 15

Back in her room at Linton Lodge, Shannon lay on the bed and cried because of everything that had happened, and everything that hadn't, and then she ran a bath and lay under the water for as long as she could hold her breath, her dyed dark brown hair fanning out around her as the wind howled outside her room.

When she got into bed, she couldn't sleep – every time she closed her eyes she relived the glass switching and the moment of the fake trip. Everything jumbled in her head and she saw her mum struggling to breathe. She switched the side light on and scrolled through her phone. The latest updated message on the Fengari app was bordered in red. *Breaking news: Hurricane Rex has been blown off course and will not make landfall. However, bad weather is still likely for the next couple of days, so residents and tourists are asked to take care when out and about on the island. The ferries and helicopter are due to be operating as normal by Tuesday.*

Even Hurricane Rex didn't have what it took to wreak havoc.

Shannon sent a message to Clarissa: *Mummy, no need to worry about the hurricane any more. It's not going to hit Fengari. Also, I've given it a week at Linton Lodge and it's been very lonely (but I haven't complained, have I?). The Harringtons have invited me to stay at Clifftop House so I am going to move in tomorrow for a while.*

Annabel posted in the group chat: *You seen the news? Typical. Seb could have come on Tuesday after all and now he can't get a new reservation. Life sucks.*

Monday

The next morning Clarissa tried to call while Shannon was eating breakfast in bed. Shannon answered and then let Clarissa say, "Hello? Hello? Darling, are you there?" until she hung up. She then messaged to say she couldn't hear her and that the signal was weak. A message came back to say that while Clarissa understood, she had paid Helen upfront for the summer and she didn't want the Harringtons inconvenienced. She'd already been in touch with Rosie, who had no idea the girls had issued the invitation, and frankly it was quite embarrassing.

Shannon replied the way she knew Lydia would. *I'm doing the stupid lessons and I've got a chance to have a nice time and you are being mean. I'm sure Rosie won't mind me staying.*

Towards the end of the morning, Shannon felt her phone vibrate, and as soon as Miriam was busy marking a practice paper, she looked and saw the message: *I've discussed this with Daddy and spoken to Rosie again. You can go and stay at Clifftop House. Rosie very kindly said you can arrive any time this afternoon. Aren't you lucky? Don't be cross but—* Shannon had to swipe to open the message to read the rest of it. It was long. She ignored Miriam, who had looked up.

"Lydia, you need to put your phone away. We'll have another little break soon."

Shannon kept reading: *Rosie suggested I come out. You know I've needed a break since my knee injury. I managed to squeeze on to a flight on Friday. Don't worry, darling, I will keep out of your way as I know you are having fun with the girls and their friends.* The rest of it bounced before Shannon's eyes. *I'm not sure how long I'll stay. . . I'll speak to Helen at Linton Lodge. . .*

It was Monday. Clarissa Cornwallis was coming to Fengari in four days. *Four days.* Just as Shannon was starting to find a way to salvage this mission, Clarissa would come and spoil everything. It was time to acknowledge she'd failed at what she'd come to do. The familiar emptiness she'd felt in the days after her mum died was creeping up on her again. A bleakness which might swallow her up.

It needed to be handled really carefully or the real Lydia might panic. She might contact Clarissa immediately and confess that she was travelling and Shannon – Rhiannon – had taken her place.

"Lydia, finish your essay, please," said Miriam. There was a brave crispness to her voice.

Shannon frowned. "I've had some bad news," she said.

"Oh." The furrow in Miriam's forehead deepened. "I'm sorry. Do you want to talk about it?"

"No," said Shannon. "But I need to have a break now."

Miriam blinked. "If you really need—"

Shannon didn't wait for her to finish the sentence. She walked out of the classroom and into the courtyard. The air was damp from the heavy rain the night before, but the bench that reminded her of Pigeon Park and Ela was dry enough to sit on.

When Bex had died, Ela and her family had done their best to help. They'd helped her organize a small funeral when Bex's body was flown back home. Shannon had had no idea how expensive funerals were so they'd kept it simple, not that she remembered much of the short service at the crematorium because she'd been hysterical with loss throughout it.

That night, Shannon slipped out of Ela's house and sat on the wall of Pigeon Park, looking down on the desolate open space in the half-light, and the play park, which needed a major overhaul. The swings didn't even have any seats.

She thought she'd feel closer to her mum there, because although the park was rank these days, it was a place they'd come to a lot when she was little. She'd learned to ride a bike here, which they'd kept at Nan's house, and they'd practised penalty shots, using clothing as goals, and there had been endless picnics in the summer, with orange Fanta or mini chocolate rolls as an occasional treat. Her mum had had so much energy. This was where happy memories should be, but instead she was trembling with rage.

Shannon had loved her mum with a fierceness other people didn't understand. Bex Jones had deserved more than the difficult, short life she'd had. Ever since Nan died it had been the two of them, there for each other no matter what. And now Shannon was on her own and it was so, so hard.

In the courtyard of Fengari Training College, there on her own, she whispered, "I may not have much time, but I'll make Emily and Annabel Harrington pay for what they did to you, Mum. I'll find a way." She stifled a sob by taking a deep breath. She'd come so far – literally and metaphorically. If she couldn't end their lives, she would make sure they'd be miserable ones.

Staying in Clifftop House meant she'd have a chance to find something concrete to use against them. There were things her mum had hinted at, things that might bring them down and make them suffer for years like her. Maybe that was even better than killing them.

But to only have four days...

She composed a message to Clarissa. *I'm begging you, please don't come, Mummy. I want this to be my adventure.*

She could hear Miriam calling her, saying she had a couple of minutes left until the break was over. She tucked her knees into her chest and her phone vibrated, making her jump.

Darling, I do understand, but I am overdue a little break and Rosie would love me to come. It'll be fine, I promise.

At least it had been a swift reply.

There was nothing she could do. She had to be gone before Clarissa arrived.

Miriam stood next to her. "Lydia, I don't know what's happened. Let's talk about it."

You're impossible, Mummy, Shannon messaged. *If you're going to spoil my fun, I want to take the rest of this week off to explore the island on my own before you get here.*

"I can tell you're not in the mood to work but we need to have a chat," Miriam persisted.

Shannon's phone pinged again and she swiped to read the message.

I'll see what Daddy says but I don't see any harm in that. Your teacher tells me you're making fantastic progress. Well done darling x

Shannon stood up. "I'm taking the rest of the week off," she said. "Mummy will explain."

Miriam stood there, unsure what to say. Maybe she didn't feel she could ask about the bad news again. Maybe she thought Shannon was lying. It didn't matter. Shannon was never going to see her again.

"I see," said Miriam. She didn't see at all. "I'll wait to hear from your mother." She sighed. "I'm sorry about the bad news, Lydia. I hope you have a good break, and I look forward to seeing you next week. I'm enjoying teaching you."

"You're a good teacher," Shannon said. *That was stupid and sentimental*, she told herself as she closed the door to the college. It had sounded too much like a goodbye.

At Linton Lodge, Shannon messaged Lydia saying she should carry on as normal, playing everything down as much as possible.

Shannon/Lydia: *I'll explain everything to Clarissa when she arrives and tell her it was my idea. She'll be startled at first and maybe cross. But by the time she speaks to you, she'll have calmed down. It will be fine.*

Shannon had to count on the fact Lydia was a coward and would prefer Shannon to break the news of the swap to Clarissa. Next, she packed her bags to go to Clifftop House. Linton Lodge was the most luxurious place she'd ever slept, and she walked round her room touching things she wanted to remember – the softness of the bed linen, the silky edging on a blanket she'd never needed but which had been on a shelf in the cupboard, the ripples on the bone china mug she'd made tea in, and the texture of the blinds made from fabric with a raised design. She resisted packing the complimentary shampoo and conditioner because that was a cheap move for someone like Lydia Cornwallis.

When her bags were completely packed, Shannon ordered a taxi for three o'clock, then rang down for her last Linton Lodge bar snack – a fancy burger, with all the fancy stuff removed, and bog-standard fries, not rosemary salted ones, or sweet potato. As she was eating, she messaged the group chat, telling everyone how happy she was to be moving into Clifftop House for a bit. Annabel responded with a link to a TikTok of a sped-up girl tidying her room. As if. The only person doing any preparation for her visit was Mrs Pushkin.

She shut the door to the room and went downstairs to the waiting taxi.

CHAPTER 16

"Welcome back to Clifftop House, Lydia," said Mrs Pushkin, opening the door and stepping aside for Lydia to haul in her two large suitcases. Mrs Pushkin was wearing loose black trousers, and a black top which was quite fitted, and revealed her back was slightly bent. Surely she was old enough to get a pension by now and relax in an old people's home? "Nobody is in, I'm afraid. The girls told me to tell you they've gone to the beach for a dip, if you want to join them."

"Thanks," said Shannon. She had no intention of doing that.

"Let me show you to your room. Leave your suitcases here. I'll ask the gardener to bring them upstairs in a minute." She picked something up from the chest of drawers in the hall and handed it to Shannon. It was a single key and a gate fob attached to a metal rectangular key ring on which loopy letters in red enamel said *Welcome to Fengari*. "Mrs Harrington asked me to give you these for the duration of your stay. The fob works the main gates and the side gate. Please make sure you always close the gates, or we get the occasional tourist wandering in."

Why did Mrs Pushkin have to call Rosie "Mrs Harrington"? It was too TV costume drama for words. She also pronounced *tourist* as if it was an inferior species. Shannon mentally rolled her eyes and wrapped her hand round the key ring. Now this was worth having.

Shannon left her suitcases for Finch, even though it felt wrong to have him wait on her like a servant. They *were* heavy, though.

Mrs Pushkin escorted her to the smaller of the two guest rooms Annabel had showed her before. Shannon supposed the other one was being reserved for Clarissa when she arrived.

In four days.

Mrs Pushkin pointed out two clean white towels on the bed. "Don't take those to the beach or the pool," she said. "There are blue and green ones for that, and you'll find those in the laundry room or the pool changing room." She pushed open the door to the bathroom. "Any dirty laundry may be placed in that wicker basket, or you can save my legs and bring it straight to the laundry room."

Shannon wondered if she always used that tone with guests or if it was just her. Or was she just oversensitive to it, not understanding how to interact with a housekeeper?

"I like to remind guests that this is an island," said Mrs Pushkin, "so we take water conservation very seriously. So just short showers or small baths, please."

Shannon glanced outside, where the sky was still overcast.

"A couple of days' rain doesn't alter that request," snapped Mrs Pushkin. "And sanitary products in the bin, please. This house has old plumbing. I expect you know that parts of this house date back to. . ."

"Seventeen eighty-six," said Shannon. Did this family ever shut up about how long they'd colonized the island for?

Mrs Pushkin gave a brief nod and said, "I'll leave you to settle in, then, Lydia."

Shannon went to the window and stared at the bunkhouse. It was hard to imagine how she would engineer the Harringtons' downfall, with so little time left.

There was a knock at the door and she swung round. It was Finch with her suitcases. She rushed forward to take one from him, but he carried on going forward and they bumped into each other.

"Sorry," Shannon said. "Thanks for bringing them up."

"It's no bother." His arms were so muscly, it probably *was* no bother.

"Did you get some good photos yesterday?" she asked.

"Yes, I'm really pleased with them," he said, walking towards the door but not leaving. He put his hand on the door handle. "And this will sound strange to you, but I found some indigenous grass that I've been looking for. Super-interesting, if you're a botany nerd like me!"

"Indigenous grass, no way!" Shannon laughed, but it was with him, not at him.

"You may laugh," he said, pointing a jokey finger at her, "but my sister's a biology professor and she's as excited as me. I've picked a small sample for her and she can't wait to see it!"

"Wow – a whole family of nerds!" She smiled and said, "Finch, this sounds strange too but I'd really like to see inside the bunkhouse." She clutched at the first excuse she could think of that would sound plausible in case the Harringtons found out, and which wouldn't make Finch think she was hitting on him. "My family have a place in Scotland, and we'd like to build some staff quarters. The bunkhouse was built recently, so it would be useful to have a look – if you don't mind."

He frowned slightly.

"I'm interested in architecture," she said, in an attempt to explain. "My parents say I can have a hand in the design."

"Sure, but the bunkhouse isn't a great example for staff quarters," said Finch. "It's stuffy and. . ." He paused. "The materials are quite cheap."

She nodded. "That's the sort of thing which is good to know." She went to follow him.

"Lydia," he said. "I don't want to lose my job by being unprofessional, so, er ... it's better if you come down to the bunkhouse ten minutes after me. Unless you want to organize a more formal tour through the Harringtons?"

"Oh," she said. He was right. Neither of them wanted to draw the Harringtons' attention to this. "No worries. Thanks. I only need a quick look round. I'll unpack a few things and then come down."

"OK, then," he said, and left.

She unpacked one suitcase, finding herself absent-mindedly putting them in two piles. One of clothes she liked, and one of clothes which Lydia had given Shannon for authenticity – especially for partial glimpses in the photos she would be sending Clarissa – including an out-of-shape jumper which smelled of furniture polish and dog, and a couple of tops. One of them had a rip in the armpit. When Shannon had pointed it out, Lydia had said, "Nobody will see it unless you lift your arm up." Shannon was never going to wear it. Where she came from, only someone who had no self-respect would have worn a top they knew had a rip in it. But she noticed some of the clothes she'd really liked when she bought them seemed too much now, almost as if her taste had already changed.

She placed her lighter in the drawer with her underwear and kept her passports in the lining of her suitcase and shoved that under her bed.

After a while she walked soundlessly down the stairs, stopping at the bottom to hear where Mrs Pushkin was. The clacking of plates being moved about told her that it was safe to slip into the garden, as long as she couldn't be seen from the kitchen. She walked quickly to the bunkhouse and rang the doorbell, her heart hitting painfully against her ribs. It sounded like the old-fashioned chime of her nan's house. She swayed as the door opened and Finch said with concern, "What's up with you?"

"The doorbell. It reminded me of somebody," she said, going for half of the truth. As she stepped inside, she added, "I know that sounds weird."

"Some memories can be pretty intense," he said philosophically.

Inside, it was almost just as she'd remembered seeing it on-screen when chatting with her mum. There was no hallway. She was in a gloomy living room with an L-shaped beige sofa, a very heavy-looking stone coffee table with a laptop and jumble of books and used mugs on it, a TV up on the wall, a shelf with some faded paperbacks, and that was it. There was only one window and a thick net curtain hung over it. The floor was the cheap plastic-wood strips that she and her mum had had in the London flat. Through an open door, she saw a narrow kitchen with fake wood cupboard doors, and then there were three half-open doors. A bathroom and two bedrooms. There was something shockingly brutal about the bunkhouse being built in exactly the same layout as before, albeit in brick, not wood. The pain in her chest grew worse.

"Have a look round. I'm not the tidiest of people, so you'll have to ignore my mess," said Finch.

Shannon didn't hear the rest of what he was saying because it suddenly hit her that she could smell smoke. She felt her stomach turn and her eyes smart. Panic surged through her.

"Are you OK?" he asked.

She couldn't see any smoke. Was it a hallucination? Something supernatural? Her mum sending a sign?

"You want to lie down on the sofa?" he asked, still worried, and for a moment she did. She wanted to collapse on the sofa and howl, but she was coughing now. It wasn't a cigarette smell. It was more like a bonfire, the ghostly lingering smell of the bunkhouse fire. Now there was a charred taste on her tongue.

"I'm OK," she said. "I think I'm just coming down with something. It always happens when I'm on holiday. But maybe I should splash some water on my face."

"That door there." On her way to the bathroom she glanced in Finch's room. The floor space between his bed and the wall wasn't visible because it was covered in clothes, a couple of towels and a small tower of nature books. On the chest of drawers, dirty crockery and cutlery was piled up, next to strands of dried grass. There was a photo of a smiling couple, who she guessed might be his parents.

The other bedroom was where her mum's had been. She knew it was to the left when you came into the bunkhouse

169

because its small window faced towards the west and she'd taken photos of dramatic sunsets through it. She psyched herself up in the bathroom before going to look at it. The room was furnished in exactly the same way as Finch's, but there were no belongings in it. At what point had her mum known she was going to die? She'd died trying to escape – had her bedroom door been locked from the outside? Her throat tightened, choking off her air supply. She felt hot, burning hot. The nightmares she'd suffered after her mum's death came back to her. The flames, the smoke, the heat, the struggle. The terrible, terrible panic.

"What do you think?" called Finch.

She ran from the room, into the lounge. He stared at her.

"I need some air. I don't feel well. I'm sorry," she said, and she ran to the door, gasping as she opened it, stumbling into the brightness of the afternoon. She gulped big mouthfuls of clean air and wiped away the tears which were pouring down her face.

CHAPTER 17

*She was in a burns unit, finally finding the end of a bandage of
a body which had been completely covered apart from a slit for the
mouth and nose, frantic to know if her mum was underneath.*

As she jerked out of sleep, she let go of the bit of duvet
she was clutching, the end of the bandage from her dream.

Annabel was in her room, Emily behind her. Their hair
was wet against their heads from their swim. They looked
more similar than ever. Even-featured, clear-eyed; they
were ordinary-looking monsters.

"Welcome to Clifftop House, Lyds!" trilled Annabel.

"Thanks," said Shannon, rubbing her eyes, jolting back
into being Lydia. Her clothes were sticking to her from
the heat of lying against the duvet. "Mummy has granted

me a week off lessons. I'm gassed. Finally, I get to have something like a proper holiday. I'm so tired I actually fell asleep."

"We heard she's coming to stay on Friday," said Annabel. "Seb's parents are being so lazy about re-booking his flight. I hate them." She sat on the bed, and Emily perched on the faded blue upholstered chair in the corner which had seemed to Shannon to be there as a large ornament, like the stool in Clarissa's floristry shop.

"We just got back from the beach and now we're bored. Want to hang out in the summer house? Dad's got a load of spirits we could pinch. Let's mix some together and see what happens?"

"Yuck," said Shannon. "Definitely not."

The two of them laughed. "You should have seen how messy it got when we made Piglet do that," said Emily.

"I'm glad I didn't," said Shannon, and they laughed again.

"Agghh, we need to think of something fun to do," moaned Annabel. She pulled at Shannon's arms. "Come on, get up. We need fresh blood."

Shannon shook away Annabel's grip and sat upright immediately. "What d'you mean, fresh blood?"

"New ideas," said Emily, her eyes even bluer from her deepening tan. "Fresh input."

"Then you've asked the right person to come and stay," said Shannon, lifting an eyebrow to make it seem mysterious. She searched at the side of the bed for her trainers. "Remember those fireworks you showed me, Annabel? Let's go down to the summer house and set some off."

Annabel clapped her hands. "Inspired!"

As they walked down the garden, Shannon saw how the sisters egged each other on, and how their behaviour was so much more extreme when the two of them were together. Now they were telling Shannon how they were pros at setting off fireworks, since the party they'd had at the end of last summer. She worked very hard at keeping her voice level as she said, "Didn't you have a fire in the bunkhouse last summer? I'm sure I heard that from someone."

"Yeah. And?" said Emily. "The fire wasn't started by a firework. It was started by a cigarette." She yanked open the door of the summer house. It smelled of sickly scented candles and there were shortbread biscuits spilling out of an open packet on the table. "Don't eat those, they'll be stale," she said.

Shannon watched Annabel select an armful of fireworks from the astounding collection, and they planted them in the earth at the back of the summer house. "I guess it would be better if we waited until it got dark," Shannon said.

"Nah, we're in the mood to do it now," said Emily. She was like an impulsive twelve-year-old.

Annabel produced a gas lighter gun and they took turns lighting and running away, reacting in over-the-top ways to the fireworks' bangs, screeches and sprays of coloured light – laughing and howling like wolves, acting scared and whooping. The smell of smoke and explosives hung in the air.

And all the time, Shannon thought of the fire in the bunkhouse and her mum being trapped and afraid, and her heart squeezed into a tight ball, small and hard.

When Ted the gardener came to see what was going on, Emily told him it was none of his business, and he muttered, "You girls."

After they'd finished, they lay on the sofas in the summer house, Emily smoking and tapping her ash on top of the biscuits. Shannon closed her eyes and tried to remember everything her mum had told her about the girls. Trawling her memory for anything that she could use against them. She would bring them to their knees.

She thought of the bikinis and wraps lying in plastic bags in a heap on the floor of Annabel's bedroom. The separate account Annabel had used on Instagram for her beachwear had been taken down halfway through last summer, after lots of people piled into the comments to say she'd ripped off someone else. Her mum had said there'd been a letter and Annabel had been in a massive sulk about it. How bad had it been? Was it a legal thing?

"I'm thinking of doing something like your beachwear," she said lazily to Annabel. "Maybe with jewellery. Did you, like, come up with a design and get them made somewhere? How did it work?"

Annabel screwed up her face as if she didn't really want

to think about it. "I got everything made in India – Piglet's dad sourced a company for me. To be honest, Lyds, it was fun to start with, but it was a load of hassle by the end."

Shannon noted Annabel hadn't specified how she'd come up with a design.

"You shouldn't have splashed it all on Instagram," said Emily.

"Insta was the best bit," said Annabel. Her voice was whiny. "And I got loads of sales through it. I'm still selling things privately but it's not the same."

"Why shouldn't you have put it on Insta?" asked Shannon.

Annabel smiled. "Just..." She paused. "The wrong people saw them."

Shannon waited for more, but Annabel said offhandedly, "No regrets!"

Emily smirked. Annabel threw a biscuit at her. Stray ash rained down on the sofa. "Sister code." There was a warning in her voice, then Annabel said in a sweeter tone, "You're so lucky you don't have a sister, Lyds."

"You wouldn't want a brother like Henry," said Shannon. She trotted out anecdotes that Lydia had told her, such as the countless times Henry had pinned her down and used her own hands to hit herself, and how he liked to rub her toothbrush in soap.

But apparently that wasn't enough meanness to satisfy Emily. "I'm so bored," she said. "Let's invite the others round for pizza tonight."

They wasted some time betting on who would reply first on the group chat. It was Piglet. Annabel won, and told the other two to lick their fingers and scoop up some ash and eat it.

They obliged, and Shannon, not wanting the dares to escalate, said, "What shall we do now?"

Emily nudged Annabel. "How about we find out more about the gardener. He may be fit, but he's not very friendly. I find him creepy. Always out with his camera."

"Let's go to the bunkhouse?" suggested Annabel.

The hairs stood up on the back of Shannon's neck. She wondered what they'd say if she told them she'd been in the bunkhouse earlier. What if they saw Finch and he said something to her in front of the other two? "The gardener seems nice enough to me. I don't think he's creepy."

"Ah, you're so funny, Lyds," said Annabel. "So wholesome."

"It'll be fun," said Emily. "And everyone has secrets." She winked. "Even you, I bet." She was off the sofa, pulling Shannon up. "Come on! Let's go and see where Finch is. We don't want him to catch us in the bunkhouse. Annabel, get the key."

Finch was on the tennis court, mending the net. Emily said "Finally!", then declared that the job would take at least ten minutes and it was therefore an ideal time to check out the bunkhouse. "OK, let's have a bet. On a scale of one to ten, how gross d'you think his bedroom is? Ten being the most disgusting thing you can imagine."

Shannon frowned. How gross would *their* bedrooms be if Mrs Pushkin didn't tidy up after them?

"Lydia's gone for a ten," said Annabel, misreading her face.

"At least this year's gardener is good-looking," said Emily. "You should have seen the face on last year's."

Shannon looked down at the path, so she could keep her emotion from them. They were almost at the bunkhouse and she was sweating.

Annabel said, "Yeah, and we had a woman who came here as summer staff who fancied him. She was like twice his age. It was disgusting."

It was almost impossible for Shannon to move. They were talking about her *mother*. She wanted to run back to the summer house for fireworks to aim at them both.

"Our staff are always weird," said Emily. "Apart from Mrs P, of course." She tried the door. It was locked. She held out her hand to Annabel, who placed the key in it. Shannon's head was spinning. How easily they reframed her mum's defence of Bobby. Now they were about to persecute the next person, as if last summer hadn't happened at all – just because they were bored.

The key turned easily and as the door opened, Shannon could smell the smoke again. If she went inside she'd throw up. "What's the plan if he interrupts us?" she asked.

"He won't," said Annabel.

"The net looked almost done to me," said Shannon.

177

"Are you wimping out, you scaredy-cat?" asked Emily, amused.

"I'm saying you need a lookout." Shannon stood firm. "I'm happy to keep him talking if he shows up."

"OK," said Emily. "We'll have a good look round, but we won't be long. If he turns up, get him to do an errand somewhere else."

It was quiet after they slammed the door shut, apart from the buzz of insects in the nearby plants. Shannon shifted her weight from one foot to the other.

A movement caught her eye. Finch? Like, *now*? It was. He was walking with some speed down the path. He must have worked fast. In a few seconds, he'd see her and wonder why she was standing there. He might say something about her being in the bunkhouse earlier, which Annabel and Emily would overhear through the window.

His face changed as soon as he saw her. It choked her for an instant, that look of concern for her well-being. With a backwards glance at the bunkhouse she jogged over to meet him.

"You feeling better?" he asked. "I was worried when you ran off." He was searching her face, but clearly wasn't reassured by what he saw.

She couldn't tell him what Annabel and Emily were up to. That would make her too vulnerable. She couldn't risk being exposed as being on his side rather than theirs. She said, "Yeah, I felt sick, that's all. I had a lie-down and felt way better. Did you hear us setting off fireworks?"

He grimaced. "Yes, and Ted said. . ."

She didn't want to hear what Ted had said. "Thing is, Finch. We didn't clear up the fireworks, and it would be great if you could do it." She was aware of her body going rigid with the awkwardness. He looked deeply unimpressed.

"Did Emily and Annabel make you tell me?" he asked. His eyes were wide and open. Too trusting.

"No, I just remembered we'd left everything."

Go. Just, go.

She could see he was looking beyond her and turned to see what he was looking at: Emily and Annabel leaving the bunkhouse, laughing. They looked at Shannon and Finch and laughed louder, running towards the house. Emily shouted, "You're a useless lookout, Lyds."

"Come back here!" roared Finch, but the two girls ignored him. "What's going on?" Finch asked Shannon, his eyes furious now.

Shannon shrugged. She made herself go blank. She couldn't give him any emotion, but inside she was hollow with shame.

"Unbelievable," muttered Finch, and shouted, "You're trespassing!"

"Chill," Annabel shouted back. "This is private property. *Our* private property. The police wouldn't be interested." And then, "Hurry up, Lyds."

When Shannon caught up with them, wanting to cry, Emily gestured towards the outdoor chairs on the patio outside the kitchen. "I've got a stitch," she said. "Let's sit down a moment."

"You're so unfit, Emily," said Annabel cheerfully, as she plonked herself down.

"Annabel! Never say that," hissed Emily, and Annabel went quiet. Shannon wondered why that had been such a bad thing to say. Why did she have to give the impression that she was fit if she wasn't?

Emily looked at Shannon, smiling in an attempt to cover the awkwardness. "That was so much fun. Guess what we found?"

"Er . . . dirty washing?" she ventured, reliving the hurt in Finch's eyes. She had to dismiss it.

"Yeah, so much dirty stuff. Disgusting. He even had grass in there. Grass! Bizarre. We couldn't see what photos he's been taking because we couldn't get into his laptop. We found this photo, though. Look at his mum – she obviously can't afford to get her teeth fixed. Tragic." Annabel pulled out her phone, and showed Shannon the photo she'd seen on the chest of drawers. Shannon hadn't noticed his mum's teeth when she'd seen the photo earlier. They were crooked, but not too bad.

"Why wouldn't you have the self-respect to get your teeth done?" said Emily. "You just save up."

"And don't you think his dad looks shifty?" said Annabel. "I mean, that jacket? *Please.*"

Shannon curled her toes to give her something to concentrate on that wasn't punching them in the mouth so they stopped speaking. "What if he tells your parents you were in there?" she asked.

Annabel didn't miss a beat. "You're such a worrier, Lyds. We'll tell them we were playing a game of dares with you."

"Oh," said Shannon. She couldn't quite work out whether that meant they would blame her, but she let it pass.

There was a noise behind them, and they saw Mrs Pushkin at the doors that led from the patio into the kitchen.

"It's my night off, remember, girls? And your parents are out at that charity function. D'you want me to leave you some dinner tonight, or will you get a takeaway?"

"Takeaway," said Emily. "We've invited some people over to the summer house."

"As you wish," said Mrs Pushkin. She added that setting off fireworks during the afternoon had annoyed some of their neighbours. She had smoothed it over, but she'd rather it didn't happen again.

Shannon zoned out of the conversation. Tonight, hopefully Douglas and Rosie would be sleeping soundly after their big night out.

Time was running out, and she had work to do.

CHAPTER 18

Shannon wanted to go to her room and be by herself, but the other two insisted on her hanging out with them in the garden room to watch a film.

"I heard you like anime," said Emily as she picked up a TV remote. "Let's watch one on Netflix. Which ones d'you rate?"

That was the first time Shannon had heard Lydia was into anime. "Who did you hear that from?"

"My friend who knows Crispin," said Emily.

It must have been Crispin's thing, not Lydia's. "Yeah, it was something we did together, yeah," said Shannon, forcing herself to look wistful, as if she was missing him, to buy herself time. Emily was loving her discomfort.

"Did you two have a favourite?" Emily persisted.

Shannon's mind was blank. She couldn't think of a single anime title. She thought of the manga her friend Ela had read ... *Assassination Classroom*. Had that been made into a film?

"I'm *not* watching anime," said Annabel, and Shannon said with concealed relief, "I honestly don't mind what we watch," and almost laughed when Annabel selected a true crime series.

The opening sequence began with a wide-angled shot of a house in what was clearly London.

Shannon had gone to Lydia's house twice before their plan swung into action. Lydia's parents were out, but if they'd come back without warning it wouldn't have been the end of the world. The Cornwallis family knew her as Rhiannon-who-helped-out-in-the-florist's. They'd have been surprised that Lydia was so friendly with her, but it wouldn't have been a red-flag moment.

The house in South Kensington was in a row of three-storey properties. It had freshly painted white window frames and a front door with stained-glass panels. Inside, it was far bigger than it looked from the outside. The style was upper-class rustic, despite the location of the house a few metres away from a tube station, and there were vases of flowers in every room. Obviously. There were flowery cushions and flower paintings, but it was arty, not like in Nan's house. Nan wasn't very subtle with her love of florals. She'd had a printed dress with pink roses so large, only about five and a half roses could fit on it.

Lydia had taken her into the vast kitchen, all wood and baskets and open shelves with jars with things poured into them, like rice and seeds. There was a lot of sparkling stainless steel and a large, professional-looking coffee maker. Lydia had poured her juice from the enormous fridge packed with food and alcohol, and they'd sat at the huge wooden table and Lydia had talked about her likes and dislikes, her food preferences and everything that came into her head. Then she'd taken her upstairs to show Shannon her floor of the house, which consisted of a bedroom and walk-in wardrobe, study and bathroom. "I hope you don't turn out to be a stalker," she laughed, as Shannon noted which brand of hair products and make-up she used.

Shannon laughed, and with a flash of inspiration said, "We could write up what we're doing for a newspaper or a blog afterwards," knowing that Lydia would be completely taken with that idea, and the whole thing would be less creepy for her. And that's when Lydia had said, "Crispin's cousin is a journalist for a gossip website. He's always looking for content. The juicier the better! He sometimes sells his stories to newspapers."

Shannon had tucked that bit of information away in her head, and now she was retrieving it for her new way forward.

Watching this true crime show, she saw how the

strangest things brought people down, mistakes they made in other areas of their lives or things they blurted out.

They were watching the next episode when Rosie put her head round the door and said, "Lydia, darling! I'm so pleased you said yes to coming to stay. Marvellous to have you here, and so exciting that your mama is coming on Friday. You can fend for yourselves, can't you, girls? I gather from Mrs P you've opted for a takeaway for your friends."

Shannon smiled sweetly at her and thanked her while the other two barely acknowledged her.

Rosie said, "Girls! Clarissa says Lydia is going after a tennis scholarship, so make sure you get some games in with her while she's here."

Shannon did her best to look modest while inwardly freaking. First the anime and now this. Lydia had told her she hated tennis, but that Clarissa pushed her to play. She'd been planning to say she was rubbish.

"Have fun, then!" Rosie said. All of a sudden she held up her phone. "I'm just taking a photo of you three to show Clarissa that you're safe and sound."

Shannon immediately held her hand in front of her face, but it was too late! There was a heavy brick of horror in Shannon's stomach. She could tell Rosie had taken it and was satisfied it wasn't too bad. "Please," she said, "don't send her a photo of me. I look awful."

"Your mother isn't going to think you look awful," said Rosie. She was typing a message. "There. Sent. Don't worry, Lydia. Your mum will love it."

Shannon's breathing became rapid and shallow as panic threatened to overwhelm her. Everything had been ruined in that swift, unthinkable action. She pressed the corners of her eyes, near her nose, because there was an unbearable pressure building up inside her head. What could she do, apart from wait?

Around her, life carried on as normal in Clifftop House. Emily and Annabel were bickering about who was going to steal the alcohol from the wine cellar once their parents had gone out.

"Ah, Victor says that he'll bring some," said Emily, checking her phone. "He can, quote, 'literally get his hands on anything'."

"Either of you looked his family up?" asked Annabel. "Like, exactly how rich are they?" She paused the episode.

Googling would be a distraction, as any second Clarissa would surely contact her or Rosie would come in, demanding to know who the interloper in the photo was. The three of them did it simultaneously. Up came Victor's family's art foundation. The family art-dealing business was expanding to become a visual arts centre in the south of France which would house gallery space, a restaurant and members-only lounge. There was a photo of Victor with his parents. His mum was dressed in a silvery gown that had clearly been made to measure because it fitted her curves perfectly. She had a plump, smiley face. His dad was scowling, as if he didn't like being photographed. Annabel found the net worth of the de Courtois family first: six hundred and fifty million euros.

"Wow," said Emily. "He's only here this summer because he met Ollie at that sailing competition, so we have to make the most of him while we've got him."

A couple of hours later, miraculously, Rosie's text hadn't triggered any reaction at Clifftop House. It would come at any moment, though. The temperature was cool enough for Shannon to be wearing a hoodie. The hurricane had passed, but the skies were still cloudy and threatening more rain.

The eight of them were sprawled around in the summer house. Zander sat on a chair with Maddie on his lap, Piglet was cross-legged on the floor, Ollie and Victor shared one sofa, and Annabel and Emily the other. There was just enough room for three people to sit on each sofa, Shannon had to decide which one to go for. She chose to go in between Ollie and Victor, which annoyed Emily, who told her to stop flirting with Victor. Now she knew his family's enormous net worth, she was acting differently around him.

"I'm only sitting next to him," Shannon said, trying to keep her mind off the photo.

Victor put his arm round Shannon. It felt heavy on her shoulders, but in a reassuring way. "What's wrong with flirting?" His arm pulled her round, to encourage her to look at him. "You can flirt with me all you like."

She rolled her eyes, and when he gave her a squeeze, she almost spilled her vodka and lemonade, and he looked embarrassed. She'd made sure to pour herself a really weak one, and while watching him get himself a drink had noticed he wasn't drinking alcohol at all, although he pretended he was.

Annabel read out a series of messages off her phone from Seb saying how much he missed her, her voice cracking a little, and the attention moved to her.

They decided on pizzas, none of them sticking to the menu Piglet had posted for them on the group chat, apart from Shannon. Piglet phoned over the order, giggling as she explained what needed to be taken away or added to each pizza, and ordering a load of sides which they hadn't discussed. When she finished the call, Shannon asked how much she owed, and Victor said, "Ahh, you're so sweet, Lydia." She liked how he said the name *Lydia* in his French accent.

"It all evens out in the end, doesn't it?" said Piglet.

Shannon didn't think it actually did. She hadn't seen Annabel, Emily, Maddie or Zander forking out for much. Some rich people could be so cheap.

"While we're waiting, let's play a game," said Emily, drinking straight from the Prosecco bottle she'd placed on the floor next to her. "It's called guess the objects on the gardener's chest of drawers."

"Oooh," said Ollie, fanning himself dramatically. "I'm not sure if I want to know."

188

Emily spun the game out until she showed everyone the photo, and nobody could believe the grass, and Annabel went on about how strange his parents looked. Nobody asked why or how the photo had been taken.

Maddie said, "Why does that agency always send weirdos?"

Shannon took a gulp of her drink and coughed.

Victor patted her on her back. "You OK?"

She nodded, unable to speak for a moment.

"Who knows? But thank God for Mrs P," said Emily, sounding like her mother.

Annabel nodded. "We literally couldn't function without her."

That, thought Shannon, was probably true.

"I think your Mrs Pushkin is scary," said Victor.

"Me too," said Shannon, and they shared a look. She wasn't sure what sort of a look it was, but something passed between them. He'd definitely picked up on the fact she hadn't joined in the game. In contrast, he'd been responsible for the guesses becoming more and more wild, ending with a pet snake.

"Let's go and confront your gardener," said Maddie. "Ask him to explain the grass. Maybe he smokes it, or he's into witchcraft?"

"Good idea, Mads," said Annabel. "Reminding me why you are very much my best friend on the island."

Shannon noticed Piglet looking hurt, but then Shannon's phone vibrated. Her stomach dropped as she stood up and went to read the message in private.

189

Darling, Rosie sent me. . . she read from the first line as she swiped with shaking fingers. The message loaded and she told herself to stop jiggling around. Victor was watching her.

Darling, Rosie sent me a photo of her girls with someone else on the sofa. Hilarious. She must be distracted. I won't point it out! The girl looked a little bit like what's-her-name from the florist. Rhia? I'm sure you are settled in to Clifftop House now. Hope you're having fun!

What? Clarissa was so confident that Shannon was actually Lydia that she hadn't been thrown whatsoever by that photo.

Relief surged through her veins. She sent Clarissa a laughing face emoji and a thumbs up.

There was a loud buzzing sound, and Emily got up to speak into an intercom on the wall which appeared to be linked to the side gate. She asked the pizza delivery person to walk through the gate and down the path to the summer house. The person said there was a lot to carry. "We'll give you an extra tip," said Emily, and ended the conversation.

"Some of us could go and fetch them," said Shannon.

Annabel said, "They've delivered to us here before. It's not too much to ask. It's the same as them having to carry food up to a top-floor flat." She opened the drinks fridge and asked who needed more. Ollie took another beer. Annabel poured herself another rum and Coke, spilling a lot of the Coke on the wooden floor.

"Wipe that up," said Emily. "Or it'll be sticky."

Annabel stepped over the spillage, ignoring her sister.

"You know we're supposed to be keeping the summer house clean ourselves this year," said Emily. "I threw away those shortbread biscuits, so I've done my bit."

Piglet made a sympathetic face at Annabel. "Maybe we could send one of our cleaners over sometimes."

"At the end of the summer," said Ollie. "Let's make it an utter mess first."

Everyone laughed.

When the pizza guy showed up, he was breathing heavily, muttering that he was having to make two journeys.

"Calm down," said Emily, swaying a little. She was drunk. "I said we'd give you a tip." She looked at the others. "Anyone seen my purse?"

Victor stood up and produced a few notes from his pocket. "Here," he said, offering them to the man, who was unpacking his bag on to the steps of the summer house.

The man, who was probably in his thirties, grunted his thanks.

"How much do you earn in a week?" Annabel asked him.

He looked at her as if she had two heads, then mentioned a sum that seemed low to Shannon, although she wondered if it was because she only had London to compare with . . . or if she had become too accustomed to hanging out with rich people.

Annabel's face changed; it seemed to twist. Shannon felt her stomach churn, aware she was about to witness something unpleasant. A split second later, she realized it would be an opportunity, and she covertly got her phone out and pressed record. If Annabel stayed true to form, this could be something a gossip website might like.

Annabel said to the guy, "We'll give you a week's wages as an extra tip if you lick the floor over there." She pointed to where she'd spilled the Coke. Shannon felt both sickened and elated at once – this might be exactly the footage she needed.

The man said, "You what?"

"Lick the floor. It's only Coke."

"I'm hungry," said Victor. "Let's eat."

"Hang on," said Zander. "Let's see if he'll do it."

The man was standing completely still, a frown on his face.

"He's drooling at the thought," said Annabel. "Aren't you, Pizza Man?"

He likely had kids, Shannon thought, as she moved to a better position. Was he actually thinking about doing it?

"I don't have enough cash on me, Annabel, for that big a tip," said Victor.

"We can transfer the money," said Annabel softly, her eyes never leaving the man's face. "Straight into his account. Easy."

Eventually the man spoke. "I'll get the rest of the delivery for you, miss."

"And then you'll do it?" she persisted, but he didn't reply as he walked away.

Victor picked up the cardboard boxes of pizzas and the paper-wrapped sides of garlic bread and fries. "I think you over-ordered, Piglet."

"She does that," said Ollie. He was on the edge of the sofa. "D'you think the guy will actually do it?"

"Hope so," said Annabel, swirling the ice cube in her drink so that it clinked against the glass over and over. "People usually do what I tell them."

"True that," said Emily. She held her phone up. "We could film it."

Shannon said nothing as she leaned against the kitchen work surface. This bunch felt so untouchable, so invincible, that they would even suggest filming it themselves. Unbelievable.

"You'd get him the sack," said Ollie.

Emily shrugged. "That's on him."

"You two are really terrible when you're together," said Maddie, but she was laughing.

"Don't let him dump the rest of the order and run," said Piglet. "Make him tell you yes or no."

"You shouldn't have given him the first tip, Victor," said Annabel.

"Apologies," said Victor, "but you didn't tell me your master plan." He sounded sarcastic but it was hard to tell.

Annabel hovered at the doors of the summer house. "He better come back," said Piglet.

"If he doesn't, he's definitely getting fired," said Maddie. "I know we ordered a lot, but Zander is a big eater, aren't you, hun?"

"Here he is!" Annabel actually clapped her hands with excitement. It was grotesque.

All of them were watching the guy now. He strode to the steps.

"Place the food on the table inside," ordered Annabel.

He did as he was told without comment. He went to leave quickly after he'd done it, but Annabel and Emily stood by the doors, barring his way.

Shannon couldn't bear it any longer. She left her phone on the side, propped up. "Let the guy go," she said.

Annabel shot back, "For God's sake, Lydia. You can be such a drag with your nicey-niceness."

While she was talking, the guy barged through their barricade.

Annabel moved immediately, towards the table, where Zander and Maddie were opening the boxes. She picked up a couple of large slices of pizza, shoved one in Shannon's hand, the hot melted cheese burning her, and said, "We're going to chuck these at him." She ran in bare feet and Shannon had a micro-second to decide what to do. She had a new lifeline as Lydia and she had to seize it. If she alienated the sisters now it would be harder later.

"This is so Annabel," said Emily, holding up her phone to film.

Shannon pulled her up hoodie so her face wouldn't be caught on film.

Annabel yelled, "Now!" and she hurled her pizza slice

at the man's neck. It thumped against him and slid down to the grass. Shannon threw hers with less force, making sure it fell short of his shoulder.

The guy turned round, roaring with outrage, lunging for Annabel. He caught up with her easily and gripped her wrist, swearing into her face. She screamed loud and long as Shannon stepped away. As Annabel went to punch him in the face, he caught her other wrist, and Victor was the first to reach them as she was haphazardly kicking the man, Ollie close behind.

The guy dropped Annabel's wrists, and Victor escorted him down the path towards the side gate. Shannon and Ollie walked back to the summer house with Annabel, who was rubbing her wrists and shouting to the others still in the summer house, "Did you see that? What an animal. He was about to attack me." She was all hyped up, her eyes glowing.

"So funny seeing him snap," called Emily.

Shannon wanted to pick up one of the empty bottles of champagne lying on the floor and crack it round their heads. Would she ever have it in her to stop them?

"I'm ravenous," Annabel said as she stepped inside, and grabbed a handful of fries.

CHAPTER 19

Shannon lay in bed and went back over the strange evening in her mind. They'd played card games after eating, and when the others decided they'd go home, nobody did anything about the leftover food, apart from Shannon, who gathered it up.

"Little Miss Sensible," said Emily, leaning against her drunkenly while smoking, as Shannon carried the pile of boxes and tubs to the kitchen.

"You'll get mice," Shannon said, and then was immediately cross with herself. It's what her mum would have said, and she shouldn't have saved the food. Lydia wouldn't have done. But now she'd carried them into the house she'd ram them into the enormous fridge.

Emily stood laughing at her, running cold water over the stub of her cigarette before putting it in the bin. "Mrs P will hate you for messing up her fridge. She's fussy like that."

Annabel was pouring herself a glass of water. "I've been thinking about the gardener and how weird he is. I'm going to order a spy cam for the bunkhouse," she said.

Shannon would warn Finch, after she'd left. By the time she'd finished with them, they would think twice about tormenting him again, but she owed him a heads up.

"One day your schemes will get you into trouble," she said lightly as she slammed a tub of coleslaw into the fridge.

Now in bed, she made sure the footage she'd got had been saved to the Cloud. It showed the sisters behaving appallingly, but would anyone else care? She needed more. Something bigger. Later tonight she'd look for it, and if it brought down the whole family, so much the better.

At three a.m. exactly, Shannon decided it was time to go downstairs. She'd heard Rosie and Douglas come back a couple of hours ago and was certain they were asleep. She hadn't heard Mrs Pushkin come in after her night off, but since the housekeeper had her own entrance at the side of the house, Shannon hadn't expected to, and given that Mrs Pushkin had to be up early for work the next morning, it was unlikely she'd have been late.

Shannon slipped her phone into the pocket of the silk dressing gown she hadn't been able to resist buying for the trip. Opening her door very slowly, she came out on to the landing. Glancing out of the big window towards the back garden and the sea, Shannon saw there was enough light from the moon to differentiate the glittering water from the sky. She drew a quiet breath. Everything in Fengari was extreme: the ugliness and the beauty.

The stairs made no noise as she hurried down them in bare feet. She entered the study from the hallway, the closed door making a loud click as she opened it. For a moment she stood, listening for sound in the house. There was nothing, apart from the hum of appliances in the kitchen next door and the steady ticking of a clock on Douglas's untidy desk. The piles of books and magazines around the room must have frustrated her mum when she had to clean in here.

Her breath caught in her throat as she thought about her mum cleaning in here last summer. She looked round quickly. There were a few lever arch files on a shelf, but when she went through them they were all to do with Clifftop House – bills and reports about the roof and the bunkhouse. Shannon lingered on a document from the insurance company about the fire. The fire had been attributed to human error. Her mum wasn't even named. She was called *the deceased*. Shannon had been sent a slew of similar documents as next of kin, until people realized she wasn't legally an adult.

She'd felt like one, though. The weight of everything had been on her shoulders, with no one to help her. Ela's mum had tried, but it had been beyond her.

The filing cabinet was locked. Where would Douglas

keep the key? Somewhere nearby ... the desk drawer was the obvious place. It was stiff. She yanked it, but it was stuck on one side. Shannon crouched down to see what was in the way. It looked like a piece of paper had become caught. She peered on top of the desk for something long and flat enough to push it down. A silver thing – a letter opener? – was sticking out of a mug of pens and scissors. She grabbed it, and as she pushed it into the drawer, she heard a noise in the hallway. She moved as quietly as she could through the door that led to the kitchen, listening. If she was caught, she'd rather it be in the kitchen.

It was nothing, she told herself. Just a creak in a house.

Then the door to the kitchen swung open dramatically and Mrs Pushkin stood there in a quilted peach-coloured dressing gown. She had a shoe in her hand, holding it up like a weapon. In any other circumstance, Shannon might have laughed.

"Lydia, what are you doing?" Mrs Pushkin's voice was devoid of any warmth.

Shannon made a show of breathing out slowly. "Thank God it's you. I heard some noises and I came down to see who it was."

Mrs Pushkin looked sceptical.

"You were out," said Shannon quickly, glad she had prepared an excuse. "There was some trouble with the pizza delivery guy, and when I heard some noise down here, I was scared it was him. Annabel will tell you – he got really angry with us."

"So you came downstairs on your own?"

"I'm tougher than I look," said Shannon. It was true. She was.

"And that?" Mrs Pushkin asked, her lips thinned, pointing at Shannon's side, at the silver letter opener. "You took that from the study?" She held out her hand, palm upwards. "I need to ask this, Lydia. Are you short of money?"

"What? No! Of course not. I got this for self-defence!" Shannon handed over the letter opener, and her horror was genuine as she noticed there was a little silver sculpted owl at the end of it. It was probably valuable. "The noise – you must have heard the creaking?"

"I heard you, that's all," said Mrs Pushkin. "I'm sorry, I should have warned you, there's usually an alarm on downstairs. Mr and Mrs Harrington must have forgotten to set it before they went to bed. If they had, the whole household would be awake now."

"Oh," said Shannon.

"Well, you know now," said Mrs Pushkin. "I think we should both go back to bed, don't you?"

Tuesday

Shannon woke early with a sense of desperation. Her big chance had been thwarted. She wouldn't be able to go into the study again at night now she knew an alarm was usually set and Mrs Pushkin was suspicious of her.

It was Tuesday. In three days she had to be gone.

Out of the window, she saw Finch, already working in the garden. The thought of how she'd treated him made her want to shrivel up. He was kneeling by the edge of a flower bed near the bunkhouse, weeding and turning over the earth. She had an overwhelming urge to tell him how sorry she was. Stepping out of her room, she could hear sounds from the kitchen, which meant the alarm must be off, so once she was dressed, she slipped out of the back door into the garden.

The sky was pale grey with no hint of the sun. Out at sea there were boats in the harbour, their sails triangles of white against the inky water, and overhead she heard the fast whir of helicopter blades. Funny how if she'd heard that noise at home in London, it would have meant something bad had happened because it would have either been a police helicopter or the air ambulance.

Finch jumped when he caught sight of her – and she saw he had AirPods in. He nodded stiffly at her as a formal hello and, when she didn't move, he removed an AirPod.

"Finch, I came to apologize for yesterday." This was big-time awkward. "I wish I hadn't gone along with Annabel and Emily. It was . . . a stupid game of dares. I'm really sorry."

He stared at her. "You warned me about them, and then you act like them." He picked up some weeds he'd dislodged and threw them into his gardening tub. "You should have more guts."

"I know. I'm sorry." He probably thought she was weak for apologizing when she knew Annabel and Emily would still be in bed and out of the way.

"All right, then," he said, wiping his forehead and replacing his AirPod, and she darted back upstairs.

By the time it was breakfast, Shannon's stomach was rumbling with hunger; she'd been unable to eat after the incident with the pizza delivery guy. Mrs Pushkin served her pancakes with syrup and sliced banana, and waited until Emily and Annabel were there before asking pointedly how she was after such a busy night, and Emily had demanded to know what she was talking about.

"Lydia was roaming around downstairs saying she'd heard noises," said Mrs Pushkin. She pursed her lips together.

"God, Lyds!" said Annabel. "You need to chill out."

Emily said, "You were lucky. Mrs Pushkin might have murdered you and claimed it was in self-defence."

Mrs Pushkin said, "That's not funny, girls."

Rosie passed through the kitchen for a coffee to take with her to an appointment with a tile supplier for her en suite bathroom, followed by lunch with friends. Douglas had already gone, to play golf. Annabel and Emily bickered about who had finished the last of the fresh pineapple and mango juice, and Shannon knew that her focus today was to watch for when Mrs Pushkin was far enough away from the study to go back in there. She didn't know how long it took to play golf.

Annabel was talking about playing tennis at Ollie and Piglet's house, and Shannon said she'd stay behind to relax. No way could she let them see her play tennis if Clarissa had told them Lydia was going after a tennis scholarship.

"Oh, no. We need you to play, so you'll have to come," said Annabel. "There are eight of us. That's a good number."

"Isn't it supposed to rain today?" said Shannon. "I'm sure I saw that on the app."

"Finch mended the net yesterday. Easier to stay here, I reckon," Emily said. "We can hole up in the summer house if it rains." She flicked open the Fengari app on her phone. "Nah, I think we'll be OK with the weather until this evening."

Annabel said, "I want to swim in Piglet and Ollie's pool afterwards. They always have cool inflatables. Remember the giant unicorns last year, Em?"

"I remember you popped one during that race because you were losing," said Emily.

"My toenail was sharper than I thought," said Annabel, and grinned. "Come on, you two. Let's go to Pigs's place."

"Your parents are out," Shannon said. "That makes it more fun here."

"Yeah, that's true," said Emily. She was sprawled across two chairs, scrolling through her phone. "And I'd rather go to their house this evening for a barbecue. Let's suggest that."

"I thought you said it was going to rain this evening," said Shannon.

"Their chef does the best barbecues," said Annabel. "He can cook outside and we can eat inside."

"Your first match will be against Mads," Emily told Shannon, barging into her room without knocking, where Shannon was messaging Lydia to ask why she'd said she was bad at tennis when she clearly wasn't. "You're probably a similar standard. Mads plays for her school. The others will be here around eleven."

Saliva drained from Shannon's mouth as she said, "Sounds good, Ems." She hadn't even packed tennis gear. She could find a white sports top, but she needed a white tennis skirt. Or did people like the Harringtons wear any old sports gear for tennis? She'd have to check on her phone.

There'd been a time when she'd been good at sport, running in particular. She'd won a race at sports day and someone had said she should join an athletics club, but it would have been three buses away and her mum and Nan had both been working. She'd kept up her running until she'd gone to secondary school, and then it had turned into jogging now and then.

Shannon saw from social media accounts that while most people the Harringtons knew wore white for tennis, there were plenty who didn't, but the little flippy skirts with built-in shorts were the thing for girls. She reluctantly went to ask to borrow one of Annabel's.

Shannon stared at herself in the mirror after she'd got

changed into a white skort and sleeveless white top, plaited her hair so it was out of the way, and tucked her necklace under the neckline of her top. With her hair like that, no make-up and the tennis gear she was unrecognizable as Shannon Jones.

She looked the part, but she certainly couldn't play it. She noticed, however, that she had started to grow accustomed to the cliff-edge terror of being found out; it had bothered her less and less as the days had passed. She was good at improvising, and was growing in confidence. She didn't know how, exactly – not yet – but she would handle this challenge, too.

Maddie and Zander arrived first and immediately went to the tennis court to warm up with Annabel and Emily. Ollie and Piglet were next, dropped off by a chauffeur wearing a full uniform, including a cap. Shannon only saw that because she was back in the downstairs toilet double-checking the rules of tennis at the time and noticed them out of the window. To get out of the tournament she was weighing up an upset stomach or an ankle injury, but she still needed to understand the scoring. She hadn't yet heard from Lydia as to why she'd lied about her tennis skills. It unsettled her. What else had Lydia downplayed?

It was when Victor arrived that Shannon decided to act. As he came on to the court and kissed everyone on both cheeks in turn, she pretended to trip over a racquet on the ground and twist her ankle. He clutched at her arms as she went down with a howl, grasping her ankle. "Oh my God, are you OK?"

"I'm not sure," she said with a couple of quick intakes of breath.

"Clumsy Lydia strikes again," said Annabel.

Victor insisted on taking a look at it, even though she said it would be OK in a while.

"I've done it before," she said. "It's been a bit weak since a skiing accident in St Anton." She was pleased with that.

Victor's fingers were cool against her skin, touching her gently where she said it hurt. She winced on cue, and he pulled back, concerned. "This looks pretty bad. Are you sure you don't want to see a doctor?"

"Is it bad? I'll call Mrs P," said Emily.

"It's not swollen yet. I think it's only bruised. I'll be fine," she insisted, allowing Victor to pull her up. She liked being this close to him, even if she wasn't sure about him.

"No, no, don't be ridiculous," he said, shaking his head. "You can't play. Sit, sit on the side and rest."

It was exactly what she'd hoped he'd say. She was so grateful she had to fight back an instinct to lean forward and hug him. Instead, she hobbled to the side of the court. "Maybe I'll sit out my first match and see how I feel after that," she said in a way that she hoped looked sufficiently reluctant.

"Maybe you won't be able to play at all," said Piglet. She looked at Shannon sympathetically. "Bad luck. I heard you're good."

"I'm sure I'll be fine in a bit," said Shannon.

Victor looked around. "We need some spectator seating."

"I can ask the gardener to bring some over," said Ollie. Without waiting for an answer he went to find Finch, who came without saying anything or making eye contact and left four folding chairs against the tennis court fence.

"Lydia, sit down for now," snapped Annabel, "we'll have you as a linesman."

First up to play were Ollie and Zander. There were fast, hard-hitting strokes and grunting from both, and swearing from Zander as Ollie thrashed him in straight sets.

Straight sets. Shannon tucked that phrase away for another time. After a while, she staggered to her feet and said she needed to go to the toilet.

"Use the one here," said Annabel, jerking her head towards the pool building.

"Nah, I'll go in the house," said Shannon. "I'll get some ice when I'm there." She moved slowly, being sure to keep up a believable limp. From drama class she knew that the best way to fake one was to keep one joint from bending – her ankle, or her knee – but try to overcome it as naturally as she could anyway. It was frustrating going, but she had to think about Mrs Pushkin seeing her out of a window, and potentially Douglas if he was back.

Please let him not be back.

There was nobody in the kitchen. In excruciating slow motion, she pushed the connecting door to the study and peeked in. It was empty. Where was Mrs Pushkin?

There was no time to check – she'd have to make some outlandish excuse if she was caught. A treasure hunt? A TikTok challenge? Or maybe she could keep things simpler, focused on her injury – looking for gauze? If she hesitated now, there might not be another opportunity. She went back into the kitchen to grab a spatula from a jar by one of the double ovens to push down the paper which was jamming Douglas's desk drawer and worked as quickly as she could.

The desk drawer opened with minimal effort from the spatula, and she saw a set of keys straight away. To her enormous relief, the third key she tried opened the filing cabinet. The first drawer was everything relating to Annabel. With so much paperwork here in their holiday home, Shannon wondered how much Douglas must keep in their house in Oxfordshire. It was lucky for her he hadn't gone paperless.

There must be something incriminating in here, she knew it. There must be. She leafed through the papers ... there were invoices for riding lessons, tennis lessons, X-rays and letters about a broken finger, phone bills ... and here, oh my God, a clear plastic sleeve of letters from Poodle and Dunn, copyright lawyers.

Clear infringement of intellectual property. . . Refused to desist when asked. . . Damages sought. . . Products need to be destroyed immediately. . . No resale value. . . Client distressed. . . Matter settled. Thank you for the payment.

Annabel had blatantly ripped off someone else's fabric

design and had it printed on cheap fabric and manufactured into identical beach wraps and bikinis. In her arrogance she'd boasted about "her designs" on Instagram.

Well, the products weren't destroyed; there were at least a dozen boxes of them in her bedroom. Perhaps a photo of those with today's copy of the *Fengari Times*, which was on the table in the hall, proving the date, sent to the original designer? It could work, in combination with last night's video.

Next, Shannon found Emily's file. There were the same sort of invoices as there were in Annabel's file, and a letter following a conversation asking Emily to leave a summer art club five years ago because of bullying behaviour. There was a copy of Douglas's reply, outraged that Emily had been accused of something which he said amounted to high-spirited fun. That was interesting, but not worth sending to a gossipy website.

Both girls – ideally the whole family – were going down for what had happened to her mum. She needed more.

She sighed and glanced up: a face was staring at her.

Victor.

"I came to see if you needed help getting ice," he said. He spoke quietly, holding her gaze. "What are you doing?"

"I can't tell you," she said, because really there was no lie to cover this.

"You're looking for something," he said. A statement.

She nodded, sweat trickling down the back of her neck. "Are you going to say anything?"

"To the Harringtons?" he said. He didn't pronounce the *H* of *Harringtons*, and she found it weird that this was what she was focusing on rather than the horrendous thought that he might alert everyone to the fact that he had caught her spying in Douglas's study. That everything could be over, just out of reach of the goal.

"To anyone," she said. She held her breath and the squawk of a bird outside made her jump.

He shook his head. "I'll keep your secret, *Lydia*."

His words should have calmed her. She was grateful for them, but it was the way he pronounced *Lydia* that set off an alarm in her head. He drew out the three syllables, and it seemed less about his accent than about a slight mocking emphasis. *Lyd-ee-ah*. Was he questioning who she was?

He moved his head abruptly, indicating that they should leave the study. When she failed to react, his eyes became more urgent, and she realized his hearing was better than hers. Somebody was coming downstairs. He pushed the filing drawer in quickly and quietly, and turned the key, which he handed to her. Shannon raced across to the desk and pushed it into the open drawer, which she slammed closed, then she threw the spatula into the wastepaper basket to get it out of sight. The next thing she knew, Victor was dragging her into the kitchen, where he dropped to the floor.

"It's not looking too bad," he said loudly, holding her ankle. "But you can't run on it for a while."

"I don't think I'll be able to play tennis today," she said

in a disappointed voice.

Victor held her gaze for a moment, eyebrows raised very slightly. "It certainly looks that way."

A second later, Mrs Pushkin bustled into the kitchen with some shopping. "Are you OK?" she asked, more irritated than concerned.

"Lydia twisted her ankle." Victor stood up. "She doesn't need a doctor, but I'm hoping you have some ice?"

Mrs Pushkin didn't say anything, but she got out a bowl and filled it with ice from the icemaker in the fridge. She tipped it into a plastic freezer bag and wrapped a tea towel round it. "Here," she said.

Shannon winced at the coldness against her leg, and she thought she saw the hint of a smile on Victor's face. "Thanks," she said. "Sorry to cause a fuss."

"While you're here," said Mrs Pushkin, reaching for a notebook and pen on the work surface, "you can tell me what food your mother likes eating. I need to plan next week's menu."

"Of course." Shannon knew it didn't matter what she said. She'd be long gone by the time Clarissa was served anything. She thought back to what was in the fridge when Lydia opened it to get the milk for the tea one of the times she went round to her house in South Ken. "Vegetables," she said.

Mrs Pushkin frowned. "She's a vegetarian? No one told me that."

Shannon wasn't sure, and she couldn't risk anyone

contacting Clarissa any time soon for more details about dietary restrictions. "No, she's not, but she likes vegetarian food. She's not big on red meat." She gave a final nod. It sounded right. Very Clarissa. "And she likes herbal teas. Liquorice flavour is her absolute fave." It wasn't. Clarissa had given away a box of liquorice-flavour teabags at the florist's to Shannon, without even asking her if she'd like them. *As a gift*, Clarissa had said. It hadn't been a gift. It had been a cast-off.

Victor held out his hand to pull her up. She wiped the sweat and icy dampness from her hand on to her skort and let him. As they left the kitchen, Shannon limping more self-consciously, he offered his arm to her when they went down the steps.

"Very chivalrous," she said, as she leaned on him. He had the power now. She would have to wait to see what he decided to do with it.

"Of course," he said. "But the tournament is quite intense, so I'm happy to have a break."

"Aha," said Shannon, keeping things as light as she could. "Your true motive!" At the bottom of the steps she let go of him, and he walked at her pace until they reached the wooden table and chairs set back in a curve of the flower bed.

He pointed at a chair. "Do you want to sit down a moment?"

"Sure," she said. She was nervous; was he going to prod her for answers to what he'd just witnessed even though he said he'd keep her secret? She would deny being in the study if he told anyone, but Mrs Pushkin had seen her in there last night so they were more likely to believe him than Shannon.

They sat next to each other, looking out to sea like an old couple with nothing better to do, and Shannon waited.

"Do you want to talk about it?" Victor asked.

"No," said Shannon softly. She pushed the nails of her right hand into the palm of her left.

"OK," said Victor.

"You said you wouldn't tell anyone," she said firmly.

"I won't."

She looked at him. He was less arrogant when it was only the two of them. She much preferred it. "Thanks."

"I think you're an interesting person," he said, and it was so unexpected, she laughed properly, with her mouth open.

"I'm actually very ordinary," she said, aware she was letting him see a flash of her true self, at least the old version of herself who had a best friend and lay on sofas laughing with them about all sorts of things.

He moved his head ever so slightly, as if he was thinking about what she'd said. "I don't think so."

It was because he never mixed with people like her. He was bilingual, understood art and rich people, discussed eye-watering sums of money and travelled the world. Even Lydia was ordinary compared to that.

"I'm less exhausting than the others, I'll give you that," she said. It had been hard to believe at first, but Lydia was relatively easy-going within the circles she moved.

"Yes, but. . ." said Victor.

Piglet appeared and stood with her hands on her hips. "There you are! Victor, we're waiting for you to play your match against Emily."

CHAPTER 20

A little while later, Ollie having beaten Maddie in the tennis finals, they were all flopped out in the summer house with the doors and windows open. Outside it was overcast, but the humidity was rising like a sweaty promise of the later storm. Ollie droned on about how he'd set up his best shots.

Annabel caught Shannon's eye and they shared an eye roll. "Ollie, if your dad wasn't such a family friend and knew all our secrets, we wouldn't put up with you being such a bore," said Annabel.

Shannon perked up at this, wondering what they meant. Did Ollie and Piglet's dad really know all their secrets?

The others laughed.

Ollie said, "Can't lie. My dad's more popular than I am."

Maddie giggled. "My parents call your dad Mr Fix It."

Annabel was looking at her phone. "Seb's parents need to get on and rebook his flight. I hate that they're moaning about the cost."

Shannon, who had been sitting against a cushion up against the wall, with her "bad" leg stretched out, leaned forward to inspect a chip in the nail varnish on her big toe. She was suddenly aware of Maddie staring at her shoulder.

"Wait, Lydia," said Maddie. "Stay like that a moment. Your birthmark has faded in the sun. Let me take a look."

Shannon sat back instantly so it couldn't be seen.

"Hey, don't embarrass Lydia," said Victor. He caught her eye and her stomach jolted as she looked away. *He suspected the birthmark was fake.*

"Sorry," said Maddie without sounding sorry.

"Aw, Lyds, it's fine!" said Piglet. "Honestly, it's a tiny birthmark. I think you're beautiful." She beamed. "Inside and out."

Maddie snorted. "No need to go over the top, Piglet, you loser."

Annabel said, "Pigs and Ollie, we need cheering up. Let's do a barbecue at your house later."

Piglet blinked. "Tonight?" she said. "But there's going to be a storm."

"Don't be so wet, Pigs," said Emily, then realized what she'd said and added, "Haha."

"That's a fantastic idea," said Victor. "We don't have to eat outside."

Shannon wondered why he was so keen on the idea.

"That's what I was about to say," said Annabel triumphantly. "We can eat inside! Honestly, Pigs, your chef does the best food. We need that after those terrible pizzas."

"Yes, your chef, Duncan . . . the food is to die for," said Maddie. "Zander has to experience his cooking. His life won't be complete without it."

Ollie shrugged. "We'll do it, then." He seemed pleased in his quiet, almost emotionless way. "Pigs, give Duncan a call and tell him."

"Tell him to do those steak skewers," said Annabel. "Those are my favourite."

"And lobster tails," said Maddie. "Those are *my* favourite."

Piglet nodded, and held up her hand so she could make the call. She walked to the door of the summer house. By the end of the phone conversation, she was giving a thumbs up and Annabel shouted, "Duncan, we love you!"

"You must all stay over," said Piglet, hanging up. "You can't go home in a storm. Mummy says it would be irresponsible."

"Yes, sounds awesome, Piglet," said Victor.

"We've got three spare bedrooms," said Piglet, sitting back down in between Annabel and her brother, "so you'll have to double up." She looked round. "So, Mads and Zander . . . Emily and Annabel. . ."

"Me and Lydia?" finished Victor, with a cheeky grin. Shannon raised an eyebrow, aware that she didn't hate the idea.

Piglet was embarrassed. "Oh, that won't work. Let's say Victor and Zander, Mads and Bels, Emily and Lydia." She looked at them for confirmation.

"Sure," said Shannon. "Thanks, Piglet." She couldn't imagine having to share a room with Emily. But then again ... it could be an opportunity. She stood up because she had pins and needles, shaking out each leg.

Mrs Pushkin appeared in the doorway from nowhere with two jugs of juice and some glasses on a tray. "I have a message from Mrs Harrington," she called as she set it down on the small table outside the summer house. "Lydia, can you do some tennis volleys with the girls to practise their backhands today when everyone's gone? The tennis coach can't make it this week."

"I'd love to, but my foot—" said Shannon.

Mrs Pushkin gave a little smile. "I know you've hurt your foot, but you only need to stand still and work your upper body. I saw just now that you're fine putting weight on it."

Shannon clenched her jaw and swore repeatedly in her head. To her horror, Piglet rose and said, "Come on, Ollie, we should go," and Maddie tugged on Zander's arm and said, "Yeah, we'll leave you to your tennis practice. Victor, can we share a taxi with you?"

Emily eased herself off the sofa with a groan. "OK, let's get this practice over with."

They walked back to the tennis court together with the others carrying on to the side gate to pick up their taxis, Shannon being sure to limp.

"Go easy on that foot," said Victor as he waved goodbye.

Shannon nodded. Her throat was dry and she couldn't speak. At least the others wouldn't witness her undoing. A second, more severe, injury wouldn't be credible. She picked up a spare racquet and a couple of balls. Annabel and Emily stood sullenly one side of the net and she made her way to the other.

"We'll do a few rallies and then stop," called Emily. She dropped a tennis ball, it bounced and she hit it. Hard.

Shannon swiped at it and missed. "Sorry!" she called, sweat collecting on her forehead.

Annabel sent over a ball, less hard, and Shannon caught it on the handle of her racquet and it ricocheted into the fence. "What are you doing?" Annabel called. "You're not even playing backhand."

Shannon had to think what backhand was. She tried to drop and hit a ball over the net but missed. It was a comedy miss, like a young child would do. There was no part of her body which wasn't hot and sweaty now.

Annabel whacked another ball towards her and it hit her arm. Shannon wasn't sure if it was intentional or not but it hurt.

"I give up," said Emily. "This is hopeless." She walked up to the net. "You're really shit at tennis, aren't you?"

Shannon froze.

"You're going after a tennis scholarship?" Emily's smile grew wider.

This was it: everything was falling apart. Shannon's head was flooded with panic while her body seemed incapable of doing anything.

"Join the club," said Emily. "You don't need to pretend with me. My family knows all about the scholarship scheme. Mine's basketball." She walked away, saying, "Come on. Let's go and find something to eat."

Shannon stared after her before limping to catch up, unable just yet to drop the pretence of having hurt herself earlier, adrenaline coursing through her, a million questions buzzing through her head. Emily had got a false basketball scholarship. She had no idea how that worked. Surely she'd be expected to play for her university? The details were unimportant right now. *This* was the dynamite she needed.

Annabel had persuaded Piglet to make the dress code "barbecue smart", which everyone had to interpret for themselves. Shannon didn't have a problem with that. She had a couple of dresses that might never be worn if she didn't wear them on Fengari. One was too loose to be something she'd wear as herself, but she loved the bright orange, red and pink swirls. Her silver sandals looked good with it, and she had repaired the chip in her nail varnish with a similar colour she'd brought with her.

Rosie was concerned about the girls being away from Clifftop House during a bad storm. "Yes, it won't be a hurricane, but we don't know how bad it's going to be," she said on her return from her errands. She hadn't said anything about the backhand practice, which convinced Shannon that it had been a test from Mrs Pushkin.

"It's not even raining yet, and Hideaway Lodge is made of steel, for goodness' sake, and Peter's not going to let anything happen to us," said Emily. "We're one of his favourite families, right?"

Rosie sighed. "I suppose we are. This weather is so tedious."

The three of them took a taxi to Ollie and Piglet's house, all of them sharing the back seat, Shannon up against the window. She remembered what Annabel had said about Ollie's dad knowing their secrets, and wondered if there was any evidence in Piglet and Ollie's house about Emily's fake scholarship. It seemed a lot to hope for.

When her phone pinged, she glanced at it. It was from Lydia. It was first she'd heard from her all day, and she was desperate to hear about her tennis scholarship. She held the phone up for Face ID.

Lyra/Lydia: *I need to speak to you ASAP.*

Shannon/Lydia: *Not now. Later tonight or tomorrow?*

Lyra/Lydia: *No – ASAP.*

Shannon quickly typed: *I'll try soon*, then slipped her phone into her bag, wondering what the hell it was about. Had she done the unthinkable and confessed to Clarissa? If she'd done that, surely Clarissa would have contacted Rosie? Had something happened to Lydia or Crispin?

"Who's Lyra?" asked Annabel, next to her.

"What?" asked Shannon, flustered before she remembered that she'd put Lydia in her contacts as Lyra.

"Are you OK, Lydia?" Annabel frowned.

"Yes, I'm fine. Lyra's a mate."

Her phone was vibrating in her bag.

"How's your foot?" asked Emily with a little laugh. She poked Shannon in the side. "Come on, you weren't very convincing when you pretended to hurt it."

"I did hurt it," lied Shannon before making an embarrassed face, "but I exaggerated it because I didn't want you to find out how crap I am at tennis. But you know what it's like with the scholarship." She held her breath.

Emily sighed. "Yeah. It's so difficult." She made it sound like it was a massive burden.

"Are you going through Ollie and Piglet's dad too?" asked Annabel. "For the scholarship?"

Shannon nodded and hoped the girls might keep talking about this fake scholarship thing.

"I guess your mum knows about it from ours," said Emily. "Peter makes it really easy. His fixer fee is sky high, but it was my only chance to get into a really good uni."

"Can you imagine Emily actually having to play

222

competitive sport, though?" laughed Annabel.

"I've never even met the basketball coach," said Emily. "He's been paid off, thank God."

Shannon's phone stopped making the vibrating noise for a moment, then started up again, the noise of it worming into her brain.

As soon as the taxi arrived and Shannon had stepped out of the car, she sneaked a look at her phone. Lydia had repeatedly tried to call her and had left another message: *I've broken up with Crispin and I'm going back to London.*

Everything was about to implode. Shannon probably only had hours left. There was a pain so bad behind her eye that she had to push the heel of her hand into it to ease it.

The enormous front door opened, and Piglet stepped out wearing a pale pink dress with a ruffle at the bottom and fuchsia-coloured heeled sandals. She did look a little like a piglet.

"We're going to have the best evening," she said excitedly as the first fat raindrops began to fall.

CHAPTER 21

The inside of Hideaway Lodge was cavernous and light despite the dark grey clouds outside. In contrast to the lack of windows at the front of the house, the back was mostly glass. Any wall that wasn't a window was hung with lots of paintings, in different styles, but they all seemed to go together like patchwork. On the next floor up, there was a space Piglet called a gallery, where you could look down. The wall behind it was also lined with paintings. Even though her mind was elsewhere, Shannon loved it.

The view from the large room downstairs, and presumably the gallery, was out to sea, where two boats bobbed up and down in the same spot, but it wasn't as dramatic as Clifftop House, where you could see the arc of the harbour and some of Old Town as well.

"Want to see the food being barbecued for a moment?" asked Piglet opening a section of bifold doors, set within the huge glass wall. "The others are out there, under the awning having a drink."

Shannon stood and breathed in deeply to steady herself. Despite everything, she would miss being part of this world. She'd become used to being in beautiful surroundings and the lavish lifestyle.

Piglet handed them each a large golfing umbrella.

"Tell Lydia what those yachts are called," said Annabel in an amused voice. She pointed to the boats at sea.

"They're called *Oliver* and *Penelope*," Piglet said. "After Ollie and me. Isn't that hilarious?"

Shannon smiled politely. It didn't seem that funny to her. She wondered when a boat became a yacht. Was it when it was a certain size?

"Hope they don't get smashed to pieces in the storm," said Emily in a way that suggested she half hoped they would.

Piglet laughed. "It's a tropical storm, Ems, not a hurricane. Anyway, Daddy's got insurance."

What was Lydia doing right now? Booking a flight home? Was she already at an airport?

Shannon said she needed the loo. Piglet told the other two to carry on to the barbecue and doubled back with Shannon to show her the way to a large washroom with black-painted cabinets and towels and white everything else.

"Meet you at the barbecue," said Piglet. "It's outside to the left, by the tennis court."

The bolt on the door slid across smoothly. Shannon left her umbrella against the basin. She was relieved to be on her own, but it wasn't safe enough here to have an emotional phone conversation that might be overheard.

Shannon/Lydia: *Lydia, I'm sorry to hear about you and C. You seemed so good together. What happened?* She hit the send button as fast as she could.

Lyra/Lydia: *Crispin's so unreasonable. Thinks I'm moody.*

Shannon/Lydia: *You're not moody! You're probably tired from all that travelling. Where are you now?*

Lyra/Lydia: *In a hotel room in Florence. It should be romantic but I've got the ick now and it's so awkward. Crispin wants to go to Marbella and I'm gunna fly home. Had enough.*

Someone tried the door handle of the toilet, and Shannon called, "I'll be out in a minute." She messaged quickly: *You'll both regret it if you act too quickly. Give it until Friday? Let me speak to your mum. I reckon you and C will make up and it will end up as a funny anecdote for that article you wanted to write about this summer.*

She studied her face in the mirror as she waited for a reply. Her face had changed. It wasn't only the brown contact lenses, toning down of her make-up and the simple ponytail which she would have twisted higher for a night out in London; it was because she hadn't covered up the freckles. She peered at them. They were a goldish colour; she quite liked them, and it made her look more like Lydia, which gave her a thrill.

There was a display cabinet in this bathroom of old – probably antique – perfume bottles. The glass bottles with gold stoppers against the black of the display cabinet looked beautiful. It wasn't something the Harringtons would have had in their house. It would have been far too blingy. Ollie and Piglet's house was different. Things here were bright rather than faded. She took a selfie next to the display cabinet. Perhaps one day she would have one too. She'd start saving her perfume bottles now. The pretence of it – thinking she had any sort of future where there'd be a display cabinet like this – made her headache worse.

Her phone pinged.

Lyra/Lydia: *I don't know. It just feels so bad right now.*

Shannon/Lydia: *What about . . . you go travelling on your own for a while? That would be cool.*

She leaned against the side of the display cabinet and sank

to the white tiles on the floor. They were cold.

Lyra/Lydia: *Crispin is a dick.*

Shannon/Lydia: *Show him you don't need him to have a good time. You don't want him to think you've gone running home immediately, do you?*

Lyra/Lydia: *I don't care*

Shannon/Lydia: *You do. Think about it. Don't make any hasty decisions. Sleep on it.*

Lyra/Lydia: *OK*

Shannon/Lydia: *Tell Crispin I think he's a dick too x*

Lyra/Lydia: 😄

There was a hairpin crack of hope. But whatever Shannon was going to do, she was going to have to do it fast. She took a deep breath, grabbed the umbrella and left the toilet. She had to put Lydia out of her mind for now or she'd make a mistake.

The rain was splattering down, but since the others hadn't come back inside yet she put up her umbrella and went to find them. A large, white, sail-like awning was attached to the house and a tall metal pole. It was flapping wildly in the wind, and the others were huddled together underneath, umbrellas up, laughing about something Victor was saying. The huge barbecue was under a gazebo. It was being tended by a bearded man in chef's clothing who was darting about, turning food and moving it on to different parts of the grill. His face was wet with rain and sweat.

Shannon gave Maddie, Zander and Ollie a hug, and kissed Victor on both cheeks as usual and half expected him to whisper something in her ear. He didn't touch her shoulders either, or make searching eye contact, but she was acutely aware of something being different between them.

Duncan, the chef, offered her a cocktail from the trolley next to him. He said he'd invented it for the summer and it was called the Pen Potion. "After Penelope," he said. "It's gin-based with passion fruit, lime and strawberry."

Shannon supposed Piglet must be used to things being named after her. She noticed Victor was the only one not drinking a cocktail; he had a beer in his hands that didn't look as if it had reached his lips yet. She took a small sip of the cocktail, and pronounced it delicious, though it was too bitter for her taste. She swivelled round to look at her surroundings and noticed a basketball hoop stand in the tennis court.

Her mind was fizzing with how she could use that basketball hoop. She assumed that the whole group understood the scholarship scam if it was Piglet and Ollie's dad who masterminded it, but it was in all their interests not to talk about it with outsiders.

The rain suddenly became heavier, drumming down so loudly on the awning they couldn't hear each other speak. Ollie gestured for them to go inside, and they ran with their drinks, laughing as they got in and dumped their umbrellas, checking their clothing to see how wet they were.

"Good to see your leg's better," murmured Victor.

Shannon nodded.

As the rain came swishing down like a plastic curtain, Duncan ran in with the trolley and placed food on an enormous table in the dining area, cursing that some of it had become wet and that was going to dilute the flavours.

Two kitchen staff brought in plates, cutlery, salads, tiny chipped potatoes, and breads. Lots of sauces were next, including home-made tomato ketchup. Duncan returned, drenched, with more food. Three more staff members, all of them non-white, Shannon observed, went round securing doors, windows and shutters as the wind wailed and thunder cracked and rumbled.

"Leave one of the lower shutters open, please," said Piglet. "I love storms."

Shannon wasn't sure why she couldn't do it herself.

"Thanks, everyone," said Ollie in a lofty tone of voice to the staff as they finished up. "If you could wait in the back room until you're needed. It's not Hurricane Rex, but it still might be a busy night."

"What's the back room?" asked Shannon as they went

towards the kitchen.

Ollie looked at her as if she'd said something in a different language. "Back room? It's at the back of the house – actually it's at the side. That's what we call the staff quarters. There's a small common room the staff like to hang out in, and some bunk rooms for sleeping. Perfectly adequate in normal times. Got to hope the storm doesn't do it any damage tonight. Recent ones have been quite ferocious. It's all to do with climate change, of course."

Shannon thought of her mum. She might have been happier here, but she still would have been amongst people who were more concerned about buildings than their staff. Piglet set up a projector screen in the sitting area and Ollie played around with the mood lighting. Their parents appeared, Peter and Mel. Peter was short, with hair that was way too dark for his skin tone, and a bone-crushing handshake. Mel was tall, with the striking features of someone who might have been a model at one time, and dressed in something knee-length which was either a dressing gown or an haute-couture dress.

Peter said he and Mel would give them some space and eat in the little lounge, indicating a room off to one side. Mel said she wanted some photos of the storm for her Instagram and would join him in a bit.

The eight of them sat on the velvet-cushioned seating and ate while watching *Midsommar* and listening to the weather howling outside, and the clank of things being lifted by the wind and then dropped.

"Great night for a barbecue," said Ollie, as if it wasn't a joke that had been said five times already that evening.

"I think it was one of Duncan's best," said Piglet, ignoring his sarcasm. She tossed her plate forward, not bothering to do anything when chilli sauce dribbled off it on to the white rug, and snuggled down between Victor and Zander.

Shannon was wedged between Annabel and the arm of the sofa, next to a picture painted with oils. She wanted to touch it, to feel the rough, raised brushstrokes of it. She felt safe here in this sturdy house with its steel shutters with the storm raging outside. Safe for a moment, anyway.

Somebody chose another film. She rearranged herself on the sofa so Annabel wasn't as close to her, and let her head rest on a velvet cushion, thinking briefly of Ela, who always said velvet gave her the shivers, and let her eyes close.

She woke as everyone was getting to their feet, muttering about bed. One of their group was missing. Victor. She looked around and saw him emerge from the little lounge, shaking Peter's hand. If his hand was being crushed, Victor didn't make it obvious.

The heavy rain had stopped and there was just the slow banging of a loose shutter somewhere.

"Is it over?" she muttered.

"Yeah," said Annabel, stretching out her legs. "The worst of the storm's passed."

They followed Ollie and Piglet up some wooden stairs

232

to the gallery. Looking down, Shannon could see that all the plates, glasses and leftover food had been cleared away while she had slept.

"All the rooms are en suite," Piglet said. "There's a little kitchen in here if you wake up early and want to make yourself tea or coffee. Duncan left some mini pastries in there for you."

Shannon got Piglet on her own on the pretext of asking for a hairdryer for the morning. "I meant to ask," she said as Piglet found her one in a chest of drawers on the landing, "do you set the alarm at night? I occasionally sleepwalk."

Piglet shook her head. "No, don't worry. We only set up all that stuff when there's no one in the house."

The room Shannon was sharing with Emily was at the end of the corridor. She used the bathroom after her, keeping her brown contact lenses in for the night in case Emily noticed her blue eyes, though by the time she came out in her best pyjama shorts and Lydia's ripped T-shirt, she could hear her soft snoring. Emily was lying on her side, her face towards Shannon as she climbed into bed. Shannon studied it for a moment, fantasizing about smothering her with a pillow. No, she'd probably back out at the last second like last time, and she didn't want to imagine the fallout from something like that.

Looking for evidence that Peter had been paid bribe money from the Harringtons, and recording Emily saying something about the scholarship, was the better way. She already had the legal letters about Annabel ripping off the

233

beachwear designs, and the footage of their behaviour with the pizza man. The lovely Harringtons would be exposed as anything but. Shannon would make sure that as well as the gossip website, her evidence would be exposed on as many social media platforms as she could manage. She would set up accounts specifically for the purpose and draw it to the attention of people who liked to bring others down. Once a pack descended on social media, blood got spilled and people's lives changed for ever. She'd seen it play out before, and she'd make sure it happened to the Harringtons. Annabel and Emily would be expelled from school, they would be vilified, and all their friends would disassociate themselves from them. And Rosie and Douglas? They'd go to prison for the university admissions scandal, and Annabel and Emily would finally understand what it was like to have their world shattered into unsalvageable pieces.

She waited an hour and a half, listening to the loose shutter banging, then went barefoot into the corridor.

She walked along to the gallery. This was the point in a TV drama when someone would push her over and she would land on that white rug, sprawled out in a dead-body shape. She looked round, uneasy, but no one was there. She approached the gallery, not wanting to stand too close to the polished wooden rail, even so. Then she saw a movement on the ground floor, and had to lean over it anyway to see who it was.

Victor was coming out of the room next to the little

lounge. He was in shorts and a T-shirt, with his phone in his hand. She didn't know what made him look up at that moment. She was holding her breath and making no sound whatsoever. His face fell as he saw her, stricken for a millisecond, then he raised his hand, indicating for her to wait.

She understood: he was hiding something, just like she was. They were equals now.

She went downstairs, as lightly as possible so no one else woke, emotions tangled. What was he up to? What did it mean for her?

"Let's go into the kitchen," said Victor, meeting her at the bottom. She could smell that distinctive aftershave of his, and had an overwhelming desire to slip her hand into his, which confused her. Why was she thinking about that when there was so much else going on? "If anyone finds us, we'll say we were hungry," he added.

As they walked, it struck her: Victor had just spoken without his strong French accent. Where was he really from — who was he?!

The kitchen was large and almost industrial. Everything was stainless steel or silver, even the bench they sat on at the metal table, which had grey cushioned seating. Victor opened the enormous fridge and found the remains of the pavlova they'd had earlier for dessert. The richness of the piled-up cream had been too much for her then. Now she couldn't even look at it.

"Not that," she said. "Cheese?"

He arranged a cheese board for them. She couldn't imagine him being hungry any more than she was, but she watched him place the cheeses carefully, fan out a few crackers and find a cheese knife. It had a double point. She'd seen it on a YouTube video when she was studying how people like the Harringtons lived.

"I know you're not Lydia Cornwallis," he said when he finally positioned the cheese board on the table in front of her.

"And you're not Victor de Courtois," she said. He was a fraud, just like her. He'd seen the tells that the others hadn't, such as the time she'd been wrong-footed by the valet parking, but she'd sensed he wasn't like the others too.

"Correct." His face was more serious than she'd ever seen it.

"Are you even French?"

"French-Algerian," he said. "I like to make my accent thicker for these people. It seems to help them trust me. There's something you want from the Harringtons," he said. It was so strange, talking to him now. He seemed like a completely different person, but, oddly, one who felt even more familiar? Perhaps ironically, more honest?

"Yes," she said. "Revenge."

"I see."

"Last summer my mum worked for them. She lived in the bunkhouse. It was wooden then and dilapidated..." Saying what happened out loud was so much more painful than it being in her head, but Victor was listening to her in a way she'd rarely been listened to. He didn't try and interrupt to smooth it over. "Emily and Annabel ... they set fire to the bunkhouse and my mum ... she didn't make it out."

"Oh my God. You're serious?" He knew what they were like, but he was genuinely shocked.

She nodded.

He went to touch her hand, but she moved it away. If he touched her now, however much she wanted it, she might dissolve. There wasn't time to explain everything how she wanted to. "And there's something you want from ... Peter?"

"Yes," he said. "Money. It's what I do." He shrugged. "I figure they don't need as much as they have."

"Peter's an art collector," she said slowly.

"And he thinks my family has an art foundation which needs investing in," said Victor.

"You were in his study?"

"Yes, to see how far I can push him. I saw his laptop password yesterday evening when he was talking to me. I wanted to look over a spreadsheet he had upon his screen that he wouldn't let me see."

"Could you help me..." Was this asking too much? "I need to see if I can find evidence the Harringtons paid Peter to get Emily a basketball scholarship so she could get into her prestigious university."

"I can try," he said. "Peter has paper records, but nothing incriminating. Everything confidential is on his laptop. I can get you access to his financial documents, but not his bank account. Wait here."

Victor returned in under a minute with Peter's laptop. He showed Shannon the folders where information about the scholarships might be held, and after methodically searching, they found evidence of a company owned by Peter which had received eye-watering amounts of money from D and R Harrington. The company went by the bland name of Sure Education, and when they clicked on further documents they found Annabel's name as well as Emily's. "Looks as if Annabel is down for a basketball scholarship in a year's time too," said Victor.

Shannon looked up Sure Education on her phone. "It says it's an elite tutoring service," she said. She exited the webpage and took photo after photo on her phone of the documentation on Peter's laptop. "I'd really like some video footage of the two of them playing basketball to go with this," she said. "They're definitely not scholarship standard, are they?"

"I doubt it. They weren't any good at tennis." He winced. "Mediocre at best. You, though, were truly terrible."

"You were watching me do the backhand practice?" She clapped her hands over her eyes, then removed them to say, "You were supposed to be getting a taxi."

"I held back for a moment. I saw enough."

She winced. "Mrs Pushkin was probably watching from the bushes."

"She probably assumes you're in line for a fake

238

scholarship like everyone else round here," he said. "More importantly, isn't Lydia's mother turning up at the end of the week? I guess you need to be gone by then."

"Yes. I have two days, then she'll be on the island." The breath she exhaled wobbled in her throat. That was the best-case scenario. If Lydia went home now, she had no time at all.

"I need to leave soon too. We can help each other until then. I can cover for you." His eyes were locked on hers. That shiny brown colour reminded her of conkers in Pigeon Park. The park reminded her of her mum and Ela, and she felt a stab in her stomach. "Yes," she whispered. "I need Annabel and Emily to keep on trusting that I'm Lydia Cornwallis."

"And I need to be Victor de Courtois until I have some signatures." He put his hand out and she took it. The handshake was formal, but the heat of his skin against hers was thrilling. This was a connection unlike any she'd ever experienced. Two con artists finding each other in a fake world.

"You're very believable," she said in a low voice.

"Thanks." But his smile faded quickly. "I have a problem, though. I've run out of money."

CHAPTER 22

"What d'you mean?" asked Shannon. "No money at all?"

Victor sighed. "Very little. When I told you this is what I do, I should have said I'm quite new to it." He grimaced. "I'm still learning – my cousin is teaching me."

"How are you going to pay your hotel bill?"

Victor rolled his eyes. "Precisely. I didn't think I'd be on Fengari so long. Marco wouldn't let me reserve a table in the Anchor Room because I'd built up such a bill at the Maritime, but he thinks my dad is wealthy enough to pay it off eventually. That's why he got us the reservation at the Castle on the Hill. I owe Ollie money for that. He's going to ask soon, and I need to stall."

"I can't bail you out," said Shannon. "If I put it on Lydia's mum's credit card, she'd know immediately."

"That's not why I'm telling you," he said. "I wanted to be ... what's the word? Honest."

They both laughed, albeit quietly. It was proper laughter, not the put-on version she'd been coming up with when she was around Emily, Annabel and the others. It made her touch the edges of happiness.

In a low voice, Victor told her about his family. "I don't know if you've seen the art foundation website. I expect you have. That photo of me with my parents is genuine. We were dressed up for my cousin's wedding. My father is a tailor and he made that suit in the photo, and my mother's dress. My mother's jewellery isn't real. She has an eye for what rich people wear because she studies magazines when she isn't cutting or styling people's hair. But she can't read, and my father doesn't like technology. He doesn't ever go online. My cousin does the website and mocked up all the articles."

He looked at his hands and stretched out his long fingers with neat fingernails. "I am a good tailor too, but I won't work all hours to be ripped off by my snake of a boss and sweat with fear whenever he calls my name. My cousin, he's the same as me. We are like brothers. He helps me with the business side and he pretends to be my father when it's necessary. We're a team." He paused. "We're a team that needs money to keep going."

Shannon held on to her necklace. "Thanks for telling me."

"I hope we can trust each other?" He was looking beyond her eyes into the real her.

"You can trust me," she said. She wanted to touch the side of his face, to lean in and smell that aftershave.

"We should get some sleep." He stood up and they put away the cheese and crackers. At the top of the stairs, they hugged, and Shannon closed her eyes and pretended that the circumstances were different – that she had met someone who wasn't going to disappear from her life within the next day or so. It had been so long since she could be totally herself with someone.

Back in the room with Emily, Shannon dozed on and off, her thoughts when awake veering between her encounter with Victor, and the relief of having a partner in crime, and how she didn't quite have enough evidence against the Harringtons yet. One more piece of video evidence and she'd be there – but how to get it? She dreamed the real Lydia was shaking her awake, and when she woke properly, she could hear heavy rainfall again, Emily wasn't in her bed and it was nearly eleven o'clock.

Wednesday

Shannon pulled on scruffy jogging bottoms and an expensive knitted top (spotted on a friend of Annabel's Insta feed in April) and went downstairs to see what she was missing.

Everyone apart from Maddie and Zander were standing by the glass wall that separated the lounge area from the garden, watching people rushing about in the pouring rain. "What's going on?" she asked.

"Oh, hi, Lyds. Come and watch," said Emily. "It's hysterical. There's been a massive leak in the staff quarters and they are swarming about like ants out there, rescuing their things."

"They're moving things to the garage," explained Piglet. "There are heaters in there so everything will dry out in no time. I do feel sorry for them."

But not sorry enough to help them, thought Shannon. "How about," she began, but Victor trod on her foot. He didn't think she should volunteer. It wasn't something these people did.

"Luka – our premises manager – is organizing everything," said Piglet, half anticipating what she was about to say. "No need to worry." She gestured to the kitchen. "Ollie's gone to round up some people to make us brunch."

There was pressure again on her foot, perhaps telling her not to suggest they got their own food.

Annabel was pointing at someone carrying clothes on hangers. "Look at that woman's shirt. It's yellow under the arms."

"Ew. And so frumpy," agreed Emily. "Where would she even wear that?"

Shannon imagined snatching that shirt and winding it tightly first round Annabel's neck, then Emily's.

Mel popped her head out of the little lounge. "Everyone OK this morning?" She glanced out of the window. "Oh, look what's happening to our poor lawn."

"Mads and Zander aren't up yet, but Ollie's taking charge of brunch," said Piglet, and her mum nodded and went back into the room.

Taking charge of brunch was a grand way of saying *finding staff to tell them to make some food*, thought Shannon.

Someone fell over in the mud, and everyone except for her burst out laughing. She turned away and, as she did, her phone pinged quietly. She saw the name Lyra and hurried to the toilet.

Lyra/Lydia: *I'm on the early train to Geneva to see my godmother for a few days. Have told her not to tell Mummy and I'll explain when I get there — I definitely think it's better that you speak to Mummy before I do x*

OK... It was definitely better than Lydia going straight home to London, but her godmother might easily send a message to Clarissa on the quiet and that would be it.

Shannon typed: *Sounds brilliant. Hope you are feeling OK?* She added a hug emoji, although an uneasy-face one would have been more accurate.

When she returned to the others, Annabel was telling Piglet her parents were paying their staff too much because she knew for a fact how much the PlayStation cost that a guy barely older than them had under his arm.

"Assuming he bought it," Zander said, raising his eyebrows meaningfully.

"Brunch won't be long," said Ollie. He was carrying a plate of the mini pastries that had been in the little kitchen upstairs. "Duncan apologizes for the delay. It's not usually this chaotic. We got more staff in to help with all you guests. Some of our staff usually live out, and now there's the business with the staff quarters. Seems the roof hadn't been patched recently."

Shannon wanted to run outside and tell everyone how sorry she was that she'd caused more of them to be here and have their things ruined. She had a sudden feeling of spiralling out of control, that she was reaching a breaking point.

"What sort of hot drink would you like, miss?" A girl about her own age, dressed in black, was standing with an iPad taking orders. Her hair was damp in patches. She was calm and expressionless. Professional. She suggested various different coffees and teas.

Shannon asked for breakfast tea.

Maddie and Zander appeared in the gallery and the girl waited until they'd come downstairs and hugged everyone and exchanged stories of the noisy weather outside before stepping forward and asking what drinks they wanted.

"Dark-roasted coffee for me," said Mads. "With extra-hot coconut milk. Zander will have the same, but with medium-roast coffee. Ethiopian for us both, if you've got it?"

The girl murmured that she would check.

"Tastes much better," said Maddie with the sort of friendliness she thought equated to being nice to the staff. "You should do a taste test sometime. Drink it alongside Colombian. Let me know what you think!"

The drinks appeared and orders were taken for hot food, the staff eager to please. Shannon took her tea and curled up in one of the velvety armchairs, her chin on her knees, and tried to remember what her mum had told her about Bobby, and what had happened after his death.

Bobby had come from the mainland – it had always been his dream to work on Fengari because his grandmother had once told him it was the most beautiful place on earth.

He'd come to the island with good references. He was big and strong, but vulnerable. Too eager to please his boss's daughters. Not sharp enough to know the difference between friendship and being taken advantage of.

When his body was found, Shannon's mum went straight to Rosie and said she thought Emily and Annabel might know what had happened. Rosie was horrified at what was being insinuated. Neither she nor her daughters could be held responsible for someone else's mental health. However, she would speak to the girls to set Shannon's mum's mind at ease.

Shannon's mum had told Shannon what happened next, and she could remember the thunder on her mother's face, painful to see even through a mobile phone. "A word, please," Rosie had said, summoning her mum for a talk the day after his body was found. Emily and Annabel were out somewhere, and the two of them had sat on chairs in the garden.

"I spoke to the girls," Rosie told Shannon's mum. "They say they had very little to do with poor Bobby. They took him swimming once, but that seems to be it. I don't want to hear anything more about this unfortunate incident."

"That was the time they took his clothes and left him, and he had to walk home in the full sun in nothing but his swimming shorts," said Shannon's mum. "I told you about it the day after it happened and you said it was young people having a joke."

"I think it was more about poor communication," Rosie said. "And the young man was clearly lacking in common sense."

Shannon remembered wincing when her mum had told her that. Rosie sounded cruel; the guy was dead.

Her mum had said Rosie needed to understand what had been going on. "I told her I'd seen the girls giving him dares, confusing and bullying him, making him think he'd done things wrong. I think drowning might have been a dare that got out of hand. Or he couldn't take the bullying any more."

Rosie's voice had been razor-sharp in reply. "You're saying my girls are liars? Anyone suggesting my family did anything malicious needs to be extremely careful. We would fight an allegation like that, and not just through the courts." She'd fixed her eyes on Shannon's mum at that point and said, "Am I making myself understood?"

"Honestly, Shan, she sounded like the mafia," said her mum. "You should have seen the look in her eyes. I've seen the same in the girls. They're capable of anything."

Shannon shivered as she remembered it. She had thought it was all so far away and irrelevant.

And then, one evening, her mum had found a note which Bobby had placed in the bathroom cabinet, in between a box of her hair dye and a spare toilet roll. *I didn't steal the monster. I don't know how it got into my room.*

It finally made sense to her mum. She phoned up Shannon and said there was a statue of a strange terracotta animal in a display cabinet in the main house which the girls had told Bobby was worth a fortune. It had gone missing and Rosie and Douglas had spoken to Shannon's mum and Bobby, saying if they knew what had happened to it, they should speak up before the police were involved. Shannon's mum said the girls must have planted it in his room, and told him he was going to be in big trouble to see his reaction, and that was the final straw for him.

"You don't know that for sure, Mum," Shannon had said. She'd been shaping her eyebrows at the time, her mum on speakerphone.

"Maybe not," said her mum. "But somebody needs to look into it." She sighed. "Bobby hid the monster in my box of hair dye. I put it back in the display cabinet. Rosie and Douglas think I'm covering for him, of course."

She'd gone to the police with the note. The police station was tiny and the two police officers on duty said they knew the Harrington family well. They played golf with Douglas Harrington. They said they couldn't be sure Bobby had written the note, and the wording was odd for a grown man, but of course they would investigate.

One of the police officers came to the house to talk to Annabel and Emily over a cup of tea and slice of Mrs Pushkin's coffee and walnut cake. A few days later, they invited Shannon's mum to the police station, where they thanked her for her concern about Bobby and told her there would naturally be a full inquest into his death, but they were satisfied that no crime had been committed.

That same day, her mum had found a note on her bed saying, *We know you snitched on us. You'd better watch your back.* She had been incandescent with anger.

"Mum, you need to calm down," Shannon had said. "Those girls are obnoxious and they're trying to scare you. Act as if you don't care. Finish your contract and get the hell out of there."

Her mum had made a frustrated noise, and said she'd call back in a couple of days. But she never did, because a fire had ripped through the bunkhouse and she had been asleep inside.

After the funeral, Rosie Harrington sent a message to Shannon via the agency. Her mum had been smoking in the bunkhouse, which was strictly forbidden. The building was so badly damaged it would have to be rebuilt at considerable cost, which meant regrettably they wouldn't be paying her mum's wages; however, there would be no lawsuit. If Shannon had any questions, she should contact the Harringtons' lawyer.

There was absolutely no way her anti-smoking mum had burned down the bunkhouse with a carelessly placed cigarette. She had been murdered.

Shannon cradled her mug of tea and repositioned herself on Piglet and Ollie's velvety sofa. Having Victor on her side was a comforting thought, but the window of opportunity to properly wreak her revenge was closing rapidly.

CHAPTER 23

The eight of them sat round the big dining table for brunch, and staff kept bringing out more and more food. Outside, the rain continued to lash down. Shannon thought of the basketball hoop in the tennis court, probably battered or blown away by now. Even if Emily had loved basketball, Shannon would never have been able to get her outdoors in this weather to shoot hoops anyway.

"Exciting news, everyone," said Annabel, looking at her phone. "My spy cam for the creepy gardener is on its way. Can't wait to set that up. We'll have a viewing night where we can watch the footage." She grinned at their faces. "Come on, guys. It'll be hilarious."

Zander groaned. "I'm still hungover." He pushed away his plate.

Maddie rubbed his shoulder.

"Hey, Victor," said Ollie, slapping him lightly on the shoulder. "Can you pay me back for the Castle on the Hill meal?"

Victor nodded. "Of course. Send me your bank details. I'll have my dad wire you the money. I've spent over my allowance this month." He said it breezily, but Shannon saw him carefully control his breath, in out, in out, and then take a sip of freshly squeezed orange juice.

Peter emerged from the study with a couple of ring binders. He grunted hello to everyone, stared out of the window and tutted a few times, then said to Victor he'd like a quiet word with him. "Can I show you some of my collection?" he asked, holding up the ring binders, when Victor had leapt to his feet and wiped his mouth with the heavy cloth napkin. As they went into the study, Shannon heard Peter say, "I'd like your opinion on a couple of paintings. You might have to ask your old man if you don't know for sure," he said.

As the door closed, Shannon heard Victor say, "Actually, my mother is the best at knowing the potential of artwork," and Peter, clearing his throat, say, "Ah yes, I've heard she's a formidable person."

"What time is everyone leaving?" asked Maddie. "I said I'd let my folks know when I'd be home."

Annabel looked at the time on her phone. "Soon, I guess."

"I've got a personal training session in a couple of hours," said Ollie. He recited his daily gym routine to no one in particular and it was suddenly apparent to Shannon that he gymed in the house.

"You have an indoor gym?" she asked, toning down her incredulity.

"Ollie spends hours in there," said Piglet. "Lifting weights, all the machines, shooting hoops."

Shooting hoops?

"Want to see it after we've eaten?" asked Ollie.

"Sure," said Shannon.

She was being given a chance by the gods of revenge. If she could get some basketball footage, it would reinforce the evidence she already had of large sums of money being given to Sure Education in Emily and Annabel's names. With that, the legal letters about Annabel ripping off the beachwear designer, and some of the pizza man footage, she hoped it would add up to enough to destroy the Harringtons.

She could engineer a game of forfeits, but shooting a hoop as a forfeit was super-lame. She had to come up with something that the girls wanted. Like really, really wanted. Nobody here would care about the fake scholarships, but Shannon could imagine that neither sister would want to expose herself willingly.

The key was not to spook them. She pretended to scroll through her phone, as if she was catching up with her socials. In fact she was checking Emily's university term dates. She'd heard Rosie tell someone at the drinks party that the family would be spending Christmas in London this year.

"Oh wow!" she said. "My mate Ela's offered me her tickets to see Harry Styles in his Christmas show in London with backstage pass. She can't go any more."

Emily lifted her head from her own phone. "What? He's doing a Christmas show?" She went back on her phone and said, "There's nothing online about it."

"It hasn't been officially announced yet, but it's on the twenty-first of December. A charity gig," lied Shannon. "Ela's dad works on the staging concepts so he knows before anyone else and gets first dibs on tickets." She liked how she'd got the word *concepts* in. An authentic touch. Ela's dad *did* stage events, but only down the local pub.

"He'd be great to see live," said Annabel. "What's the venue?"

Shannon shrugged. "I don't know, other than that it'll be central. A regular theatre, not a big venue."

"I can be in London in December," said Maddie. "Hint. Hint."

"I'm going to buy both tickets off her so I have a spare one if anyone wants to come with me," said Shannon. She held up her index finger quickly as if she'd just had a brilliant idea. "We'll rock, paper, scissors it. Who's in?"

"Me, me, me," said Maddie.

"Me," said Annabel. "I'm your old family friend, remember." She winked.

"I'll be back for the Christmas holidays," said Emily. "So yeah, definitely. And Annabel got the bangle, remember."

Shannon smiled and breathed out slowly. Hallelujah. The gods were definitely smiling on her.

"I'm in," said Zander. "I'll give my ticket to Maddie if I win."

"No," said Shannon. "Everyone has to play for themselves. No ticket transfers. And you've got to be in London on the twenty-first of December."

"That rules me and Ollie out, then," said Piglet. "We'll be in Switzerland. Skiing."

Zander brushed some crumbs on to the spotless polished wood floor. "No offence, but I don't want to go to a Harry Styles gig, Lydia."

"None taken," said Shannon lightly. She had to stop herself from smiling. She had three of them competing. That was ideal.

"Names in a hat is better than rock, paper, scissors," said Maddie. "Pigs, can I have some paper, a pen and some scissors?"

"Hold up," said Shannon. "I want to make this more competitive."

Ollie said, "Oooh. I'm all for some competition."

"Some challenges in the gym," said Shannon.

Emily, Annabel and Maddie groaned. "We've just eaten," said Emily. "We can't do any sport until our food goes down."

"OK," said Shannon. "Well, I want to see the gym

anyway, so it should be something in there." She looked at Piglet. "What d'you recommend that's not going to make our contestants vomit?"

Piglet looked delighted to be asked. "We've got this golf putting trainer. You decide on the slope and see if you can whack the ball into the hole."

"Cool," said Shannon. "Anything else?" She needed Victor here for backup, but he was still with Peter.

"See how long they can keep their arms up in the air?" said Zander. "It's a form of torture."

"Not feeling that," said Shannon. "It's also got to be something that doesn't need gym gear."

"Everyone's got to have bare feet unless they have non-marking trainers," said Ollie. "The floor is new this summer."

There was money for a new floor in the gym but not for a decent roof for the staff quarters. *Noted*, thought Shannon. This family deserved to have a large chunk of their money taken by Victor.

"Oh, Victor!" said Maddie. She'd spotted him leaving the study. "Lydia's organizing the Hunger Games here."

Victor made a surprised face. "Tell me more. Sounds fantastic!" He pronounced it *fantastique* and Shannon had to keep a straight face.

"I've got a spare gig ticket for Harry Styles in London. I don't want to pull names out of a hat," Shannon said.

"God no," said Victor. He'd caught on quickly. "You want to do something a lot more interesting. Who's taking part? What's the challenge?"

"Emily, Bels and me," said Maddie. "Something in the gym that requires skill and minimal scope for puking, and no gym gear."

"Hmm," said Victor. "Didn't know you guys had an indoor gym. Nice. D'you have a basketball hoop, Ollie?"

"Yes," said Ollie. "I'm in the A team at school."

"Perfect," said Shannon before anyone else could interfere. "Three tries on the golf machine, three attempts to shoot a hoop. Six points up for grabs. In the event of a tie, we keep going until the winner is two clear points ahead."

Emily moaned that she couldn't shoot hoops in bare feet. "It's only for fun," said Victor, deliberately avoiding Shannon's eye. "Come on, Ollie, show us where your gym is. I want a go on the golf machine."

The gym was in a whole separate area of the house that Shannon hadn't noticed when she'd been in the garden because it had its own garden. She suppressed a gasp as Ollie pushed open the door. It was nearly as big as her college gym and about one hundred times more up to date and clean. The floor was pale cream and shiny, and Ollie wouldn't let anyone in until he'd checked they weren't wearing the wrong footwear.

To make it fairer, Ollie suggested the three competing girls had bare feet. To start with, everyone had a go on the golf machine, screaming when they got a ball in the hole, and whooping when the auto-return shot it back out again.

While Zander was lining up a shot with jeering from the others for taking so long, Shannon said under her

257

breath to Victor, "I'll film. Can you keep everyone from noticing?"

"Yes," he said without further comment, and she was grateful for his cool detachment, as she felt her whole body vibrating with nerves. Emily knew Shannon was aware she had a fraudulent basketball scholarship and she didn't want to think about what would happen to her if Emily or Annabel realized she was filming.

"Basketball next," said Ollie after each girl had a full three points owing to the easy gradient Piglet had set on the golf machine. He picked up the basketball by the side of the gym and shot a hoop easily.

"Show-off!" said Piglet, and he glared at her. "Competition time, part two!" she sang. "And there's everything to play for. Who's first?"

"Me!" said Maddie. Her ball hit the backboard behind the net and missed.

"Not bad, Mads," said Ollie. "That was nearly a bank shot."

Nobody could be bothered to ask what a bank shot was.

"Bad luck, babe," said Zander.

Annabel said she'd go next, and Shannon got her phone out of her jogging trouser pocket and held it by her side, slightly tilted, as if she were simply casually holding it, maybe waiting for a message to come through. Annabel lined up her shot and it bounced off the rim. "Close," she said. "I get half a point for that." She looked at Shannon, whose mouth went dry.

"No half points," called Victor. "Em's next."

Annabel fetched the ball and threw it hard at Emily. "Let's see what you can do, you *basketball prodigy*," she said.

Emily glared at her.

"Come on," Ollie said. "Use those muscles."

"Stop putting me off," said Emily, and threw the ball before she'd finished talking. It fell way short. It was almost as if she didn't have enough strength in her arms. Shannon felt a swell of satisfaction. That would definitely go towards showing Emily hadn't won her scholarship fairly.

Maddie scored on her second try. "I'm going to meet Harry Styles!" she yelled.

Annabel scored too, dancing round the tennis court with glee. "Bit flukey," she said. "I'm normally hopeless. Go me!"

Shannon smiled to herself.

On her second go, Emily jumped half-heartedly towards the hoop, but the ball was never going to go in. In the final round, Maddie and Annabel missed their third tries. They both had four points each.

"Time to even it up, Ems," called Victor.

Emily made another feeble attempt, then caught the ball as it bounced and hurled it against the wall in anger.

"Now it's between Maddie and Annabel!" said Victor.

Shannon tucked her phone away a fraction too late.

"Were you filming me?" Emily asked Shannon, moving towards her, kicking the ball out of her way. Her voice was hard. She whipped round. "Why was Lydia filming us?"

Shannon stepped back. "I wasn't filming. It was a photo. To send to Ela. I'm showing her how I was deciding who to give the second gig ticket to." She let out a breath.

"I don't like being filmed when I haven't given permission. I thought you'd understand that, not liking being photographed yourself," said Emily. Her blue eyes flashed with an unspoken threat.

"It was only a few photos," said Shannon.

"Delete them," said Emily.

"What's the problem?" asked Victor, making his way over. "Lydia, you'll delete the photos, won't you?"

"Course," said Shannon. She pulled the phone out of her pocket and held it up to her face so it opened. "Look, I'm doing it now." She swivelled her body sightly so Emily couldn't see that her finger wasn't quite touching the screen.

Suddenly her phone was no longer in her hand. Annabel had come up behind her and snatched it. "You lying cow," she called, poking her finger at the phone. "You did take a video. I've deleted it now."

Emily was immediately in her face. "What were you thinking?" she hissed. "I have to be really careful. If that video had got out, I'd have slaughtered you."

Shannon swallowed so hard her throat hurt. "Did I video accidentally? Oh, I'm sorry. I thought I had it on portrait mode." The shock and bleakness in her voice was real. That footage had been perfect – of both girls.

"Maddie and Annabel still need to battle it out," called Zander.

Shannon watched Maddie win and do a victory dance while Annabel sulked and Emily stared coldly at her. She went through the pretence of saying she'd let her know the details of the gig as soon as she could, while she felt sick for letting the footage slip through her fingers. Emily was still glaring at her and she felt a cold unease creep into her chest.

"Anyone want a drink, or food, before they go home?" asked Piglet in a cheery voice.

Everyone murmured that they'd eaten and drunk enough, and they packed up their things. As they waited for taxis, Annabel said, "We should plan our trip to the mainland."

"Oh yes!" Shannon forced a smile. She'd forgotten she'd agreed to pay for that. She'd book, then cancel after she'd left Fengari.

"I found a really nice place," said Maddie. "It has a balcony overlooking the harbour. I'll send you the link."

Victor was looking at his phone. "Yeah, sure. I'm in," he said, without looking up. "Hey, did you see that some flights are scheduled to come in this evening? Ferries and the helicopter start again tomorrow morning. They're going to be crowded." He was letting her know she had to book now if she wanted to get away by Friday when Clarissa came.

Peter came out of his study to say goodbye. He slapped Victor on the back and said he'd draw up the paperwork.

"Had an email from your old man. Wants me to tie it up in the next couple of days. Why the rush?"

"There's only one spot left for a named sponsor. He has someone else sniffing around and wants to settle everything before it becomes awkward. He hates overpromising." Victor picked up his Louis Vuitton holdall. "Do you want me to see if I can catch him now? Double-check?" He looked at his phone. "We could probably catch him before he flies to Muscat."

Peter paused. "Nah, let's not disturb him now, but I'll give him a ring if I need to later."

"Sure. I'll message."

Peter slapped him on the back again and they shook hands. Shannon wondered how sweat patches weren't appearing under Victor's arms. Peter did the same to Zander, then said, "Goodbye, ladies. Be good," to the rest of them.

Outside, the air smelled earthy and damp, and the pale grey sky at sea had merged with the water like a foggy filter. The tropical storm was over and everything was still.

In the taxi, Emily sat in between Annabel and Shannon. "I still can't believe you were stupid enough to take a video," snarled Emily.

"It was a mistake," said Shannon. "I'm sorry. It's been deleted." She felt the weight of that loss in her body, which was aching all over.

"It was a pretty big mistake," said Annabel.

It made Shannon want to gag when she thought about

what Annabel might have seen on her phone had she looked beyond the video footage. She would tread very carefully in these last few hours on the island. Her priority now was to get off the island. She'd go back to Clifftop House, pack and book herself on to whichever form of transport had space first.

Annabel pulled at her seat belt so she could perch at the edge of the seat and look at them both. She held up her phone. "Seb's cheapskate parents have finally paid extra for him to get here on Friday!"

"Couldn't care less," said Emily. She was pressing against Shannon, so that Shannon's shoulder was jammed against the window. When Shannon tried to move, Emily applied more pressure. It was starting to hurt.

Annabel laughed. "You're jealous he's going to take me away from you. You like hanging out with me on Fengari."

Shannon would be gone by then. Seb could watch the fallout when Clarissa arrived.

"So there'll be nine of us for our trip to the mainland," said Annabel. "I'll check if the accommodation Maddie's found sleeps nine. If not, we'll have to look for another one. I'm not sharing a room with anyone other than Seb."

Shannon gazed out of the window, at the flooding on the road and the tree debris, and let Annabel witter on. None of this was any of her concern. Her phone vibrated several times.

She looked at it as she got out of the taxi at Clifftop House. There were a string of messages from Crispin's mum.

Lydia, I need to talk to you urgently.

Have you gone away with Crispin? I don't know why he lied and told me he'd gone with Benedict and Ollie. I saw Ollie in Pret today and he looked very startled to see me.

Tell Crispin he promised to check in with me every third day. It's been five days now.

Call me as soon as you get this.

Emily accidentally bumped her hip into Shannon so she fell against the taxi as it drove off.

"Careful!" said Shannon.

"My mistake," said Emily, making slow and deliberate eye contact, and then, "I'm watching you, Lydia."

Shannon bit down hard on the inside of her lip. Her phone was vibrating again. It was Crispin's mum, still hounding her. Everything felt as if it was sliding out of control.

CHAPTER 24

Mrs Pushkin came into the hall as they arrived back at Clifftop House, her finger to her lips. "Girls, your father is in bed, so you need to be quiet."

"What's wrong with him?" demanded Emily.

"He's feeling exhausted and has a bad back. Nothing to worry about," said Mrs Pushkin. "He'll be as good as new after he's had some sleep." She made him sound like a baby.

"Is he ill, or are you just fussing?" asked Annabel.

"He's had a tiring morning," said Mrs Pushkin. "I'd like it if you were more respectful of your father. He does so much for you girls. He's tired because he insisted on going outside this morning to help sort out the garden."

"The gardeners shouldn't have let him help," said Annabel.

"It's their job, isn't it? That reminds me, I'm waiting for a package. Can you let me know when it arrives?"

Emily said, "Dad's not the only one who's tired." She went upstairs.

Shannon excused herself, muttering she'd go upstairs for a while too, while Annabel said she was going to call Seb. "Did you know he's coming to stay on Friday, Mrs P?"

"I didn't," said Mrs Pushkin when Shannon was near the top of the stairs. "It's lucky I take everything in my stride and put up with everyone's nonsense, isn't it?"

"It is!" said Annabel. "You're the best!"

Shannon looked down and saw her blow a kiss to Mrs P. She wasn't the sort of woman you hugged.

In her room she looked out at the garden, more damaged than Ollie and Piglet's, presumably because it was more exposed. Trees were missing branches, and one was down completely. Smashed patio pots had been swept up into a wheelbarrow. Some plants were still covered in mud, and others were lying in a soggy heap, waiting to be removed. Had Douglas needed a lie-down after Bobby disappeared or when his body was found? When her mother's body was pulled from the bunkhouse fire?

As she stood at the window, she composed a message to Crispin's mum.

Shannon/Lydia: *Don't be upset. We wanted to have a secret adventure! We're having so much fun but it's busy. We're in Marbella now. The beach is amazing. Crispin has a hangover but he says he'll phone you soon when we get a better signal.*

Hopefully that would keep her from contacting Clarissa for a day or so.

She would leave the island tomorrow, Thursday, and go back to being ordinary Shannon Jones, who liked tight, garish clothes, glittery heels and lots of make-up. Except she wasn't sure she did like those things any more. Not as much as she used to. She had no plans for when she returned to London. She couldn't go back to Ela's family, the flat she'd shared with her mum had other people living in it now, and she wasn't sure her elderly neighbour would want her back to stay. Anyway, who knew how resourceful the Harringtons and Cornwallises might be, in trying to work out who Rhiannon had really been? Would they make the connection to her mum? Maybe she shouldn't even stay in London, then. She would go somewhere else, to a hostel, and find a job immediately. Any job. It would be OK, she told herself. She came from a line of strong women.

She found the private ferry website on her phone. A banner came up saying that they were experiencing a high volume of traffic and there was a queue to get on to the ticket-buying part of the site.

Fifteen minutes of virtual queuing later, she was able to see there were no tickets left for the next three days. *Sold out.* Panic pounding in her ears, she found the regular ferry service. Nothing for four days.

She googled *Fengari helicopter*. Selected flights were available from Friday morning and that was the best she was going to get. As long as she left before Clarissa arrived on the ferry... The flights were hideously expensive, and she couldn't put it on Lydia's credit card because Clarissa would find out straightaway and wonder what the hell she was doing. She'd reached the limit on her own card. It could go on Margot's debit card, but it would wipe everything from that account.

She had no choice. The question was whether she should book under her own name so there was no risk of it leaking back to the Harringtons that their guest was planning to go, or Lydia's. There was also the worry that the authorities might cross-check it with people coming in and find she wasn't on the list because she'd come in as Lydia Cornwallis. On balance, she decided it was safer to leave under her own name. She booked the first flight of the morning and ticked the box to confirm that she understood the ticket could only be refunded if the helicopter couldn't fly because of the weather. It was such a large chunk of money she felt sick. Next, she went online and found her prepaid open ticket and booked the return part of her flight from the mainland back to London.

Shannon lay on the bed. If only she hadn't messed up with the basketball footage. The evidence she had didn't feel like enough. She wanted the Harringtons to suffer like her mum had, to lose everything like she had. That meant their freedom, their money, their beloved house, their friends and – more importantly – their reputation.

A thought came to her. She grabbed her phone and wriggled up on to an elbow. What if she pitted one sister against the other? Got them so paranoid they tore each other down? It would make perfect footage for a gossip site.

It took minutes to write a direct message from one of her fake Instagram accounts.

Hi Emily – you don't know me, but I met your sister at a party and we had an interesting discussion. How much are you willing to pay me to keep quiet about last summer?

She sent the same message to Annabel, swapping her name in place of Emily's, and sent it from the other fake account.

The wording was deliberately ambiguous, not spelling out exactly what had happened last summer, but she hoped the implication was clear: the other sister had snitched, and even if they worked out that they'd both got the same message, they'd know someone was on to them.

There was a hammering noise outside. She went to the window and saw Finch, fixing stakes in the ground to lift up plants which had been flattened in the storm. He didn't work quickly but he was steady and methodical. There was a wheelbarrow next to him, in which he was putting broken-off pieces of foliage, twigs, and flower stems. She noticed he'd kept the flowers in a separate pile from the rest.

She leaned against the window. She thought about the

helicopter she would take on Friday morning. She could almost hear the judder of the blades turning, the backdrop to her escape. A flash of colour by the bunkhouse caught her eye. It was the flowers from the wheelbarrow, tied together with string or wire. Finch had left them by the door, like a little floral tribute. It jolted her, and before she'd really registered what she was doing, she'd slipped her feet into her Nikes and was making her way outside.

Finch was raking leaves when she reached him. He looked up when he saw her. "Hi, Lydia," he said warily, and carried on raking.

"I saw the flowers you left outside the bunkhouse," she said. "I wondered what they were for. If there was any reason you'd left them there?" She winced. The words sounded peculiar now they were out of her mouth. She supposed she wanted him to say he'd heard that someone had died in the bunkhouse and he'd left them there in their memory.

"Oh." He looked surprised. "They were broken stems from the storm. I thought I'd put them together and give them to Ted for his wife. She's not well. I didn't think anyone would miss them. They'd only end up on the compost heap."

"Oh," she said. She realized how much it mattered to her that her mum wasn't forgotten.

"You can take them if you want them," said Finch. "I genuinely thought no one would want them."

"It's fine," she said. "Forget I mentioned them." She

270

should walk away, but now she was here and he already thought she was weird and she was leaving the island soon, she'd ask something that had been bothering her. "Why does the bunkhouse smell of smoke? That time I was in there, it was really strong? Could you smell it too?"

Finch stopped raking and stared at her. "I don't know if you knew this, but there was a fire last year and the previous bunkhouse burned down."

Shannon nodded, but she guessed he hadn't been told that a person had been in the building at the time.

"Rosie Harrington told me that one piece of furniture was saved," he said. "The stone coffee table. That's what smells. I should give the whole thing another scrub down, but I'm used to it now."

It wasn't a ghostly smell, then. If her mum was going to send her a sign, it was better that it wasn't a reminder of the way she'd died. Even so, loneliness crept through her.

"Are you OK?" Finch snapped her out of her thoughts.

"Yes," she said. "Thank you."

He nodded and lifted a load of leaves and shoved them in a large green bag and placed his booted foot on them to pack them down, conversation over.

She was restless. There was no point wasting her last few hours on the island lying in bed. She went back upstairs for her key, changed into her scruffier trainers, swapped her thin knitted jumper for a hoodie and her joggers for black jeans. She'd go for a walk. It wasn't a very Lydia thing to do, but she wouldn't go far.

Opening the main gate, she chose to go down the hill to the first viewing point where cars pulled in for people to take photos of the view.

When she reached it, she sat on the wall for a while, looking out to sea. She felt sure her mum must have done this. As she reached up to hold the hearts on her necklace, her phone vibrated.

It was a message from Victor: *Only just had a chance to send this. You're back in the game.* Attached was a video, taken from where he'd been standing in the gym, of Emily and Annabel playing basketball – badly.

CHAPTER 25

Shannon almost fell to her knees as she viewed the footage. It wasn't as close-up as hers had been, but it was exactly what she needed. Full of energy now, she carried on walking, reaching a footpath which led her along the cliff. It was hard to imagine she'd soon be back in London with its cars and bus fumes and crowds.

When she returned to Clifftop House, she took a running leap on to the bed, and attached the video to the email, which she would send as soon as the helicopter engine started up on Friday morning. Then she prepared messages for social media. She only had two evenings and one whole day to get through and she would add any last pieces of footage her fake Insta messages had provoked.

Emily and Annabel arrived at the table separately for dinner, both of them dressed as casually as her. In fact, Emily looked as if she was wearing a pyjama top. Before she'd come here she'd assumed the Harringtons changed for dinner, like she knew people did in expensive hotels, but it seemed they only got dressed up when it was a proper dinner party or they went out. She cringed when she thought how dressed up she'd been when she first came here for dinner.

The girls were twitchy as they sat down, Annabel playing with her hair, Emily biting a thumbnail, neither of them hearing Mrs Pushkin ask for a mat to be placed on the table before she burned her fingers holding the dish of tiny roast potatoes. Shannon went to fetch one.

"Thanks," said Mrs Pushkin briskly, then, "Oh, I forgot to put out fish knives. Will you get them, Lydia, since you're up?"

Shannon knew where the cutlery drawer was. The problem was she wasn't a hundred per cent sure what a fish knife looked like. She'd know it when she saw it, though – was it flat but curved? She'd watched a YouTube video about cutlery. It would come back to her. There were several kinds of knives, lined up in velvet-lined compartments. Returning to the table, she was fairly sure of her choice, and hoped she hadn't taken too long.

Rosie appeared with Douglas, who was suggesting they might have to cancel a summer party they were having in a week's time because of the mess of the garden.

"Harringtons never accept defeat. That's our unofficial family motto, Lydia," said Rosie, leaning back to allow Mrs Pushkin to place the plate of fish in a white sauce in front of her for her to serve. She said it half-jokingly, but her mouth was set in a determined line. "We'll get the gardeners to make up some magnificent pots and place them strategically around the garden."

"The staff quarters were pretty much washed away at Ollie and Piglet's," said Annabel. "It was quite funny, actually."

Mrs Pushkin placed a heaped bowl of steaming green vegetables on the table and then discreetly disappeared.

"Really?" said Rosie. "How very unfortunate."

Douglas stared at the table, as if in a trance. "I say," he said finally, "why have I got a butter knife instead of a fish knife?"

"That was Lydia!" said Emily, and Annabel said, "They're so tiny compared to fish knives."

Shannon couldn't stop the blush. "I'm so stupid. I was thinking about something else."

"Butter?" suggested Emily, and Annabel laughed. They exchanged glances, too relaxed for people who were effectively being blackmailed online.

"Mummy's visit," said Shannon, unnerved. It was the first thing she thought of; Clarissa's impending presence on the island was certainly on her mind. "I'll get the proper ones."

"No need," said Rosie, getting up and replacing them

swiftly. "You must be looking forward to seeing your mama."

Shannon said, "Kind of," and out of the corner of her eye thought she saw Emily and Annabel exchange another look. What was going on?

"Oh, I forgot to say," said Rosie, frowning. "I missed a call from her earlier. She said she'd phone back this evening."

Shannon said, "She was supposed to be leaving me alone this holiday."

Rosie gave a patronizing little shake of her head. "Us mothers can't help wanting to know our babies are doing all right. I don't know what's gone on between the pair of you, but you and Clarissa are going to have a marvellous time together. Fengari is just the most healing place. You wait and see."

There was a pudding of sponge cake on top of stewed peaches. Conversation returned to the garden, and only changed when Annabel asked if she and Seb could hire jet skis when he was staying. Douglas said he didn't see why not, as long as they didn't run anyone over. "I'll clarify that," he said in his ponderous way. "Don't run over any islanders. I don't care about the tourists."

Everyone laughed, especially Shannon, who wanted to throw a fish knife at every single one of them like a dart.

As dinner came to an end, Emily suggested the three of them went down to the summer house to sort out the trip to the mainland.

"Lydia has offered to pay for the accommodation," said Annabel.

"Oh gosh, how kind," said Rosie as Douglas poured her another glass of wine. "Doug, let's take your mind off the garden and watch some TV?" She smiled at Shannon. "He likes a psychological thriller, don't you, darling? Always guesses the baddie."

Shannon would put the deposit on the Cornwallis credit card. "I'll go and get my card."

Her bedroom felt different. Something wasn't right. She wondered if Mrs Pushkin had cleaned it while she was on her walk and she had been too busy looking at Victor's video when she came back to notice.

"Are you coming?" called Annabel from downstairs.

Shannon found the credit card in her wallet and checked her phone for messages – Piglet had spammed the group chat with suggestions of different quizzes they should do that evening, and Maddie had sent links to loads of Airbnb places on the mainland. "Coming!" she shouted, checked her phone was ready to record if she needed it to, and raced down the stairs.

"Are you two OK?" she asked, as they walked down to the summer house together, neither of them saying a word. "You seem . . . weird?"

"I had a weird afternoon," said Emily. She had pulled on a baggy cardigan over her pyjama top since dinner. It looked ancient. She had things in both pockets dragging it lower at the front.

277

"Yeah?" said Shannon.

"Fengari's like that," said Annabel. "The strangest things go down here."

The girls were acting differently, but they were lacking the appetite to tear each other down. She was going to have to nudge things along.

"I got an odd DM today. . ." Shannon said, waiting for them to bite. With luck, they'd chip in with their direct messages.

Annabel pushed open the door of the summer house and suddenly Shannon was pinned against the wall by Emily.

"Look what I've got," said Emily, pulling something from her pocket with the hand that wasn't against Shannon's chest. Two passports. One for Shannon Jones and one for Lydia Cornwallis.

Shannon's body temperature went haywire and sweat sprang from her armpits and forehead. She thought she might be sick, and placed her clammy palms against the wall to dry them. She'd been right about her room. The two of them had been in there, poring over her things. The passports had been under the bed, in the lining of her suitcase. Well-hidden. Or so she'd thought.

"You're Shannon Jones," said Emily, with a hint of contempt. "You're Shannon Jones pretending to be Lydia Cornwallis. I knew something was off about you."

Annabel stepped forward into her personal space. "You're behind those messages we got, aren't you?" She looked round at Emily. "I know she is, Ems. Trust me. She's here to cause trouble. Videoing the basketball wasn't an accident."

Emily frowned. She kicked out casually and her hard trainer made contact with Shannon's calf. "Go on then, speak." The pain was sharp and it made Shannon cry out. She had been so, so foolish to think they wouldn't snoop on her like they had Finch.

But she was Shannon Jones. She was clever and strong. They would not bring her down.

"I'm Lydia," she said as haughtily as she could manage. "And I have Shannon Jones's passport."

Emily stood back and flipped through Shannon's passport and ripped out the photo page.

Shit.

"That's you." She shoved it in Shannon's face.

"It's someone who looks very like me," said Shannon. Her brain was working feverishly. "I stole Shannon's passport."

Emily ripped the photo page out of the fake passport, and that's when Shannon did cry out. Both passports were ruined. "This is a fake. It's the same person as Shannon Jones."

Annabel said to Emily, "Lydia's Insta is the dullest thing on the planet – not many photos of her." One of the first things Shannon and Lydia had done was go through her accounts and delete images of her. Lydia even had access to Clarissa's Facebook page, and had done the same there.

And there were many Shannon Joneses on the internet, but none of them were her. She had no social media and no mentions on her college website. She was a digital ghost.

They weren't sure who she was.

"We'll go to the police," said Emily. "They can work it out."

Shannon could feel her phone in the back pocket of her jeans. Her evidence was automatically backed up on the cloud. She could show it to the police, but the ones on the island would hush it up, like they hushed up her mum's and Bobby's deaths, and the Harringtons (and possibly Clarissa Cornwallis too) would destroy her.

"OK," she said, as if they'd cracked her. "Crispin – you know Crispin?"

Emily grinned. "Lydia's ex."

"*My* ex," said Shannon. "He was seeing someone called Shannon Jones. He wanted to go travelling with her. She was a friend, someone I *thought* was a friend. I tricked her into giving me her passport so she wouldn't be able to go. Crispin has a type. We look very similar. Seriously, I can't believe you just destroyed my passport over this, you psycho!"

Annabel came up so close, Shannon could smell the fish from dinner on her breath. "I think you're lying."

Shannon pushed her away and made for the open door. "I'm not listening to any more of this rubbish. Is this how you treat all your guests?"

"Only the ones who are hiding things from us," called

Emily, waving the vandalized passports. "If you're Lydia Cornwallis, 'Mummy' can buy you a new one."

Behind her Annabel said, "Phone Crispin's friend. See what he knows."

Shannon strode across the decking and on to the path, her heart pounding, her leg hurting where Emily had kicked it. If she hadn't sent those messages, she might not have provoked the girls in this way. She'd pushed her luck, and now she had no passports to leave the island with.

She had to get out of this evil house. She'd grab a few things and leave – it didn't matter where she went. She'd contact Crispin's cousin at the gossip website and tell him she had an explosive story for him. She'd ask him for help and if he refused – because after all she couldn't forget he was loosely connected to the Cornwallis family – she would find another website or a newspaper. She would demand to speak to police who weren't based on the island.

It wasn't much of a plan.

The garden still had a bitter smell in the air from the aftermath of the storm. There was an eerie silence. Drops of rain from still-wet leaves fell on her as she walked past the bunkhouse. She thought of Finch in there, and the spyware that Annabel was about to set up for entertainment. Of Bobby. Of her precious mum. Of Nan, who had held them both together. Three strong women.

Anger surged so rapidly she was certain her ribcage expanded. She wasn't going to be another victim. She would do what she came to do: bring the Harringtons down.

She pushed her thumb into the pointy part of the biggest heart on her necklace, turned round and walked back the way she'd come. With her other hand, she reached into her back pocket, got out her phone and hit record, slipping it back into her jeans.

Emily and Annabel were standing at the door of the summer house with flushed faces, talking to each other, pumped up with the drama of what had just occurred.

But a lot more drama was about to go down.

The two of them spotted her immediately and stopped talking. Shannon kept back from them, keeping the decking between them, and said, "OK, I'll tell you who I am. I am your worst nightmare. I know what you did last summer. You bullied the previous gardener until a twisted game went wrong, or he couldn't face living any more. And then you set fire to the bunkhouse and killed someone." She wanted to let the words sink in, but the girls simply stared at her, not giving her any reaction at all.

And then Emily spoke. "What happened last summer is none of your business," she hissed.

"You don't know what they were like," said Annabel. "The gardener had something wrong with him and the woman had a crush on him."

"She accused us of ridiculous stuff like you're doing now," said Emily. Her eyes narrowed. "You wrote those Insta messages to us, didn't you? Who are you?"

Shannon ignored her. "You let her burn to death. Her body was unrecognizable when she was pulled out."

"She interfered in things which were none of her business," said Annabel. "She needed taking care of."

There it was – the admission, and Shannon hoped her phone recording had caught it. Her voice rose. "Needed taking care of? You killed her. You took her *life*."

"No, we didn't," said Emily. "Mrs P did what needed to be done. We don't let people go round saying things like that about us, especially nobodies."

For a moment, Shannon couldn't speak. Mrs Pushkin had started the fire. She pictured that vile woman's pinched face. Emily and Annabel were still guilty. Emily had probably given Mrs Pushkin the cigarette which started it. Yet they showed a casual indifference. The horror of it burned through her like a flame ripping through the bunkhouse.

"That 'nobody' was a person!" screamed Shannon. "She was *my mum*!"

She only caught a glimpse of their shocked faces before she turned and ran back to the house.

"You can't get away," shouted Emily from behind. "We have the passports and everyone will be looking for you."

"I can't believe that loser was your mum!" shouted Annabel.

It was suddenly clear what she had to do. The thing that had been obvious from the start, which she had shied away from until now.

Their voices were closer behind her than she'd like but she wouldn't look round. She ran into the house, hardly registering anything her body was feeling because her head was so loud. Mrs Pushkin had done the dirty work for the family, and the rest of them had let her. To them it was no big deal.

She could hear Mrs Pushkin in the kitchen and the TV from the garden room where Rosie and Douglas were. There would be a reckoning and she would make it happen. Her plan had always needed to be adaptable; she saw that now.

In her bedroom, she went straight for the silver lighter she had tucked in with her underwear. She curled her hand round it, reassured by the smoothness of it. The only other thing she took from the room was the Clifftop House key ring, but she dived into Annabel's room and took a handful of notes which were lying in a crumpled heap on top of her chest of drawers. Low denominations, but better than her cards, which would no longer get her anywhere.

She wouldn't think about the helicopter flight. The likelihood of her being allowed to board was zero. Soon everyone would be looking for her at the heliport and ferry terminals. Getting off the island had become an impossible goal. She no longer had anything to lose.

Before, she had thought she could never actually kill them.

Well, maybe she could after all.

She knew there would be petrol in the shed where the ride-on mower was kept. Annabel had told her the first evening she was here that it wasn't locked. The

Harringtons banged on about the low crime rate on the island but the truth was they were just careless, stupid rich people. She probably only had seconds to do this, a few minutes at most. As she ran downstairs lightly, she heard Emily and Annabel shouting at their parents, telling them they had to call Clarissa, and Rosie saying, "This is Clarissa calling me back now. Shush." And then, "Hello, Clarissa? I have to stop you there because. . ."

Her head pounded as she ran to the shed. There was a huge tank with a tap on it and assorted cans near it. She selected one which she'd be able to carry when full and filled it up, leaping back as it splashed over the neck of the can – careful not to let it splash on her as the powerful smell of it hit the back of her nose.

Hurry, hurry.

As soon as she turned off the tap, she was moving. She ran to the summer house first, where nobody was. She sprinkled a trail of petrol over the sofas and the dry timber floor. She opened the doors to the cupboards where the remaining fireworks were and extended the shaky petrol path in there. This would be spectacular. To be sure the fire would take hold, she lit the petrol in two places, watching as it whooshed along the trail and licked up against the fireworks, and then she sprinted to the house, pausing momentarily by the bunkhouse. She could never set light to that building, and not just because Finch would be in there.

I love you, Mum.

Shannon had never felt so light and free as she entered Clifftop House through the back entrance. She wouldn't go upstairs because she didn't want to be trapped by either flames or the Harringtons. From their voices it seemed they were still in the garden room, talking to Clarissa on speakerphone. Mrs Pushkin was there too, adding her thoughts on someone who didn't know a butter knife from a fish knife. Emily cut in and said they should go out looking for her. Douglas said, "Don't get over-involved. She might be dangerous. The police will pick her up soon enough."

It was helpful having them all in one place like that. It would make what she wanted to do so much more efficient.

She jerked the petrol can around as the first fireworks went off. Faster and faster she moved through the ground floor, leaving extra petrol underneath the beam in the kitchen, making a ring of petrol around the garden room. She heard Rosie say loudly, "Listen! What's that noise? What's going on?" Shannon imagined the energy in the room changing, the hunters becoming the prey.

She held out her lighter. The fireworks screeched, flared, thud-thudded and crackled outside. It was about eight thirty by now, and the last bit of daylight had disappeared. Prime time for a firework display.

This was it. Let them burn. She touched her necklace and thought of her mum.

She flicked the lighter and let the flame jump to the

286

petrol. The blaze of colour thrilled her. Yellow, orange and a line of red. She locked the outside doors with her house key – she didn't really believe it would trap them, but she hoped it would slow them down, at least – and ran to the ran to the patch of plants outside the garden room. They were damp from the storm, but some of the woody stems were dry and that would be enough. Shannon tipped out the rest of the petrol and set light to it, and that's when she heard Emily and Annabel's screams, and Douglas shouting about their beloved beam in the kitchen.

They had phones. Emergency services would roll up. She hoped that at some point, as the flames swooped closer to them and the smoke entered their nostrils, they would think of the woman in the wooden bunkhouse, the woman whose name they couldn't even remember.

CHAPTER 26

Before Shannon fled the garden, she hammered on the bunkhouse door. Finch might think the exuberant firework show was simply the Harringtons going over the top. She needed to know he would be OK. She watched the fireworks for a moment – multicoloured streaks and swirls soaring and squealing, scattering drops of piercing brightness before fading into darkness. As she heard Finch unlock the door, she ran as fast as she could along the path to the side gate and out through main gates. It was dark but there were intermittent street lamps along the road.

She allowed herself one last look back. The fireworks had finished and now there was thick black smoke spiralling from the summer house, dense against the night sky. There was smoke from the main house too, but it hadn't risen as high yet. Guilt filled her head. She'd crossed a terrible line, from fraud to arson – or worse – and there was no going back. She shook the feeling off. Of course, with all the warning from the summer house, the Harringtons and Mrs Pushkin had probably escaped the fire. But at the very least, Clifftop House would be a smouldering ruin, and their precious beam destroyed.

As she ran along the road, she said out loud, "I did it." She felt an energy and strength she'd never experienced before. It made her want to whoop and scream, and tell someone what she'd done.

She wanted, more than anything, to tell Victor. As she thought of his beautiful face and his old-soul eyes which hid so many secrets, she realized with a sudden jolt that he might not want anything to do with her after what she'd done. She could ruin everything for him, with so many people after her. He had his own issues on the island, and there was a high chance he'd think she was as bad as Emily and Annabel now.

Instinctively she'd headed towards Fengari Old Town – it was where the Maritime Hotel was, and near where the ferries came and went, except she had no means of getting on to a ferry or helicopter without a passport. Soon there'd be fire engines and police cars along this road, and she didn't want to be seen. She was nearly at the viewpoint she'd been to earlier. It would be a sensible place to call a taxi from. Feasibly she could have walked there from town and then not wanted to walk all the way back again. As soon as it was within sight, she searched Fengari taxis on her mobile. She just had to make sure she didn't use the companies that the Harringtons and the Fengari Training College did, in case she got a taxi driver who recognized her. She withheld her number before calling, and when the operator asked for her number, she put on an American drawl and said, "My parents don't let me give out my number. I'm on vacation and I've walked too far out of town. My name is Cady."

By the time the taxi had arrived, Shannon had plaited her hair either side of her face to look younger and more vulnerable, although she only had one hair elastic from her ponytail so one side was coming undone. Her hoodie smelled slightly of smoke, but not too badly. It was as if, say, she'd been to a barbecue earlier in the evening. "I went walking after dinner and didn't realize how far I'd got because I was listening to music," she told the taxi driver, who, happily, was more interested in the commentary of a cricket match on his radio. "Please can you drop me by the marina?"

He grunted and said nothing until he heard a siren. A fire engine came up the road and he looked in the rear-view mirror. "Guess there's a fire up there," he said.

"I can't see anything," she said. She hoped that meant they were too far away, not that the fires had burned out.

A few minutes later a police car and an ambulance came past. "Oh man," he said. "That looks like a bad situation."

He looked at Shannon. "You saw nothing up there?"

Shannon held on to her plait and said, "No. It must have been further up the road."

"We don't get many bad incidents on Fengari," said the driver. "Though there was a fire last summer at one of the fancy properties on the cliff." He looked at her, as if assessing how old she was and whether he should tell her any details. "A member of the family's staff died. She'd been smoking in bed."

Her name was Bex Jones. She was murdered.

"Drop me here, please," said Shannon, counting out Annabel's notes. They were at the edge of Fengari Old Town. She couldn't tip much, but perhaps it was better to be tight-fisted like a teenager who wasn't used to paying her own cab fares.

"You sure you're OK getting to your hotel?" asked the driver, suddenly taking an interest. "I don't mind taking you directly there."

"It's fine," drawled Shannon. "I'm meeting my parents near here. We're going for a hot chocolate by the marina."

"All righty," said the driver, pulling over. He took her cash, smoothing out the crumpled notes on his thigh. "You take care now, young lady. This is a very safe island, but you never know. No more walks at night on your own."

"Thanks," said Shannon. As soon as she'd slammed the door shut and the driver was on his way, she pulled up her hood. If any of the Harringtons or Mrs Pushkin were conscious, they would have given a description of her to the police and people would be looking out for her.

A message appeared as she was looking at her phone. It was from Clarissa: *Shannon Jones — give yourself up immediately. You are the scum of the earth.*

She walked quickly towards the Maritime as she called Victor's number. It was only fair to contact him before she brought trouble to his door.

It was several rings before he answered. "Lydia? How can I help?"

His voice, normal and calm, centred her. "I've done something bad and I need to hide out somewhere. Can I come to your hotel? I'll explain when I get there." She bit her lip. "But say if you don't want me to. If it's too dangerous for you. People will be searching for me."

"Sure. Come to the Maritime." He hushed her thanks and continued. "Fourth floor. Suite three. Sneak into the lift with someone else because you need a room card to work it. I'm getting hassle over my bill so it's easier if I don't come down." He added, "You might want to think about getting rid of your phone so it can't be traced. Dump it away from the Maritime."

Her phone signal would be bouncing off mobile towers. She'd compromised Victor by calling him on this phone. That was stupid. She forced herself to walk at a normal pace to the harbour. She saw the group chat was kicking off – Maddie asking if Annabel, Emily and Lydia were OK because her mum had heard there was a fire on their road. Zander, Ollie, Piglet and Victor had commented, echoing concern, but there was no word from Annabel or Emily – or her, obviously.

The most important thing she had to do now was send the email to Crispin's cousin at the gossip website, adding her recording of the girls from earlier that evening, admitting their and Mrs Pushkin's part in her mum's death. She didn't have time to say all she wanted to. She'd have to hope the evidence spoke for itself. After she'd sent it, she double-checked her outbox. It was gone. Then she added the same recording to the messages she had prepared from her fake social media accounts. She exhaled as she released them, publicly and direct to all the sisters' friends. There would be no stopping this from spreading.

She made sure she wasn't being watched before she dropped the phone unobtrusively into the water. It dropped down into the depths with the quietest of splashes. Now she wasn't holding on to it, she became aware that she was shaking.

The last time Shannon had been to the Maritime she'd only properly taken notice of the roof terrace where she'd had lunch with Victor and the infinity pool on the floor below. This time she noted exactly where the reception desk was in relation to the two sets of shiny brass front doors, one revolving, the other automatic. A doorman in uniform stood by, ready to help anyone. She purposely didn't catch his eye and she took her time.

She made her way to the lifts and hovered, as if she was waiting for someone, until a couple called the lift. She asked them to press the button for the fourth floor, looking at her face in the mirror as the doors closed silently. It was shiny and her eyes were bright.

It was the face of an arsonist. Maybe a murderer. Was she the scum of the earth? The adrenaline of revenge was wearing off and her emotions were too tangled to pull apart. Were Annabel and Emily . . . dead?

The lift opened on to a corridor with a thick blue and white patterned carpet and nautical pictures on the pristine white wall. When she knocked on Victor's door, he opened it immediately.

"Lydia!" He ushered her in. It was like a small flat, full of varnished wood furniture, lamps with shiny brass bases and an L-shaped white leather sofa. There was a huge anchor attached to the wall above a sideboard, which was artily rusty on one side. She could see a balcony behind a gauze net curtain. He landed a kiss of greeting on her cheek, holding her hair loosely, almost massaging the back of her head as he did so. They free-fell into a proper kiss. It was urgent from the start as they found their way to their real selves, their tongues pushing harder and deeper. When they eventually stopped, they kept their faces close, studying each other in a way they hadn't been able to until now that they were on their own.

Shannon pulled away. "My real name is Shannon Jones, but I can't be her either or I'll end up in prison for the rest of my life."

Victor nodded. He held up his phone. "I think I know some of it. A dramatic fire at Clifftop House."

Shannon didn't know what she wanted to hear, whether ... *any* of them had survived or not.

"Maddie says everyone has been pulled alive from the fire," said Victor, "but Emily, Annabel and Rosie have been taken to hospital."

Tears streamed down Shannon's cheeks and she wiped them away with her hands, not fully understanding them. All five of them – the Harringtons and Mrs Pushkin – would be exposed in due course, when everything came out into the open. This outcome was all right. She knew in her heart her mum wouldn't have wished anyone dead.

Victor threw his phone on to the low coffee table, on top of a stack of glossy magazines. "What happened?" He gestured at his phone. "I've been writing appropriate responses on the group chat but I'll need to go off grid soon too."

Shannon told him her story – she spared him nothing. Let him know who the real Shannon Jones was. He sat on the leather sofa while she paced the room.

"I don't want to go down for this," she told Victor as she stood in front of him. "But I have no passport or money other than this –" she pulled the few notes of Annabel's she had left out of her pocket – "and no way of getting off the island without either."

Shannon thought of the freedom she'd had on Fengari – the warmth of the sun on her skin, the sights and experiences that she could never have imagined for herself a few years ago. "I want to leave here and keep going. Can

I stay with you until I work out what to do?" She turned away slightly so she couldn't see Victor's face if it didn't react the way she wanted it to. "Even though you know what I've done."

He stood up and came towards her. She bit her lip as he took her hands. Was this the kind but firm brush-off?

"Join the team," he said.

"What?"

"Join me and my cousin. You have what it takes." He let go of her hands. "It's an invitation; you don't have to accept."

"Are you serious?" She leaned against him. He was slim, but he felt so solid. Like the anchor on the wall.

"I wouldn't joke about something like that," he said.

She breathed in the smell of his neck, and felt the soft fine cotton of his shirt and, underneath it, the hard muscles in his back. "I accept," she said. "Thank you."

"We can't stay here," he said. "Everyone's looking for you, but any minute now they'll be looking for me too. Peter's getting suspicious." He pulled an exasperated face. "I've been working on this project for months. But a big part of this . . . this job is knowing when to bail. The hotel staff are circling because of the unpaid bill too." He nodded his head towards a Louis Vuitton suitcase by the door. "I can't risk taking everything, but I want to take that case."

"I'll take it out of here," said Shannon. She knew Victor couldn't be seen with a suitcase or they would know he was doing a runner. She took hold of the handle.

"Check inside," he said. His face was serious. "You should never take someone's luggage unless you're confident about what's inside."

"Are there drugs in there?" she asked.

He was unlocking it and he looked up. "No, that's not what I do. Look." He flipped back the lid. It looked like a heap of clothing. "Take a proper look. Shannon – or whoever you are now – you have to know what you're taking on."

She squatted and lifted up the different layers of clothes. There was something rigid amongst the shirts. She lifted out a rectangle the size of a big picture book, wrapped up in a super-soft sweater. As she unwrapped it, she saw it was a small oil painting of a fragmented person and a tree in an ornate gilded frame. The colours were bold and harsh. "Why have you got this?"

"It was hanging in one of the hallways at Ollie and Piglet's. It's worth a lot of money."

"You stole it?"

"Yes. They have so many paintings, don't they? I doubt they've noticed it's gone yet."

She laughed. This was surreal. She stopped. "I hope the staff don't get into trouble."

"They'll work out it was me soon enough. But I know a fair bit about art. It's a Léger, a lovely example of cubism. So, you see why you might want to know what's in the case?"

"I'll look after it," said Shannon as she wrapped the painting back up. "Where can we go?"

297

"There's a hotel called the Old Custom House. It's opposite the marina and has no doorman. I've been scoping it out. They should have a room for tonight. If we get a sea view we'll be able to watch the yachts." He looked at her. "The security in that part of the marina is intense, but that's our only way off the island."

The landline in the bedroom rang, and Victor ignored it. A couple of seconds later his phone on the coffee table rang. It lit up with *Carlos, Reception Manager.*

"It's time we left," said Victor. "No time for hair dye. Come with me."

Shannon followed him into the bedroom, where he slid open the wardrobe. It still had clothes in it. It reminded Shannon of all the things she'd left behind at Clifftop House. He selected a shirt with a striking geometric pattern in black, orange and yellow. It reminded Shannon of the painting. He ripped it width-ways so he had a band of material. He tucked in the frayed ends and made it into a band, which he expertly tied round her head, like a fancy Alice band. He told her to ditch the hoodie, which she removed carefully so it didn't dislodge the hairband. He handed her a shirt with a small red-and-yellow pattern, and a black jacket. "Your black jeans will do, and so will the Nikes. A sleek leather boot would be better, though." He dived into another bag. "I nearly forgot to pack this. It's my make-up kit. I never know when it's going to come in handy."

She raised an eyebrow.

"That birthmark you drew on yourself was amateur. Here, you need bright red lipstick." He handed her the lipstick and pointed at the mirror. She applied it carefully, removed her brown contact lenses to reveal her blue eyes, and turned to face him. "So?"

"Perfect. Who are you going to be now that you're not Lydia or Shannon?"

She knew right away: she was Margot Bonvalier.

CHAPTER 27

Shannon went down in the lift on her own with one of Victor's room cards. He had kissed her and said he would take the next one down and meet her at the Old Custom House Hotel. The suitcase was small enough that she could be going for a meeting with some important materials. Except it was very late on a Wednesday evening. In the lift mirror she looked at her hair with material tied round it. It made her look more "arty, rich tourist" than "teenager on the run". Her heart was beating too fast and she was sure she could still smell smoke on her skin. Word must be getting out about the fire and her disappearance.

There was undoubtedly CCTV in this lift, otherwise she might have practised saying *I am Margot Bonvalier,* but she could hear it in her head, with the slight French intonation. Not that she would overdo it. She certainly didn't want anyone breaking into French. Her GCSE French wasn't enough for anything other than a chat about hobbies or the fictional places she had been on holiday.

The staff on the desk were busy with guests, but the doorman was standing to attention, looking for someone to help or engage with. She moved swiftly towards the doors.

He smiled at her. "May I get you a taxi, miss?"

"I am fine, thanks," she said. It was her first sentence as Margot and the accent could have been better.

He gave a dip of his head and behind her she heard, "Mr de Courtois! I urgently need to speak to you. Come with me, please."

Shannon kept on walking, her hand sweaty on the handle of the suitcase. She heard Victor say, "Of course. What can I help you with?" and when she was outside the Maritime, in the dark cover of night, she glanced back in through the floor to ceiling glass exterior and Victor was gone, having been taken into an office out of sight. The night-time air was relatively warm, but she shivered.

All she had to do was walk down the main street of Fengari Old Town and up a small side road and she would be there. Victor had told her to stick to the main route because she would be giving off nothing-to-hide vibes.

It was hard not to think the occasional person she passed was scanning her face to see if she was Shannon Jones. There was plenty of light from the shop displays and the street lamps for them to have a good look at her. She thought of drama club, and how her teacher had encouraged them to inhabit their characters. Margot Bonvalier had come to Fengari with her boyfriend – he was here on business and asked if she'd like to come along. After the summer, Margot would be travelling before she applied to university. She was thinking of studying law. She was young, but you patronized her at your peril; she could stick up for herself and was well connected.

Her trainers made no noise on the pavement, but the suitcase rumbled. The smell of barbecued food wafted out of a restaurant. The fire at Clifftop House would be completely out by now. She wondered how badly the house had been damaged – now that she knew everyone was alive, she allowed herself to imagine the irreplaceable old beam as a pile of ash and the little monster statue cracked and scorched beyond recognition.

A police car swung into the high street and made her jump. The whole time she'd been in Fengari, Shannon hadn't seen a single police car. She held on to the suitcase with one hand and her mum's necklace with the other, and clung on until the car had gone by.

The Old Custom House Hotel was back to front. The back of the building faced the marina and the entrance was down a small street. There was no doorman, but there was a marble floor, cream sofas and a huge vase of purple and cream flowers on a polished wood table in an area next to the check-in desk.

The woman on duty was probably in her early thirties, and with her smart navy uniform and hair in a bun she looked like one of the cabin crew on Shannon's flight over. "Hi there," she said in a sing-song voice. "How can I help?"

Shannon smiled and said, "My boyfriend said he'd meet me here – but he's still out with his client. He hasn't made a reservation. I'm sorry, I know it's late; we were staying the other side of the island." The accent was starting to fall into place.

"Let me see," said the receptionist. She tapped on a screen. "We do have rooms because a lot of people left after the hurricane warning. Would you like a room with a sea view or without?" She handed Shannon a menu of costs. They were even more extortionate than Shannon had been expecting.

"Sea view, please," said Shannon.

"No problem, I can sort that out for you," said the receptionist. "May I have your passport, please, and a card, which won't be debited until you check out?"

Shannon's heart bounced against her ribcage. "My boyfriend has my passport, but I can give you a card." As she said that, she realized how easily traced her cards would be: Clarissa's credit card in an instant, and the Margot Bonvalier debit card as soon as they saw how it was linked to payments going back and forth between her accounts. "Ah, he has that too," she said, her shoulders sagging with real emotion. "That's embarrassing."

"Don't worry," said the woman. "Ask him to give us a ring with payment details and we'll soon have you settled in your room."

Shannon bit her lip. She hated playing the subservient girlfriend, but she'd have to. "I can't disturb him. He's with a client."

The woman looked at her with pity. "Tell you what. Have a seat until he gets here, and I'll bring over a tea or coffee on the house."

"That is so kind," said Shannon. "Decaf coffee, please." She settled in a chair, lost without her phone, and wondered if Victor had been handed over to the police. She was safe in this moment, but soon there would be a photo of her circulating. Rosie had taken a photo of her that time, and of course there were her passport photos.

She had no money, bank cards, passport or even clothes apart from a few of Victor's. She pulled the suitcase closer to her. There was a hugely valuable painting in her possession, but she hadn't got the faintest idea of how to sell it.

The receptionist placed the coffee in front of her, and Shannon smiled graciously.

A little while later, a cleaner came to empty the bin behind the reception desk and said in a low voice as she placed a new bag inside it, "Did you hear on the news there was a fire bombing in one of the grand houses on the clifftop? There were people inside and everything. They haven't caught the person who did it yet."

"Oh no," murmured the receptionist.

"It was a family feud," said the cleaner confidently. "Terrible."

The door burst open and cooler air wafted over them. "Ah, there you are!" Victor spoke in a flawless English accent. He looked rumpled but otherwise his smooth self as he came over to kiss Shannon. His lips touched hers and grounded her once more. "Everything took longer than I'd anticipated." He handed the receptionist a card and a passport. "Please can we check in? Sea view. Ground or first floor. Stuart Perkins and Margot Bonvalier."

Victor had turned off the lights, so they wouldn't get glare on the windows. The room had a perfect view of the yachts the other side of the main road, and the bright night-time security lights in the marina meant they could see the security guard standing outside the wire fence next to the heavy-duty metal gate, which had a keypad next to it. There was a small building set back behind the fence which Shannon guessed was for customs and passport control.

She rubbed at the headache forming on one side of her head as she watched the guard patrol the area. "I bet that guy already has my details," she said.

"And we don't have long until people start putting me on the wanted list too," said Victor. "Let's hope Stuart Perkins doesn't notice his credit card and passport have been stolen for a while. He was very drunk when I bumped into him on the way here. His friends were trying to get him back to their hotel."

The first floor room was small and minimalist, but Shannon imagined that it was tastefully done if you were a certain sort of person. She'd have added a few more touches and some real flowers. Gerberas, perhaps in different pinks, and definitely more toiletries. They were stingy with the shampoo and there was no conditioner. Not that she cared at that moment. She was grateful to be lying on top of the duvet with Victor, listening to him tell her he'd had his cousin on the phone with the hotel, pretending to be his dad's accountant and giving them a reference number for the money that had been allegedly wired over from Paris.

"That hotel is part of a huge chain," he said. "I don't feel bad. This hotel is family run. Maybe when we sell the painting we'll wire them what we owe." He squeezed her shoulder and kissed her cheek. "Are you OK?"

"I'm not sure," she answered truthfully, and she found herself crying, big heavy tears streaming down her face.

He hugged her gently before she climbed off the bed to find tissues in the bathroom.

"I don't know who I am any more," she said. "I've been so focused on destroying Emily and Annabel. I don't even know if I managed that. I wanted to do this for my mum and now it's all over." She shrugged. "Everything is over."

"You pulled off something audacious," he said. "I don't know if that's the word I mean. Brave, daring and bold." Shannon nodded. She wanted him to pull her back on to the bed, and he did. He positioned himself in front of her so he was looking directly into her eyes. "You have a choice. You give up now, or you become a new person. Move forward. You can definitely do this."

Maybe she would process what had happened to the Harringtons some other time. Victor was right. She couldn't fall apart now.

He pressed the TV remote and channel hopped until he found the local news. They waited through a report about the weather and then it switched back to the presenter and the words *Arson Attack* came up on the screen. "A local family was subjected to a terrifying attack by a house guest who was not who they thought she was. Details are still emerging, but police are urging Fengari residents and tourists to be on the lookout for Shannon Jones, who should be approached with extreme caution." They'd used the photo of her from her passport. She looked scary.

Beside her, Victor laughed. "No one will recognize you from that." But then they flashed up the photo that Rosie had taken. It had been cropped and enlarged so it was pixelated, but that was a much better likeness. Victor sat up as footage was shown of firefighters tackling the blaze. Shannon waited for more information, aware she was holding her breath. "Fortunately, the family got away with minor injuries," the reporter said, "but the house has been badly damaged and the family are said to be devastated about the loss of an ancient part of the kitchen."

The beam. The beam had been destroyed. It felt like something important.

The programme cut back to the presenter in the studio.

"It's believed that Shannon Jones assumed the identity of London teenager Lydia Cornwallis. Lydia has not yet been located and her mother, Clarissa Cornwallis, made this appeal." The presenter stared at the screen until the footage appeared.

Clarissa looked as if she was at an airport. Her face was shrunken but her hair was puffed up away from her face, as neat as ever. "I'm asking anybody who knows where my daughter is to get in touch," she said in a quivery voice. "I'm very worried about what might have happened to her. I don't understand how this fraud took place – I was tricked into believing I'd been messaging my own daughter for the last week and a half."

Lydia would soon be in touch with her mum. She'd see Clarissa's frantic messages on Insta. Shannon didn't feel the slightest bit sorry for Clarissa. "I'm going to have a shower," she said.

CHAPTER 28

When she came out of the bathroom, wrapped in a towel, Victor threw one of his T-shirts at her. She saw the TV was still on and he'd drawn the curtains, but not completely. "We'll sleep in shifts," he said. "To keep an eye on the news and to watch the yachts. We need to note which boats are occupied and the shift patterns of the security people."

Shannon went back into the bathroom to put the T-shirt on and asked him to throw her a pair of boxers. "How do you start a boat without a key?" she called.

"It's surprisingly easy to steal a boat," said Victor. "It's because once you've stolen it, it's hard to get rid of. Much easier to steal than a car. People are careless with the keys. They chuck them on the chart table or leave them in the engine panel. Or they have keyless ignition. Not many people would be confident sailing a yacht away, either – you need to know what you're doing."

"And you do?" asked Shannon.

"Of course," said Victor. "I won silver in the sailing race, remember?"

She badly wanted to kiss him again, but when she touched his arm, he took her hand. "You should sleep. I'll wake you in a few hours."

Five hours later, she woke to him whispering in her ear that it was her turn to be on watch. He'd made her a cup of tea. She hadn't even heard the kettle boiling.

He'd kept notes on a piece of hotel-headed paper which he'd found in a plastic wallet in a drawer, numbering the yachts, crossing out the ones he'd seen people on, noting which had lights on, though he said they could also be security lights. He'd watched the security guard, and noted how many times he questioned people going in (only people who hadn't known the keypad code). He hadn't yet changed shift.

"I've tried to take videos when people put in the code, so I could zoom in to see what it was, but it's too dark, and impossible because of the angle," he said. He held his phone up. "And this burner phone is rubbish. I did a factory reset on my other one and left it at the Maritime. We'll probably end up having to run for the gate when someone else comes in or out, but if there's anything we can do to minimize the chances of getting caught, we need to do it. Little observations now might make a big difference later." He looked up at the TV, which was on mute. "They're looking for me now too."

Shannon watched him crawl into bed and heard his breathing deepen almost immediately. The yachts were dark shapes on the water, their masts clanking. The security guard walked up and down endlessly. Shannon wondered what he did when he needed the toilet, and her question was answered when she saw him on his radio and a man from inside the building came to take over for a few minutes. When the original guy came back, the two of them stood chatting for a while, and the sky started to brighten. Shannon yawned and looked at the TV. The twenty-four-hour news channel was showing a documentary on ship building. Scrolling text along the bottom said the next bulletin would be on the hour.

A police car cruised almost silently along the main street, past the marina, and Shannon wondered when they would start looking at hotel registers. She and Victor had to leave today, before the noose tightened. She made herself another tea, ate an individually wrapped plain biscuit on the tray, and waited for the news.

The words "Arson Attack" had changed to "Hunt for Fugitives". The presenter said, "Shannon Jones and another individual, using the name Victor de Courtois, are believed to be on the run together. They are wanted for arson, theft and fraud." There was a photo of Victor. They were still working on his true identity, but the presenter said he was

311

believed to be a French national. A police officer with a huge red face and small eyes said, "I can assure the public that we will find this pair and they will be put behind bars for a long time. We are particularly interested in the sighting of a small Louis Vuitton suitcase like this." On the screen there was a photo of a case exactly the same as Victor's – and a photo from a CCTV image of her with the suitcase, wearing the outfit which Victor had fashioned for her. She prayed that the receptionist wasn't watching the news.

Next up was Maddie, who said she'd been suspicious of Shannon from the moment she'd met her, and she couldn't believe how anyone would want to target such a lovely Fengari family. "As for Victor," she said, "that's blown me away. He was charming. A real gentleman." Then there was Finch, who looked utterly dazed, answering questions from an excitable reporter. "No, I wouldn't call Shannon, or Lydia as I knew her, evil," he said. "I think she was obsessed with Emily and Annabel Harrington. I'm not sure why. I hope we find some answers soon."

Thursday

With the morning light, the yachts came to life. People came on shore with rubbish bags or to pick up a delivery at the gate. Six of the yachts Victor had pinpointed still showed no signs of occupancy. The security guard changed. This one seemed to enjoy interaction with people who went in and out of the gate, high-fiving a teenager, and taking a pastry from a big bag when offered by a little girl with her parents. Watching it made Shannon's mouth water. She noticed after a call on his radio, he started to request bag checks from everyone going in and out. He was apologetic about it, bobbing his head and placing his hand on his chest as he spoke, but he did it all the same.

Victor's alarm went off and he sat bolt upright, his clothes from yesterday creased from being slept in. He took a moment to orientate himself. "What's happened?" he asked.

After she'd filled him in, she said, "We need to ditch the suitcase and find ourselves new looks. We've got to look older."

He moved his head up and down, thinking. "First off, we need to cut and dye your hair. I've got hair dye and scissors."

"We can use my cut-off hair to make you a man bun?" said Shannon.

He grinned. "Genius."

He opened his suitcase and found the dye. "An all-black outfit with some statement jewellery for you? I've a great silver necklace from a guest of the Maritime. And I'll smear dye on your trainers. They might not turn black, but they'll definitely change colour."

Shannon sat on the bed. "But I need a passport most of all."

"That's hard," said Victor. He climbed out of bed. "And the painting is small, but we still need to get it past the security guard without drawing attention to it. I have a laptop bag." He unwrapped the painting, but it was still too big to fit inside the bag.

"Let's work on changing ourselves first," said Shannon.

It took less than an hour for them to alter their appearances as much as they could. Shannon didn't particularly like the version of herself with short black hair, black T-shirt, heavy eye make-up, her black jeans and brown trainers with stick figures that she'd drawn on herself with black eyeliner from Victor's make-up kit, but she liked how different she looked. She could pass for ten years older.

"You need a tattoo," said Victor. He took her wrist and drew an infinity symbol with a marker. When he finished, he said, "If things don't work out today. . ." He swallowed, unable to say more.

She didn't want tears in her eyes. Her eye make-up was too good.

She pulled his face towards her and looked at his earring and the man bun, a slightly different shade of brown to his hair, and kissed him. He kissed her back. They pulled away at the same time, aware the clock was ticking.

"I need to go out. To get some food," said Shannon. "We can't have room service." She looked at the painting, which was still on the bed where Victor had tried to jam it into the laptop case. She measured it against her arm. "And I have an idea for this."

"It's too risky to go out," said Victor. "And we've only got one phone between us."

"I'll be quick," said Shannon.

Victor reached for Stuart Perkins's credit card. "Keep the amounts low."

Shannon placed the card in her back pocket, pushing it right down so it couldn't be lost. "I will." Her eyes flickered to the TV news channel, where there was a breaking-news banner along the bottom. *Local businessman Peter Dunn is being questioned by police about a company called Sure Education.*

"Get through the reception area as quickly as possible," said Victor.

"Don't worry." Shannon's stomach twisted.

"I'll worry until you're back."

Shannon left the room before she could change her mind. If her plan worked, it might save them. She walked down one flight of stairs instead of taking the lift, and at the bottom saw there was a different person on duty. A man this time. She waited until he was talking to a guest, and then she lifted her head up high and walked out into the street.

But coming towards her, her mouth set in an angry, determined line, was Clarissa Cornwallis.

CHAPTER 29

Shannon took in a breath, but her body forgot to release it. For a long moment she was light-headed. Clarissa was maybe ten seconds away, now eight, now six. She must have got on a plane immediately after that appeal and taken the first helicopter of the day from the mainland.

There was nowhere to go – no shops to dive into, or even doorways on this stretch of pavement. If Shannon stopped or turned round that would draw attention to herself.

Clarissa would soon be level with her. She was pulling a suitcase with one hand and was on her phone with the other but looking right at Shannon. "What d'you mean Lydia took a flight to Marbella instead of London?" she said into her phone. Shannon kept her eyes straight ahead as they passed each other and she reminded herself that they'd only ever seen each other a few times when she'd wafted into the shop, and Shannon – or Rhiannon, as she'd been – had been almost insignificant to her.

Shannon waited. For a gasp or a shout. A firm hand on her shoulder.

Nothing.

She itched to turn round and check Clarissa hadn't given her a second look, but that would have been peak foolishness. Her legs were shaking now the crisis was receding and she wanted to stop and find a more normal breathing pattern, but she had to keep going. This was what she was good at – not giving up.

She made her way to the supermarket at the end of the high street. It was more of a delicatessen, but Stuart Perkins was paying anyway. She moved through the aisles without checking the prices, picking up a bag of fresh croissants, orange juice, bottled water, fruit, cheese and chocolate. At the self-checkout she concentrated on doing everything carefully so that an assistant wouldn't need to come over, and she slipped everything plus a spare plastic bag inside another bag.

She was Margot's older sister Gabriella. More fiery and creative. A singer-songwriter on the come up. She went into her next and final shop. The toy shop.

There were a variety of board games to choose from, but Shannon required one with the right depth and length.

She discreetly measured them against her arm and decided a deluxe version of Cluedo was what she needed. It was first thing in the morning and already there were several families in there, and children running up and down the main aisles. She waited at the till to be served, cursing the two assistants for still chatting among themselves even though they must have seen her. Causing a fuss would only draw attention to herself. Then she realized with a stomach lurch the guy was talking about her.

"Still missing. . ." he said.

"Surely Zak and Shannon can't have left the island. . ." the girl said.

Shannon blinked. *Zak?* It would be hard not to think of him as Victor. The girl spoke as if she knew them both.

The guy lowered his voice and Shannon moved slightly to hear what he was imparting with such excitement. "Sister's friend . . . she works at the Old Custom House and thinks they might be there."

"You serious?" The girl's jaw dropped a little.

The guy nodded, waved at Shannon, and said, "Love a bit of Cluedo," and wanted to talk about his favourite board games, not reading the room and seeing that she was desperate to leave.

"This is a gift," she said, her voice strangled by anxiety. "I'm not that into board games."

"Fair enough," he said easily.

She waited until the credit card payment was approved, then left, walking as quickly as she dared.

318

"Hey!" the guy called after her. "Miss?"

She didn't turn round. She was just out of the door when she felt his panting breath on her cheek. "Here's your receipt. You said it was for a gift. You might need it."

It was hard to look grateful, but she tried. It required restraint not to sprint back to the Old Custom House. She needed to warn Victor (to her he might always be Victor). She quickened her pace, certain that if anyone was to look at her face they would see nothing but panic. As she got within sight of the hotel she saw three police cars in the side street. That was that, then. She could already see a small crowd. There would be camera crews next.

Tears stung her eyes as she walked down to the water's edge. If it wasn't for her, Victor might have been able to slip away from Fengari with the painting. Her stomach ached and her shopping was heavy in her arms. There was no plan now. Stuart Perkins's credit card would be stopped any moment and she would have to give herself up. But not yet. She would keep going until the bitter end. Along from the marina, there were benches to sit on which might be safe enough if she didn't stay for too long.

She had her eye on the fifth bench along, which was empty. On the fourth one a person sat hunched over on his phone. That man bun! She noticed how he was holding a jacket awkwardly across his lap. He'd managed to get the painting out.

"Hi!" she said as she sat down. She loved how Victor's face changed on seeing her, from concern to utter delight.

"I hoped you'd see me," said Victor in her ear as they hugged. "We should have discussed where we'd meet if anything happened."

"How did you know the police were coming?" she asked as they moved apart again. "How did you get out without them seeing you?"

"I was keeping watch. All three cars drove along the main street and I could see them turn into the side street. So I jumped out of the window."

"From the first floor?"

"Yep, that's why I asked for the ground or first floor," said Victor. He raised an eyebrow. "It was lucky I was dressed."

Shannon held up her board game. "Here." She checked no one was watching them, then discreetly removed the cellophane packaging and tipped the contents into the spare plastic bag. "We'll put this in the bin over there in a minute." She indicated that Victor should place the painting inside. It fit snugly, and as she placed the lid on top, she said, "Clever me."

"And clever me for stealing a small, highly valuable painting," said Victor. He opened his burner phone and found a clip on the Fengari app. "There's something you should see. It's really quick."

It was Lydia with Crispin in a poolside bar. Both of them looked bemused and as if they had been awake too long.

"You did an impressive job of making yourself look like Lydia," said Victor.

A warning came on the screen for flash photography. A voiceover said, "Lydia Cornwallis has been found alive and well in Marbella with her boyfriend, Crispin Taylor. It seems the seventeen-year-old was aware that her identity was being used."

"Yes, I agreed to this person taking my place," said Lydia indignantly to a reporter, "but I didn't know she had a vendetta against the Harringtons, did I? At first when I heard, I thought she was a psychopath, but you've shown me some of the stuff on social media and now I don't know. I mean, bad stuff happened at Clifftop House last summer, right? I need to speak to my parents."

Shannon looked at Victor. "People are talking about the things I posted already?" For the first time since her mum had died, she felt a small sense of peace.

He nodded. "Yes, but we're still wanted criminals."

"I have a plan," said Shannon. "Have a croissant if you aren't too stressed to eat and I'll tell you."

Shannon would have liked sunglasses, but they only had what they were standing up in, Stuart Perkins's credit card, a burner phone, a bit of food and drink in a plastic bag and an extremely valuable stolen painting in a Cluedo box. The two of them walked towards the marina.

"I shoved this in my pocket before I jumped out of the window," said Victor, unfolding the piece of paper where he'd identified the yachts which he thought were empty. "I also think the PIN for the gate has a four in it."

There were three strong contenders for empty yachts. One was moored on the nearest part of the jetty to the shore, and its name was visible: *Wild Spirit*. Victor looked it up on his burner phone. It was a charter boat. "No details about availability. Just says contact the broker," said Victor. He showed Shannon the photos.

"Oooh, very nice," she said.

"I'm showing you so we can memorize the layout," he said. She sensed he might have smiled if they hadn't been in such danger. He was gripping his phone tightly and his voice had a strained quality to it.

They carried on a little further. The security guard who'd come on shift when she was on watch was still there – the one who liked children.

All they needed were children.

They needed the right family: kids who were interested in boats and old enough to be apart from their parents without getting anxious, and relaxed parents.

"We can wait," said Victor. "But not for long, or we'll look suspicious. The police will fan out from the hotel to see if we're still in the area. It makes sense we'd be loitering by the boats."

"We can't ask more than one family either," said Shannon. "Or that will be noticed. I think I'll know the family when I see them, though."

As they waited, they pretended to be discussing something important. They gesticulated towards *Wild Spirit*, and Victor consulted his phone. The day was beginning to heat up and Shannon felt too hot in her jeans.

A bunch of tourists arrived at once, so many of them that Shannon thought they must have come off a tourist bus. This gave her a few families to choose from. She honed in on one with two boys, aged about ten and seven. The boys ran to the fence and pressed their faces up against it while the parents sipped coffee from takeaway cups.

Shannon said, "Let's go," and she and Victor wandered towards the gate. She stopped next to the boys and said in Gabriella's voice, which was a little like Margot's but more animated, "You guys like the yachts, yes?"

The younger boy nodded; the older one said, "Yeah."

"You see our one? *Wild Spirit*?" She looked round at the parents. "We can take a photo of your boys next to our yacht if you like?"

"That would be cool, Mom," said the old boy.

The mum said, "Sure." She hoiked her canvas tote bag up her arm.

"Under-eighteens are fine to come into the marina without a day pass," said Shannon, hoping the mum got the hint without her having to spell it out. She and the dad were not going to go through that gate. She switched to the older boy. "You want to take your mum's phone so we can get a photo for you?"

He held his hand out for his mum's phone.

"Take care of it, Felix," the dad said. "Lucas, are you going too? We can wave at you from here, buddy."

This was it. Shannon and Victor took the kids to the

323

gate, the board game casually under her arm. "Hey," she said to the security guard. "Our friends told me the PIN but I've gone and forgotten it. I know it had a four in it." She made an embarrassed face. "I had it on my phone but I left it in the hotel. We've got the entertainment!" She held up the board game.

The guy smiled. "Your friends, ma'am?"

Lucas was rattling the gate. "I want to go through. I want to see the boats."

"In a minute, sweetie," said Shannon, channelling Gabriella Bonvalier.

Victor said, "Andre and Fabien."

The security guy nodded. He couldn't possibly know everyone, and he was enjoying the boys' excitement.

They looked good together, her and Victor, Shannon thought as the guy opened the gate and the boys rushed through.

"Wait for your daddy," the security guard called out.

Felix turned round. "He's not my daddy," he called. "I only just met him."

The security guard's smile faded. Victor seemed to stumble. Shannon said, "The boys will warm to you, don't worry." She said in a low voice to the security guard, "He's my new boyfriend. It's not easy for them, all this change." And carried on walking with Victor slightly behind her. "Boys, wait for me!"

Victor caught her up at *Wild Spirit*. "Good save," he murmured, taking the painting from her. "I'll check out the engine. You take the photos."

Shannon said, "Right, boys, where shall we take the photo of you two?" She lined them up and took various shots. Lucas waved to his parents, who waved back. They moved towards the gate. Were they going to engage the security guard in conversation?

"Victor?" she called. "How's it going?"

A middle-aged man in navy shorts and a pink T-shirt stretched over his large stomach walked by. "Are you taking *Spirit* out?"

Shannon nodded.

The man shot out his hand. "Bruce Kingston-Lawson. You're?"

"Gabriella Bonvalier," said Shannon. "Lovely to meet you. Excuse me," she said. "I need to finish this little photo shoot."

"Big westerly out there today, but the waves should die down by the afternoon," he said as he ambled further along the dock, presumably to his own boat.

She glanced at the boys' parents. They were talking to the security guard and he was looking at them. Frowning.

"Here," she said to Felix. "Here's your mum's phone. You take it back to her now. Have a lovely day." She gave a wave and climbed on to the yacht as the engine started. The boat was all shiny wood and gleaming technology. Through a window she glimpsed a kitchen which was bigger than the one in her old flat.

She could have knelt down and kissed the decking, but she had to find Victor. He was at the huge wheel.

"We need to hurry," she said. "The security guy's on his radio."

The yacht was nosing out of its space now. "This beauty started like a dream," said Victor. "Keyless ignition."

"How fast does it go?" asked Shannon. "What if someone comes after us?" She ran to a window. The parents were hugging their boys and watching the yacht. The security guard in the building had joined the other one and seemed to be shouting at him. "Oh." Shannon was light-headed. "A police car has just pulled up outside the marina fence."

"It's OK," said Victor. "There's a speedboat on the back we can use."

"You know how to get it off the back?"

"Of course. But the wind's up now. This yacht will pick up speed, and it won't take long to get to the mainland. I think we'll save the speedboat for the last bit. Find a more secluded cove for going ashore, because they'll have radioed ahead. I've sailed that coastline – there are loads of places we can duck into." He smiled. "You can breathe out. It's going to be OK."

"I can?" She exhaled loudly and put her arm around his shoulder.

Her put his arm around her waist and kissed her briefly before returning both hands to the wheel. "Welcome to your new life."

ACKNOWLEDGEMENTS

Thank you to Linas Alsenas, Pete Matthews and Sarah Dutton for invaluable editing expertise; Jess White and Arub Ahmed for copy-editing and proofreading skills. You guided me through the Fengari storms!

Thank you to so many other talented people at Scholastic who have worked on this and other books of mine, including Liam Drane who designed the gripping cover, Harriet Dunlea in PR, Ella Probert in marketing and Lucy Page in sales.

Thank you to my agent Becky Bagnell for being helpful, fun and fearless!

Thank you to my colleagues at Teddington School, who have taught me a lot and who work incredibly hard. An especially loud whoop for the support staff.

Thank you to Emma O'Brien for introducing me to a fabulous network of fellow secondary school librarians. May we continue to convince people that a school library is so much more than a room full of books.

To my friends, near and far, thanks for being there.

Finally, thank you to Mum, Dad, the Mudies, the Franklins, Phoebe, Maia, Sophie and Tim for understanding all the hours I put into writing and being proud of me.

ALSO BY
SUE WALLMAN

LYING
ABOUT
LAST
SUMMER

Skye's sister died last
year. So who is sending
texts now, pretending
to be her?

SEE
HOW
THEY
LIE

Mae feels lucky to grow up in her father's elite wellness facility. But then she breaks the rules.

YOUR
TURN
TO
DIE

Leah used to love the old house her parents rent with friends for a week every year. Until a body is found in the garden.

DEAD POPULAR

Kate knows you don't become the most powerful girl at school by playing nice. But someone is playing a far more dangerous game.

I KNOW YOU DID IT

Ruby hopes no one at her new school will uncover her terrible secret. But she soon realizes she's not the only killer there.